THE GIFT OF
THE MAGPIE

A MEG LANGSLOW MYSTERY

THE GIFT OF THE MAGPIE

DONNA ANDREWS

THORNDIKE PRESS
A part of Gale, a Cengage Company

Copyright © 2020 by Donna Andrews.
Thorndike Press, a part of Gale, a Cengage Company.

Thorndike Press® Large Print Mystery.
The text of this Large Print edition is unabridged.
Other aspects of the book may vary from the original edition.
Set in 16 pt. Plantin.

LIBRARY OF CONGRESS CIP DATA ON FILE.
CATALOGUING IN PUBLICATION FOR THIS BOOK
IS AVAILABLE FROM THE LIBRARY OF CONGRESS.

ISBN-13: 978-1-4328-8478-9 (hardcover alk. paper)

Published in 2021 by arrangement with St. Martin's Publishing

Printed in Mexico
Print Number: 01   Print Year: 2021

THE GIFT OF
THE MAGPIE

CHAPTER 1

Monday, December 21

"Cow manure?"

I was talking into my cell phone, but my friend Caroline Willner, who'd just popped into the kitchen with an armload of brightly wrapped presents, must have thought I was talking to her.

"Is this part of the whole not-swearing-in-front-of-the-boys thing?" she asked. "And what did I do to deserve — oops!" Her voice sank to a whisper. "Sorry! Didn't realize you were on the phone."

Although I could see that her curiosity was aroused.

"We have access to a variety of manures — cow, horse, sheep, goat, and llama," I said into the phone. "Much of it's even organic. Is there a particular reason you want cow manure?"

"Well, any of those would be acceptable," my caller said. "Especially the organic ones.

7

I just don't want chicken manure."

"Of course not," I said. "It's so apt to be infected with salmonella. Give me your address and let me know when I can drop by — would sometime later today work? If you can show me the area you want fertilized, I can figure out how much manure is required and how many volunteers we'll need to spread it."

"I'll be home all day putting up the tree." She rattled off her address. When I'd jotted it down, we wished each other a Merry Christmas and signed off.

"And a Merry Christmas to you," I said, turning to Caroline and accompanying the greeting with a hug.

"Likewise." She set the presents down on the table and began to pry her small, round form out of a bright turquoise down jacket. "Your mother sent me in here to see how I could help out with this noble, heartwarming holiday endeavor you're in charge of. And it turns out to be a manure-delivery service? I can see why she told me to ask you, instead of explaining it herself."

I could see her point — I wasn't sure Mother had ever actually uttered the word "manure" in her life — she preferred "natural fertilizer."

"And it's certainly not very Christmas-y,

is it?" she added. "Not exactly festive."

I sighed.

"Manure can be pretty festive if you're a die-hard gardener," I pointed out.

"Ooh — I have an idea," she exclaimed. "How about some exotic manure? Much more festive. And I've got a lot of it down at the sanctuary. Zebra manure, wildebeest manure, yak manure — lots of options. I'm very careful about their feed, so it's all completely organic. You're welcome to as much of it as you'd like."

"I'll suggest that to Dad," I said. "He's the manure expert." And I could let him explain that we probably had more than enough suitable manure right here in Caerphilly County, thanks to the growing number of local farmers who'd taken up organic farming. Although if too many of them had figured out that they could actually sell their organic manure, nice to know we could trek down to the Willner Wildlife Refuge for a supply — it was only an hour or so southwest of us. "Most of our projects aren't that weird, and so far this is the only one involving manure. It's called Helping Hands for the Holidays."

"And just what does Helping Hands do when it's not delivering manure?"

"Well, it all started out this fall, after the

hurricane," I said. "For a while everywhere you went you saw blue tarps, boarded-up windows, and piles of branches and other debris. The Ladies' Interfaith Council figured out that some people couldn't do the cleanup and repairs themselves and couldn't afford to hire anyone. So they decided to help out."

"If I try very hard, I can see the members of the Ladies' Interfaith Council picking up fallen branches," Caroline said. "Small, graceful ones. But shingling roofs? Do they wear white gloves, or is that just for the tea parties?"

"Clearly it's been a while since you went to a Council meeting." I had to laugh. "Robyn Smith started shaking things up when she took over as rector at Trinity, and ever since they let in the Wiccans and the atheists, things have been downright lively."

"Is your mother okay with all of this?" Caroline looked anxious.

"Mother's fine with it," I said. "They haven't done away with the tea parties and cucumber sandwiches — they've just added a whole lot of other things, most of which she approves of, as long as other people do the heavy lifting. Anyway, the Council decided to fix things up for a couple of the neediest cases — a few retired folks on limited income and a young woman who was recently widowed and is trying to work full time while raising three kids. They negotiated a deal with Randall Shiffley — his construction company provided the supplies at cost and he donated the services of a few skilled workers. The Council raised the money to pay for the supplies and recruited volunteers to perform the manual labor under the supervision of Randall's workers. And stuff got done for people who couldn't otherwise afford it. The ladies of the Council saw that it was good, so they got all excited and decided we should do a lot more of this helping our neighbors."

"And that's not a good thing?" She must have picked up on my tone.

"It's a wonderful thing," I said. "But this is absolutely the wrong time of year to be doing it. Everybody's calendars are already bursting at the seams, and the weather hasn't exactly been helpful."

"Really?" She cocked her head in puzzlement, rather like a bird. "I thought you hadn't had any snow? We haven't down my way."

"We haven't," I said. "Snow isn't the only kind of weather that can complicate things. The last few months we've had unseasonably warm weather and torrential rain —

Caerphilly Creek has flooded three times already this month. But whenever the thermometer plunges into the sub-freezing zone, the atmosphere's dry as a bone. We've had nothing for weeks but warm wet days and bright sunny deep-freeze days. Everyone's mourning the likelihood that we won't have a white Christmas."

"Maybe Rose Noire should do her snow-summoning dance," Caroline suggested. "It could help — it was a lot of fun last year."

"Oh, so that's what happened?" I said. "No, thank you. Breaking the all-time snowfall record last year was interesting, but we don't need to go for two Christmas blizzards in a row. And a snowfall could bring all the Helping Hands projects to a complete halt, instead of just making everyone who's working on them miserable. At least the people working on the outdoors projects — fortunately we do have some indoor projects. In addition to roofs, furnaces, insulation, wiring, and plumbing we started getting other kinds of requests. Car repairs. Accounting woes. Medical issues. Helping Hands turned into a sort of Make-A-Wish program for grown-ups. And then —"

My phone rang. It was Randall Shiffley. I should probably answer. With luck he was wearing his mayor's hat and calling me, his part-time special assistant, on some official business. But the odds were it would be Helping Hands business. I could at least hope he was calling with a progress report on an existing project, not enlisting me for a new one.

"Hey, Randall," I said. "What's up?"

"Hey, Meg," he said. "Got a couple new ones for you."

I tried to sigh too softly for him to hear. Then I put the phone on speaker. Hearing our discussion of whatever new projects Randall was about to dump on me would probably do more than any amount of explaining to help Caroline understand Helping Hands for the Holidays.

"First one's a no-brainer. Couple over on Bland Street whose grandmother is coming to live with them, and she's in a wheelchair. They've asked if we can build them a ramp."

"Refreshingly straightforward." I was scribbling in my notebook-that-tells-me-when-to-breathe, as I called my voluminous to-do list. "You want me to go over and kick things off?"

"No need," Randall said. "I'll send one of my men over to scope it out. If their granny needs a wheelchair ramp, odds are she'll also need a whole host of other accommodations they haven't even thought of yet. Once we know what-all they need, I'll let you know how many helpers to send. Meanwhile, do you have some time today? Got a new possible project that requires your touch."

This time Randall could probably hear my sigh. Requiring my touch usually meant that either the project or the person requesting it was difficult. Possibly both.

"You know Mr. Dunlop?" he asked. "Harvey Dunlop, over on the south side of town?"

The name sounded familiar. I frowned in an effort to place him. Enlightenment struck.

"Harvey the Hoarder?" I asked.

"That's him." Randall chuckled. "Good old Harvey."

"Are his neighbors complaining again? I thought that yard cleanup we talked him into doing last summer shut them up."

"The cleanup *you* talked him into," Randall said. "I like to give credit where it's due. Yes, they shut up for a while, but now they're back, complaining about rodents, and smell, and what an eyesore the house itself is. On top of that, this time Mr. Dunlop's relatives have gotten into the act and are threatening to sic Adult Protective

Services on him. And you know what Meredith's like."

Yes, I did. Here in Caerphilly, Adult Protective Services — or Child Protective Services, or any other kind of town or county social work — meant Meredith Flugleman. Which wasn't a bad thing — she was highly skilled, passionately dedicated, and without a doubt one of the best-hearted people in the county. But she was also annoyingly perky and persistent. Once she decided that Something Must Be Done, having her around was like having a small, yappy terrier nipping at — or worse, attaching itself to — your ankles. I didn't think her approach would work well with Mr. Dunlop.

"So he's asked for our help?" I said.

"Not exactly," Randall said. "But he needs it. And I figure if anyone can talk him into asking for help, you can."

I took several of the deep, calming yoga breaths my cousin Rose Noire was always nagging me to try when stressed.

"Meg?"

"Just checking my schedule," I said. "I should be able to get over to Mr. Dunlop's house a little later this morning. I'm assuming time is of the essence."

"I can only do so much to slow down the

town building inspector," Randall said. "And you know Meredith. Luckily Meredith's on a cruise till after New Year's, and the inspector's off deer hunting for the time being. But still — the sooner the better."

"I'll see what I can do."

CHAPTER 2

"Looks as if Randall just rearranged your day," Caroline said as I was hanging up.

"And I'll have to desert you," I replied.

"Not necessarily," she said. "Do you mind if I come along? I confess, I'm a little curious to see this Harvey the Hoarder. And while I do plan to spend some time out at the zoo helping your grandfather with whatever he's up to, if I'm staying here through the holidays, I'm probably going to get sucked into your Helping Hands thing as well, so maybe I should start looking for a project that matches my skill set. This sounds a lot more interesting than plumbing and carpentry."

"Are you sure?" I asked. "The place could be pretty awful. And there could be more than just inanimate objects — there could be cockroaches. Rats."

"I've done first aid on wounded badgers," she said with a laugh. "I'm not afraid of a little old *Rattus norvegicus.* In fact, if we do find rats, I could take charge of humanely trapping and disposing of them. Right in my wheelhouse. Just give me a hand bringing in my suitcase and the rest of the presents from my car and I'll be at your service."

"Let's get the boys to help." I led the way out into the hall, reached for the cord attached to a large wall-mounted dinner bell, and gave it a brisk jingle.

"This is new," Caroline said.

"We installed it a few months ago, when Michael and I both had laryngitis," I said. "Josh and Jamie seem to find it entertaining, so we've kept it around."

From somewhere upstairs came the sound of pounding feet, then a pair of faces peered over the railing around the second-floor landing. No, make that a trio of faces. I'd only been trying to train my not-quite-teenaged sons to answer the bell, but apparently it worked on my brother, Rob, and many of the visiting family as well — probably because a reasonably high percentage of the time, whoever was ringing the bell was announcing the availability of either a meal or some fresh-baked treat that should be eaten hot.

"Can you guys carry in all the presents

and treats from Aunt Caroline's car?" I asked.

They stampeded downstairs, each pausing to give Caroline a hug. Then Caroline handed her keys to Rob and the trio raced outside. Caroline stepped into the living room to admire the Christmas tree. The main Christmas tree, anyway — every year Mother seemed to up the ante in the Christmas tree department. This year she'd affixed tiny ones festooned with gold glitter to the tank tops of all the downstairs toilets.

"Lovely," Caroline said, gazing around the room as she paused by the tree, still holding her stack of presents.

I was opening my mouth to say something offhand, like "well, of course" or "as usual" and felt suddenly guilty. The room *was* lovely. Watching Caroline enjoy it brought that home to me, and I made a mental note to say something appreciative about the decor to Mother. I'd long since let her take charge of decorating the entire downstairs of our house. Left to my own devices, I'd probably have done a decent tree and a modest wreath on the door, but that would be about it. I was too busy during the holiday season — and besides, I hadn't inherited the decorating gene.

This year's new addition to the decor was

a wide panel made of evergreen branches braided with red velvet ribbon and matte gold metallic ribbon that went all the way around the walls on top of the crown molding. Initially I was appalled to think how much painstaking hand labor must have gone into it — but then I found out that Mother had started hiring the residents of the Caerphilly Women's Shelter to do such handiwork, at generous rates that helped them build nest eggs for starting their new lives much sooner. Now when I looked up at the beautiful, intricate woven branches, one of my favorite quotes from *A Christmas Carol* tended to pop into my mind: "At this festive season of the year, it is more than usually desirable that we should make some slight provision for the poor and destitute. . . ."

And all Mother's other holiday favorites were back. Intricate blown glass ornaments catching the light in all the windows — but high up, where they'd have better odds of escaping the roughhousing that was sure to take place when cousins and friends came over to visit Josh and Jamie. Multiple trees — the music-themed one in the front hall, the food-themed one in the dining room. Even a literary-themed one in our library — who knew there were so many book-shaped

Christmas ornaments in existence?

"Should we put all these under the tree?" Rob and the boys were back, each having to peer around a stack of presents higher than his head.

"Or as close as you can get them," I said. "Caroline, just give me a few minutes to change into something presentable and we can take off."

"I'm going to run out and see Rose Noire," Caroline said. "I'm dying to see her new herb-drying shed."

I resigned myself to the possibility that Caroline might not be accompanying me to see Harvey the Hoarder. I didn't share Rose Noire's fascination with all things New Age, but even so I enjoyed visiting the herb-drying shed — which also doubled as a yoga studio and meditation room and housed her collection of crystals and other minerals. Maybe —

"Mom?" Jamie looked worried about something. Josh was frowning, too. Since the twins, in spite of being boon companions, usually worked hard on doing everything differently from each other, something serious must be going on. "Aunt Caroline brought a lot of presents."

I glanced over to the tree. Yes, the present stash was looking much more robust.

To make room for the new additions, they'd had to relocate the dogs' Christmas beds, elegant red velvet cushions with green-and-gold bows that Mother had set on either side of the fire. Tinkerbell, my brother's Irish wolfhound, had already adjusted to her new location and was dozing contentedly. Spike, our eight-and-a-half-pound fur ball, was sniffing at the new presents and uttering the occasional growl of suspicion and resentment.

"There are a lot of people here," I said.

"But she brought at least two for me," Josh said. "And probably two for Jamie."

"And she gives good presents," Jamie added.

"We need to think of something really good for her." Josh folded his arms as if expecting me to protest.

I stifled a sigh. It was nice that they'd become focused on giving in addition to receiving presents. I just wished they'd relax a little about picking their outgoing presents. We'd been agonizing over what to give various friends and family members since before Halloween.

"Good idea," I said aloud. "I'll pick her brain and see if I can come up with any suggestions while we're driving around."

"Don't forget," Josh said. "We need those

suggestions."

They dashed upstairs again, still looking worried.

"Going someplace interesting?" My grandmother Cordelia strode in. Her tall, imposing figure was clad in jeans, a plaid flannel shirt, and disreputable sneakers. Work clothes, obviously.

"What if I told you I was having tea with the president of the garden club?" I asked.

"Then I'd wish you joy of it and look around for someone who's doing something that's either useful or enjoyable. But you don't look dressed for a tea party. Got any Helping Hands projects going? I'm dressed for that."

I filled her in on Harvey the Hoarder, and as I could have predicted, she immediately volunteered to help out.

"Much more my cup of tea than the garden club," she said. "I can't wait to get this Harvey decluttered and organized."

"Remember, we have to go gently," I said. "He hasn't even agreed yet to let us help him."

"We'll charm him into it."

When we got to my car, I shouted for Caroline, who came running over to join the party. The two of them hadn't seen each other in some weeks, so they chatted happily, catching up. Which was fine with me, since it left me free to think about how to tackle Mr. Dunlop.

Although I suspected they hadn't forgotten the purpose of our trip.

"Probably a good thing Randall has you to deal with this Harvey the Hoarder character," Caroline said at one point during our drive. "After all, you have experience dealing with hoarded houses."

"Only one." I hoped that didn't sound too curt, but I wasn't fond of remembering that experience. Mrs. Edwina Sprocket, the previous owner of our beloved house, had been a hoarder, and we'd bought the house as is — meaning we, rather than her surviving family, had to deal with the cleanout.

"Yes, but your mother has told us all about how well you dealt with it." Cordelia nodded with approval. "She said you were wonderfully efficient."

"Maybe," I said. "But even a house chock-full of stuff can only be so bad. We just had to deal with the stuff — not with Mrs. Sprocket fighting tooth and nail to hang on to every bit of junk."

"True." Cordelia set her jaw. "But however bad it is, we'll deal with it."

"Absolutely!" Caroline chimed in. "Do you know if it's a big house?"

"I don't think so," I said. "The neighborhood runs to small lots. And small houses, for the most part. But I'm afraid the only times I was there before, I was focused on the yard. Anyway, we'll see in a minute — we're almost there."

Harvey Dunlop's house was on Beau Street — which local wags preferred to call The Street Formerly Known as Beauregard. Several years ago, after much debate, the town council had agreed to rechristen the half-dozen streets in town that carried the names of Confederate luminaries — but they hadn't yet agreed on what the new names would be. Eventually, Randall had sent two of his workmen around with buckets of paint to give the streets in question provisional new names. In addition to the Beauregard to Beau change, Jeb Stuart Street had become Stuart Street easily enough, and Forrest Lane — named after Nathan Bedford Forrest — had only taken a small stroke of the paint brush to become Forest Lane. Jefferson Davis Avenue had become Davis Avenue, since we already had a Jefferson Street. Robert E. Lee Street had become L Street, which was no doubt highly confusing to tourists who expected to find K and M Streets nearby. The only real problem had arisen when the two workmen nearly came to blows over how to modify Stonewall Jackson Street. They finally agreed to disagree, which was why all the signs along the northern side of the road in question identified it as Stone Street, while across the way on the southern side it had become Jackson Street. People eventually got used to it. Locals knew where they were going anyway, and luckily it wasn't a street most tourists would ever need to find.

Strange that I remembered so little about Mr. Dunlop's house from the time Randall and I had browbeaten him into cleaning up his yard — was it only a year and a half ago? No, come to think of it, more likely two and a half. I'd look it up later. The yard had been filled with pots and planters — some broken, some intact but empty, and others nourishing healthy stands of ragweed, stinging nettles, poison ivy, purple loosestrife, crabgrass, jimson weed, and who knows how many other undesirable bits of greenery. We even found a small stand of kudzu near the house, getting ready to make its play for world domination. He also had several defunct cars on cinder blocks in various parts of the yard, along with enough scattered car parts to assemble at least another half-dozen rusty vehicles. He was apparently fond of birdbaths and garden statuary — the more battered or incomplete the better — beehives, fish tanks, well-weathered lumber, and random bits of plumbing gear. He'd tried to screen the whole thing from neighbors and passersby by planting a tall boxwood hedge, but apparently his green thumb only worked on weeds. A lot of the boxwoods had died and been replaced at random intervals with smaller boxwoods, and last I'd seen it many of the surviving ones didn't look as if they planned to hang on much longer. If you asked me, the wildly variable boxwoods added another whole level of chaos and disorganization that far outweighed any contribution they made toward screening the mess.

Horrible as his yard had been, according to him, every single object in it was something he wanted to keep. A few things he was planning to use "one of these days," or at least might need at some future date. Most of the junk items were, according to him, either valuable heirlooms or family mementos of great sentimental value.

I'd finally gotten him to agree to the cleanup by offering to give him an itemized receipt for every single thing we hauled to the dump, plus a signed promise from

Randall that if at any time he actually did need any of it — or found a buyer for it — Randall would haul it back from the dump himself. There were rumors that in the months following the cleanup he'd gone up to the dump a time or two to peer through the chain-link fence at his stuff, but Randall hadn't gotten any requests to haul any of it back. Maybe that boded well for cleaning out the inside of his house.

Well, I could hope.

And then again, maybe he hadn't called to have anything brought back because he'd managed to reclutter his yard again all by himself.

As we drew near the house, I could see that the hedges were, if possible, even more bedraggled and unhealthy than I remembered. But at least the yard was still mainly clear. He'd started a new and much smaller collection of weeds and flowerpots, but apart from that it didn't look too bad.

The house, on the other hand, was a disaster. Had it been that bad a couple of years ago? Surely I'd have remembered if it had been. Maybe it had taken a lot of damage from this fall's storms.

Or maybe we'd been so focused on the yard that we'd turned a blind eye to how awful the house was.

At least it was relatively small: a modest frame bungalow with wide front porch running its entire length and a matching detached one-car garage to the right and a little behind the main house. I couldn't tell if the siding had originally been painted white or pale gray. It was all gray now; peeling paint and weathered wood underneath. The roof was more blue tarp than shingle. The porch listed downhill toward the left side of the house, and I hoped there was something to hold the porch roof up other than the six dilapidated pillars I could see. It looked as if Mr. Dunlop was trying to keep the porch clear, or at least methodically organized — there was actually a wicker rocking chair that, unlike every other possible seat within sight, was not filled with pillows, empty flowerpots, deceased houseplants, empty popcorn tins, small garden tools, milk crates of recyclables, and who knows what else. But all of it was neatly stacked, as if he hoped that with enough organization he could ward off the neighbors' complaints.

Most of the windows had at least one pane of glass that was cracked or replaced with plywood. And inside, I could see venetian blinds tightly closed, no doubt to shield the mess inside from prying eyes.

"This one's going to be a big project," Cordelia remarked.

I parked in front of the cracked concrete walkway that led to the porch. We all got out and stood for a few moments, looking at the house.

"At least it's one story," Caroline said.

"There could be a basement," Cordelia countered.

I spotted a flicker of movement in the house to the left of Mr. Dunlop's. A curtain in one of the front windows opened a crack and I saw first a face and then the twin lenses of a pair of binoculars as one of Mr. Dunlop's neighbors inspected us.

The front door of the house to the right opened and a portly man in a plaid jacket came out and stared at us with undisguised curiosity.

"Excuse me."

CHAPTER 3

We turned to see that someone had come up behind us, a tall, thin man in a baggy gray suit and a fussy little blue bow tie. He strode forward with an awkward, jerky gait and planted himself between us and Mr. Dunlop's house.

Where had he come from? And why was he blocking our path?

"What are you doing here?" He had folded his arms and was frowning at us. Combined with his bad posture and stick-thin, angular shape, the gesture made me think of a praying mantis. A very large praying mantis that had been carelessly transformed into human shape by a lazy or incompetent wizard.

"I could ask you the same thing," I said. "I'm with the county."

Sometimes saying that impressed people. Apparently this was one of those times. The man's face brightened and he rubbed his hands together.

31

"Are you here from Adult Protective Services?" He sounded eager.

"From the mayor's office." I reached into my purse, pulled out one of my business cards — not the blacksmith one, but the one that proclaimed me as Special Assistant to the Mayor — and handed it to him.

His face brightened even more.

"Morris Haverhill," he said, offering me his hand. "Representing the family. Harvey's my cousin."

We all shook his hand solemnly. His hand was bony and oddly dry.

"I'm glad to see the county's finally taking this seriously," Mr. Haverhill said. "Want me to brief you before we go in?"

Behind Haverhill I could see a small flicker at one of the venetian blinds in Mr. Dunlop's house. He was watching us: Mr. Dunlop, who was protective of his property to the point of paranoia. And I had the sneaking feeling that if he liked and trusted his relatives, Mr. Haverhill would be inside, not out here lurking on the sidewalk. Entering in Mr. Haverhill's company might not go over all that well.

I arranged my face in a stern expression.

"Mr. Haverhill, I appreciate your willingness to help," I said. "But I'm afraid I'll have to insist that you stay out here. In fact, it would be much better if you could go home and leave this to us."

"Nonsense! How can you expect —"

"Mr. Haverhill, I have previous experience with Mr. Dunlop," I said. "Not to mention extensive experience with hoarding situations."

To my relief, neither Caroline nor Cordelia laughed. In fact, they nodded and mirrored my stern expression.

"In situations like these, the hoarder often comes to resent the very friends and family members who are trying to help them," I said in the most solemn tone I could manage. "When that happens, the best thing is to back off and bring in the authorities — which you've done. So now you need to step away and let us do our job."

"It's the best thing, believe me," Cordelia said.

Caroline merely nodded emphatically.

"But I need to — I want to help."

"And you can help," I said. "It's a big job, and we'll need all the help we can get. But for right now, the best way you can help is to let us get on with our job."

It must have sounded plausible — and reassuring. His eyes flicked back and forth, studying our faces briefly. Then he blew out a long breath.

"Well, you're the experts. Just keep me informed, will you? We want to do anything we can to help out poor old Harvey."

He handed me a business card, which I tucked in my pocket without even looking at it. Not that I wasn't curious, but I was playing to an audience of one right now — Mr. Dunlop.

Caroline, Cordelia, and I watched while Haverhill went back across the street where several cars were parked. He got into the nearest one, a light blue sedan. And then he sat there, watching us.

"Troublemaker, if you ask me," Caroline said. "We'll need to keep our eye on him."

I wasn't sure what trouble Haverhill could cause, but I agreed with her assessment. So I nodded, and headed up the driveway toward Mr. Dunlop's front door. And then, realizing how treacherous the sidewalk was, with its broken concrete slabs and places where tree roots were heaving slabs into the air, I hurried back to take Cordelia's arm and keep an eye on Caroline, to make sure we all got safely to the door.

The porch steps were unsteady, and several porch boards were alarmingly spongy. I wasn't keen on standing under that dramatically slanting porch roof, but there was no way around it. A paper Christmas wreath was taped to his door — a very familiar-looking wreath, since I could tell it had been cut out of one of the gaily printed bags that the Caerphilly Market used in place of plain brown paper during the holiday season.

I reached out to ring the doorbell, then noticed that it seemed to have been rewired on the outside, with an old and rather frayed power cord that ran up to the top of the doorframe, then over to disappear inside the nearest window. The whole jerry-rigged contraption looked like an accidental electrocution waiting to happen.

I looked around, picked up a fallen stick, and pushed the doorbell with that.

I could hear a melodious "ding-dong" inside.

Nothing else happened.

I rang twice more before finally getting a reaction.

The section of wood on which the door knocker rested suddenly swung out, revealing a hole about two inches wide by three tall. A watery blue eye appeared in the opening and then disappeared.

"Go away!"

I could see fingers groping toward a leather strap attached to the trapdoor. Before he could pull it closed, I grabbed the door knocker and held on tight.

"Mr. Dunlop! It's Meg Langslow."

He gave up trying to grab the strap but he didn't answer.

"Remember me? A while back Randall Shiffley and I helped you get your yard in shape."

"And now you're back for the rest of my stuff, I suppose."

I couldn't exactly argue with that.

"Mr. Dunlop, it's really cold out here, and it's kind of hard shouting through that little hole in the door. Why don't you let us in so we can talk more comfortably?"

"Who's that with you? Did you bring the cops to strong-arm me?" His tone reminded me of Spike, who barked all the louder when something frightened him.

"This is my grandmother, Cordelia Mason." I stepped aside so Cordelia could smile at the trapdoor.

"And this is a friend of ours, Caroline Willner."

Caroline followed Cordelia's example. And they were both on their best behavior, trying to look like harmless little old ladies.

"We just want to talk to you," I said, returning to my place in front of the peephole.

At first I didn't think he was going to react.

"Just you," he said. "If the o— If the ladies are cold, they can wait in the car. And you're not coming in here — back away and I'll come out."

Caroline, Cordelia, and I retreated to stand by the car. Then the door opened, hesitantly. Mr. Dunlop stepped out and then immediately turned to lock the door behind him.

He wasn't very tall, and he seemed even shorter, thanks to his stooped posture. Back when we'd cleaned up his yard, I'd had some reason to look him up in the town records. He'd been forty-seven then, so he'd be forty-nine now, or maybe fifty. But he looked — well, not exactly older, but a lot more faded than you'd expect from someone his age.

He came down the walkway toward us, favoring his right leg slightly, and stopped a few feet away from us.

"I want to show you something." He turned and limped along the inside of the hedge until he reached the gravel driveway, then led the way not to the garage door but around the corner to the smaller side door. He stopped beside the door and pointed to the doorknob. That and the dead bolt above it were both bright, shiny, and probably decades newer than anything else on his property.

Caroline and Cordelia had decided to ignore the "just you" part, and were following us, though at a discreet distance.

"I put that in after what they did to me last fall," he said. "Before, I only had a padlock on the door. They just pried it right off."

"Oh, dear." I wasn't sure where this was headed, but I didn't think a sympathetic attitude would hurt.

He pulled a key ring out of his pocket, unlocked the door, flung it open, and gestured as if to invite us to enter.

"Look at it!" His voice shook with . . . rage? Pain? Something, anyway.

I braced myself and stepped in.

It wasn't cluttered.

I was so surprised that I stopped in the doorway, and Cordelia bumped into me.

"Sorry!" she said.

"My fault," I said as I stepped aside to let her and Caroline enter.

We gazed around at the interior of the garage, collectively puzzled. It wasn't empty. He had parked his car in it, which was more than a lot of people could manage. Compared to the house — well, at least the porch, which was the only part we'd seen — it was downright minimalist. There were more tools hanging on the walls than seemed quite necessary, but they were all hanging on the walls. One corner held a dusty clump of patio furniture that didn't look as if it had seen the light of day in years. The bags of grass seed and fertilizer had cobwebs on them. But it mostly looked like a perfectly normal garage. The only odd part was that he'd rigged up some extra storage overhead, hanging random things from the joists with hooks or ropes and storing larger things by balancing them across the joists. I spotted a moose head, a brass spittoon, a sled, a couple of crab pots, and yes, an oversized kitchen sink. But even the overhead storage area fell short of my definition of cluttered.

"You see!" Mr. Dunlop was clearly feeling outraged about something.

"I'm not really sure I understand," I said. "What happened?"

"They broke in while I wasn't home and took things."

"Who broke in?" I asked. "And what did they take?"

"My so-called loved ones." His voice was hard. "My three greedy cousins. And the neighbors helped them. They broke in and took everything except what you see here!"

I had to bite my tongue to keep from saying "How nice of them!"

"I had a carousel horse that my great-grandfather made, that I was going to restore." He pointed to an empty corner. "And three vintage pinball machines from my uncle's old grill that only needed a little tinkering to make them work again." He pointed to another corner. "A Victorian fainting couch that belonged to my grandmother. It only needed new upholstery. And her treadle sewing machine, which only needed a little work to make it good as new."

As he tallied his lost treasures, he pointed to various parts of the garage, and I realized that if I wasn't careful I could start visualizing the garage as it had been, with all his tattered treasures beginning to loom up around me, filling the open space with their bulk and weight and solid presence.

I shook myself and focused back on the matter at hand.

"What did they do with all of it?" I asked.

"A good question," he said. "They claim they donated some of it and took the rest to the dump. But I never found any of it. Not in any of the local dumps, and not at any of the nearby charities. I'm pretty sure they sold it all and kept the profits. Probably hauled it all to antique shops out of state and sold it. I gave up looking. I had my hands full keeping them from breaking into the house."

"Why didn't you report them?" Cordelia asked. "Charge them with trespassing and theft."

"I figured the authorities would side with them." Mr. Dunlop looked sullen. "Considering that everyone in the county has been trying to make me get rid of my possessions for years now."

"I'm not here to make you get rid of your possessions," I said. "I'm here to figure out how we can get everyone off your back — your relatives, your neighbors, the building inspector, and Adult Protective Services. It's probably going to mean giving up some of your stuff — but not everything. And what you give up should be your choice."

He looked uncertain.

"You should listen to her," Cordelia said.

"Because if you don't," Caroline added. "Next thing you know the relatives will show up with a dumpster and haul you off in a straightjacket."

Mr. Dunlop sighed.

"Let's go up to the house," he said. "Cold out here."

CHAPTER 4

Mr. Dunlop led the way out of the garage, stopping to relock both door locks, and then headed for the door. Morris Haverhill was still sitting in his car across the road. The neighbor on the right had gone in from his front porch, but the binoculars were still visible in the front window of the house on the left.

As Mr. Dunlop fumbled with the front door lock, I braced myself. At least it wasn't summer, I reminded myself. It probably wouldn't smell that much — right?

"I didn't pick up," Mr. Dunlop said as he swung the door open. "Wasn't expecting company."

To my relief, it only smelled a little musty. But it was every bit as cluttered as I'd expected, and I was immediately sorry we hadn't just continued our conversation in the garage, even if it wasn't heated.

Most of the floor space in the living room

was completely filled with stuff. The couch was piled high, except for a Mr. Dunlop-sized space at one end. He probably sat there to watch the television that was perched near the ceiling, atop a rather unstable-looking pile of cardboard boxes. I'd never have described myself as claustrophobic, but I could feel the surroundings starting to make me anxious. It wasn't just the piles and piles of stuff — the ceiling itself seemed lower than usual — or was that just an optical illusion because of all the places where the clutter was actually jammed up against it?

In front of us, a path led to a hallway that had been narrow even before he'd begun piling books and boxes along both sides of it. He led us to the left, down the other path, into a galley kitchen that was at least a little less overwhelmingly cluttered than the living room.

Clearly Mr. Dunlop didn't have much company. There was a small area on the kitchen table, a little clearing in the clutter, that contained only the remains of his breakfast. The rest of the table was piled two or three feet high with boxes, books, magazines, and newspapers. A relatively new-looking laptop perched atop one of the piles, and a white-painted wooden chair sat in front of the clear spot.

"I only just finished breakfast," he said, hurrying to sweep the dishes off the table and add them to the mountain of older dirty dishes in the sink. He seemed relieved when he'd done that, as if he'd restored his kitchen to company-ready condition.

It took a little bit of rearranging, but Mr. Dunlop managed to find three more chairs, and clear a space for them around his kitchen table. He put the kettle on to boil and scurried around to find enough clean teacups. Cordelia and Caroline and I all sat down and tried to pretend we weren't looking around and inventorying stuff — or, for that matter, assessing whether there was anything in the stacks looming over us that was precariously balanced and might fall down and brain us.

I was a little dubious about drinking Mr. Dunlop's tea, but I reminded myself that boiling water would probably kill most of the nasties that might be in it. We made small talk for a few minutes, mostly about whether or not there was any chance of having a white Christmas.

But after a while, Mr. Dunlop set down his teacup and looked as if he were bracing himself.

"Look — I know I have too much stuff. I

know I need to pare it down. But I want to do it myself. In my own way. I'm the only one who understands what most of these things are worth, or what sentimental value they have to me. This, for example."

He patted the kitchen table, which was made of a heavy slab of marble about an inch thick and thirty inches square, white with pale gray veins, laid atop an X-shaped wooden base. There were rough holes in all four corners of the slab, as if someone had rudely drilled through it, and one corner was broken off.

"I know it doesn't look like much," he said.

"Nice piece of marble," Caroline said. "And the contrast between the polished top and the rough-hewn parts is interesting."

"Yes, isn't it?" Mr. Dunlop's face lit up. "But it's so much more than that if you know where it came from — what it stands for. My family used to own a bank."

"Here in Caerphilly?" I didn't recall hearing of any banks in town other than the First National Bank of Caerphilly, and even that I only knew of from learning about local history — it had been bought by one of the big regional banks years before I'd come to town.

"Yes — The Farmers and Mechanics Bank

of Caerphilly. Of course, it was a long time ago. Before I was born. I'm not sure when it was founded — sometime in the eighteen hundreds. And closed in the nineteen thirties, during the Depression. Anyway — that piece of marble — it was part of the bank's counters. Just imagine what tales it could tell!"

He beamed at the marble as if he expected it to begin dictating its life history at any moment.

"Anyway, it's part of my family history. Part of the town's history. And that's only one of the treasures I have — treasures that might get thrown away if someone else just came in to clear stuff out. That's why I have to be the one to organize my things."

"I understand," I said. "The problem is that for a variety of reasons you haven't been getting that organizing done, and now you're in a crisis. Your neighbors are complaining to the county that you're blighting the neighborhood, your family —"

"Are trying to get me committed." He nodded. "Oh, don't try to deny it — Adult Protective Services is the foot in the door that leads to the loony bin."

I wasn't going to argue with him.

"Then there's the most urgent problem of all," I went on. "This house is about to fall down around your ears. A good lawyer could keep your neighbors and relatives and the county at bay for a good long time, but you need to do something to put this place back together again."

As if to emphasize my words, a small piece of plaster fell out of the ceiling and landed in Mr. Dunlop's teacup. He fished it out matter-of-factly and took a sip. Then he closed his eyes and nodded slightly.

"We can help you with that," I said. "We've got this program — Helping Hands for the Holidays."

"I've heard of it," he said. "You fixed Jeb Wilson's furnace."

Actually, we'd replaced Jeb Wilson's furnace, and his water heater besides. But he was a proud old man living on a fixed income, and we didn't want to embarrass him, so for public consumption, we'd just done minor repairs to the furnace.

"We can fix your place up, too," I said. "But we can't do it with your stuff in here. We need to do something about the stuff before the repair crew comes in."

"It sounds like a great deal," he said. "Can't you just give me a few weeks to get things organized? I'm sure I can rearrange stuff so the workmen would have enough access."

"Mr. Dunlop, I have a better idea." Cordelia set her teacup on the table with an air that suggested we'd spent far too much time on social niceties and should get down to business. "Let us help you with your stuff. Not getting rid of it," she added quickly, seeing him open his mouth to protest. "Moving it — temporarily. I'm sure Meg can find a place — I bet she can get the Spare Attic to donate a storage unit for the short time it would take to do the repairs." She glanced around and frowned slightly. "Maybe a couple of units. We help you pack up everything. We move it all to the storage unit. The Helping Hands crew comes in and fixes everything up — it will go so much faster if the place is empty. And then we can help you move your stuff back in. If you find there's some of it you don't want to bring back, we'll help you sell it or donate it or recycle it or whatever you want. But if you want every stick of it brought back here, that's what we'll do."

He actually looked as if he was considering it.

It was a crazy idea. And not very practical, either. The Spare Attic, a converted textile factory, was Caerphilly's only off-site storage business, and I knew people who had been on the waiting list there for years.

And even if we could find a space there, the other customers would probably mutiny when they heard about it, no matter how many precautions we took to ensure that we didn't move any insects or rodents along with Mr. Dunlop's stuff.

But then an idea struck me. Randall Shiffley had recently bought up an empty building in town that had once housed a furniture store. He hadn't yet figured out what to do with it — his main reason for buying it was to make sure no sneaky chain stores from outside the county got their hands on it and came barging in to put the local shops out of business. It was a free-standing building, so we were less likely to get complaints about pests — and if need be we could fumigate the whole place. Randall probably wouldn't mind, or if he did — well, he was the one who'd stuck me with handling Mr. Dunlop and his hoard.

"I have it," I said. "We can move your stuff into the vacant Caerphilly Furniture World building. I'm sure you've seen it — it's huge. You'll have plenty of room to spread your things out and sort them properly. If there's stuff that needs to be repaired or refinished, there's space to do that on-site, and we can probably find experts to help out. If there's stuff you've been meaning to sell, we can help you do that, too. It'll be great. And we can ask Ms. Ellie Draper from the library to help you start writing up the history of your valuable items, so the information won't get lost when you're no longer around to bear witness."

Mr. Dunlop looked slightly wary. But only slightly.

"You're hoping once you get all my stuff out of here you can talk me out of most of it," he said.

"Yes." I didn't think lying would work. "Definitely. But *talk* you out of it. Not grab it and stuff it in the dumpster when you're not around. We'll respect your stuff — I promise."

We sat there for what seemed like an eternity, looking at him. Finally he lifted his chin as if in determination.

"I'll do it. When were you thinking of starting?"

"I can get some volunteers over here by noon," I said.

"You've got one volunteer already," Cordelia said.

"And I can come back a little later," Caroline said. "I just need to put on some work clothes."

"Oh, my." Mr. Dunlop looked slightly stunned. He'd probably been hoping for at least a few days' reprieve.

"No time like the present," I said. "The sooner we act, the sooner you can thumb your nose at those annoying relatives and neighbors. Start packing a suitcase. And think about whether you want to sleep at the furniture store with your stuff or if you'd like me to find you a room at a nearby bed-and-breakfast. Because everything goes over to the store, as soon as we can pack it up, and this place will be a construction zone."

"Okay." He sounded a little shaky, and it was probably a good idea for Cordelia to stay and keep him feeling positive about the project.

"Don't worry," I said. "We'll get you through this."

"More tea?" Cordelia asked, lifting the teapot.

By the time I left, Cordelia had pulled out pencil and paper and was taking notes as Mr. Dunlop retold the story of the family bank in greater detail.

As soon as I was back on the crumbling front walk, I pulled out my phone. I had a lot to organize.

"I'm going to check around the foundation and out in the yard for signs of rodent activity," Caroline said. "Only take a few minutes."

I nodded. I was already calling Randall.

"How are things over at Mr. Dunlop's?" he asked.

"So far so good," I said. "You know that building you bought this summer? The old furniture store? You got any plans for it yet?"

"Not really," he said. "I assume you're asking because you do?"

"We're going to put Mr. Dunlop's stuff in it while the Helping Hands volunteers fix up his house."

Randall was briefly silent while he digested the idea.

"O-kay," he said finally. "Are you thinking it will go the way it did with his yard, and he won't want any of it back?"

"I expect it won't be nearly as easy," I said. "Because obviously he will need some of his stuff back. Furniture. Appliances. Dishes. But maybe when he sees the house all clean and repaired and empty he'll have a change of heart and be reasonable about how much he brings back. And if not, maybe we can find a therapist who specializes in OCD and hoarding to help him. But even if all we do is clean up his stuff, arrange it neatly and put it all back, he'll still be better off without the building inspector breathing down his neck."

"Agreed. Okay — what do you need from

52

me, apart from the keys to the furniture store?"

"Moving boxes. And the use of a truck. And we need it yesterday — we want to start before he changes his mind."

"I'm on it. And I should probably send Eastman over to check things out."

"Eastman?" One of the enormous Shiffley clan, no doubt, but I couldn't place him offhand.

"He just took over running Shiffley Pest Control last month, when his daddy retired."

"Good idea." I shuddered slightly. "Who knows what critters are sharing quarters with Mr. Dunlop?"

"Nothing major, unless it's changed recently. I've had Eastman out there regularly — ever since Ham Brimley next door to him began complaining about rats."

"Are there rats?" I wasn't looking forward to finding out if Caroline's matter-of-fact attitude toward rats survived a personal encounter.

"No rats anymore, and it wasn't Harvey's fault they were in the neighborhood in the first place. Seems Brimley was just throwing every kind of trash imaginable in his backyard and calling it a compost pile. Whole colony of rats had moved in. Eastman and his daddy took care of that this last spring, and they've been keeping their eyes on the place ever since."

"Is Ham Brimley the neighbor on the left or the right?"

"Right, I think. Garage side, whichever that is."

"That would be the right side." I glanced over at where the portly man — presumably Mr. Brimley — was back on his porch, glaring at me.

"Other side's Mrs. Gudgeon, who could single-handedly keep the nine-one-one line afloat if the rest of the county gave up using it," Randall said. "Keep an eye on Brimley."

"Is he dangerous? Because I was going to leave Cordelia out here to keep Mr. Dunlop on task. If there's any danger —"

"Just a blowhard, as far as I can see. But he could be part of the bunch who broke into Dunlop's garage while he was in the hospital with his gallbladder and cleaned out a bunch of his stuff."

"Mr. Dunlop mentioned that," I said. "He thinks his relatives were also involved."

"Wouldn't put it past them, either. I'd keep my eye on all of them."

"I plan to," I said. "And I also plan to keep them out of Mr. Dunlop's house."

"Good," he said.

With that we signed off. I was feeling chilled and turned to go back to my car. As I was reaching for the door handle, I heard a voice behind me — too close.

"You're not condemning the house, are you?"

CHAPTER 5

I started, and turned to find that Morris Haverhill had returned.

"No, we haven't condemned the house, Mr. Haverhill." I refrained from explaining that Randall had done his best to assure the building inspector that if he just gave us a little more time we'd have the house up to code. "I already told you —"

I suddenly realized that this wasn't Morris Haverhill — Morris was still sitting in his car, scowling at us. But the man in front of me was clearly a Haverhill. He wore a faded blue suit rather than a gray one, and his bow tie was navy rather than red, but apart from that I'd have had a hard time figuring out which was which if they were standing side by side.

"You told my brother." His voice suggested that he didn't like being mistaken for Morris. "I'm Ernest Haverhill." He held out his hand, which proved to be as dry and bony as his brother's.

"Sorry," I said. "As I told your brother, we're here to declutter the house, and then a crew will come in to fix it up. It hasn't been condemned yet, and if we can get our work done, it won't have to be."

"Well, that's not very satisfactory," he said. "When will you know?"

Not very satisfactory? I considered and rejected several snarky replies.

"That depends on what the building inspector finds when he gets here," I said finally. "I'm sure your cousin can keep you posted."

"I'm sure he could, but he won't," Ernest said. "Just hides in his house. Won't even answer the phone."

He glared at me as if this was my fault. I thought of pointing out that if his cousin refused to talk to him, maybe trying to pry information out of me was a little inappropriate. But I sensed that was a subtlety that would be lost on him.

"Let's see how it goes, shall we?" I accompanied this nonanswer with a bland smile. Realizing he wasn't going to get any information out of me, he made a "hmph" noise, turned away, and crossed the street to get in one of the cars parked there. Not the one his brother Morris was sitting in —

the one at the other end of the little line. There appeared to be a tall figure in the middle car — did they travel in threes, like the ghosts in Dickens's *A Christmas Carol*? And would I soon be meeting the Haverhill yet to come?

I got into my car and dialed Mother. When her phone went to voicemail, I called Robyn Smith — who as rector of Trinity Episcopal was one of the main instigators of Helping Hands for the Holidays.

"Meg! Your mother and I were just talking about you!" she said, once we'd exchanged Christmas wishes.

"Mother's there with you — good. I have a lot of work for both of you."

I filled them in on our latest project and then laid out my requests: willing bodies to pack Mr. Dunlop's stuff. Food and beverages to fuel the bodies.

"We can manage that," Robyn said. "Your mother wants to know if she should come over to help out."

"Good heavens, no," I said. "If she even caught a glimpse of this place she'd probably have to take to her bed with a cold compress over her forehead. Remind her that we're keeping our eyes out for rats and cockroaches, and encourage her to stay put and recruit volunteers."

"Roger."

"And see if you can get at least one volunteer who's also a deputy," I said. "Cousin Horace might be willing. Or Randall's cousin Vern. Or Aida Butler."

"That could be tough," Robyn said. "Last I heard, the chief had two officers out — Sammy Wendell with his broken leg, and poor Bethany in California, not knowing if her mother will pull through or not."

"Three actually," I said. "Four if you count civilian staff." Which meant I had to fill her in, since she hadn't heard about George, the desk clerk, having his appendix out late Sunday night, or the fact that Dad had sent another officer to the hospital with concussion — a casualty of the same obstreperous drunk-and-disorderly prisoner who was responsible for Sammy's broken leg.

"I see I should add a few hospital visits to my agenda," she said. "Getting back to your project — why do you want a deputy — are you expecting some kind of trouble?"

"I don't know. Randall says there's bad blood here." I glanced around. The binoculars were still trained on me from the house on the left. The Haverhills' cars were still parked across the street from me. Mr. Brimley had left his porch and come down to the street. In fact, he was now crossing the road and approaching one of the cars. Ernest's. "I have this creepy feeling of being watched by unsympathetic eyes," I said. Ernest Haverhill had rolled down his window, and he and Brimley were talking. They were both frowning — but were they frowning at each other, or at Mr. Dunlop's house? "And some of those eyes belong to Mr. Dunlop's relatives and neighbors," I continued to Robyn. "According to him, they've already done a vigilante decluttering on his garage and made off with a lot of valuable antiques."

"Does he actually have any valuable antiques?" Robyn asked. "I tried to make a pastoral call a couple of times — not that he's ever come to services since I've been here, but we have a bunch of Dunlops buried out in the Trinity churchyard that I'm pretty sure are his kin, so I thought I should try. The one time he let me in I couldn't see anything but rubbish."

"Who knows what's buried beneath the rubbish?" I asked. "Besides, what matters is that he *thinks* he has a house full of treasures. What if the neighbors or the relatives try to take advantage of our being here to barge in again and start throwing his stuff away? That could torpedo the whole thing."

"Somehow I think you and Cordelia could handle them." Robyn chuckled. "But yes, it would be nice to have someone who can take official action if necessary. I'll see what we can arrange."

"Thanks." We hung up, and I continued to watch Brimley and Ernest Haverhill. Now Morris Haverhill had gotten out of his car and was walking in my direction. No, not in my direction. He stayed on the opposite side of the street until he was well past my car. Then he crossed the road and hiked up the driveway of Mr. Dunlop's left-hand neighbors. I kept expecting the middle car, the one between Morris's blue sedan and Ernest's silver one, to open and reveal its third Haverhill, but it remained closed and motionless. Its windshield reflected the sun and prevented me from seeing if there was anyone inside.

I started when Caroline opened the passenger door.

"No sign of rodents," she said. "Let's go run these errands of yours so we can get back here and dig in as soon as possible."

"Good idea," I said.

But I kept checking the rearview mirror as I drove away, seeing the Haverhills and Mr. Brimley and Mrs. Gudgeon, the lady of the binoculars, all staring at Mr. Dunlop's house and talking in what their faces suggested were probably conspiratorial whispers.

"He'll be fine," Caroline said, reading my expression. "Cordelia will keep an eye on things. Your mother and Robyn will have the place crawling with volunteers in no time. And we'll be back before too long. Where to next?"

"The lady who wants the manure, I think."

"Excellent!" She settled comfortably in her seat. "I can't wait to meet the manure lady."

"Her name is Ida Diamandis," I said. "We should probably work on thinking of her as Mrs. Diamandis, not the Manure Lady. Avoid any embarrassing slips of the tongue."

"I will be the soul of discretion. Are you planning to spend all day on these projects?"

"Pretty much," I said. "Because we want to finish as much as possible before Christmas Eve. I, for one, am planning to spend Christmas Eve with family and friends — and not sorting through some packrat's clutter." As I drove, I filled her in on some of the events on my — and probably her — schedule. Tonight was the New Life Baptist Choir's annual Christmas concert for people who, not being Baptists, wouldn't be able to hear them at the actual holiday services. Tomorrow night was the first night of Michael's one-man show of *A Christmas Carol* — demand had been so high that he'd scheduled three more performances between Christmas and New Year's, but we'd bagged a ticket for her to the gala opening performance.

"And Wednesday night, the twenty-third, Mother will be holding a dinner so elegant that Michael and I aren't invited."

"Surely that's not her real reason?" Caroline said. "Because if it's that elegant, I don't think I'd fit in, either."

"Don't worry," I said. "We're actually invited but not going because we're among the chaperones for a middle-school caroling, cookie-baking, and sleepover party at Trinity."

"You're brave souls," she observed.

We were drawing near Mrs. Diamandis's house, so I broke off to concentrate on finding the right address. She lived a little closer to the center of town — although, thank goodness, well out of the touristy part. Still, even here we could catch the strains of a brass band playing "Good King Wenceslas" and see the top of the small Ferris wheel — part of the Christmas Carnival now occupying the town square, which also featured a merry-go-round and several other lesser rides. It was one of Randall's innovations for this year's Christmas in Caerphilly celebration. Like Mother with her decorating, Randall seemed to feel the need every year to top the previous year's holiday excesses. Which wouldn't have bothered me quite so much if they hadn't also felt the need to get me to help them brainstorm and make decisions. And in Randall's case, implement them. I had to give Mother credit — once she'd settled on each year's over-the-top decorating scheme, she went off and found volunteers or hired help to carry it out. All Michael and I had to do was *ooh* and *ah* on cue.

I'd already started trying to find a way to convince them that more was not necessarily better. Maybe toward the end of the season, I could say something like "I think this year everything was absolutely perfect! Let's do it all just the same way next year!"

Would they listen?

Worth trying.

I focused back on finding Mrs. Diamandis's house. And reminding myself not to call her the Manure Lady.

Mrs. Diamandis's house and lot were both small but well maintained. A neat picket fence surrounded the yard, and when I saw what was inside the fence I figured I knew why she wanted manure. The entire yard was full of what probably looked to the uninitiated eye like small dead shrubs peeking out of the tops of tiny tussocks. But since Dad was an obsessive gardener and Mother was a member in good standing of the Caerphilly Garden Club, I recognized the unprepossessing objects as dormant rosebushes, carefully mulched for the winter. There were dozens of them. Except for a narrow path from the front gate to the front door, and a few even narrower paths designed to give access for whoever tended the roses, every square inch of yard was filled with roses. For that matter, so were the side yards, although they were each less than six feet wide, and from what I could see of the backyard it contained more of the same.

In the summer it must have been magical. In fact, I was sure I'd admired it at least once, when I was driving through this part of town. Now, in the dead of winter, all I could think of was how very much work all those roses must take.

"Looks a little OCD to me," Caroline said.

"I suspect being a little OCD actually helps if you're trying to grow roses," I said. "From what I've seen, growing them requires so much work that you've got to be either OCD or just plain crazy to bother with them."

"Is that why you've got so many in your backyard?" she asked. "Who takes care of them?"

"Dad," I said. "And you'll notice they're not exactly in our backyard — they're in their own little compound in the middle of the llama pen. The llamas chase off any deer that try to get at the roses — short of an eight-foot fence, that's the only way Dad's found so far to protect them. Let's go see why Mrs. Diamandis needs the Helping Hands project to manure her roses."

As I headed for Mrs. Diamandis's front door — decorated with a small and slightly faded artificial Christmas wreath — I couldn't help thinking that in summer, even if she'd been careful to plant nothing but thornless roses next to the path, the journey would still be difficult. And if she hadn't — well, it probably discouraged annoying door-to-door solicitors.

I rang the doorbell and we waited. And waited. I was about to try again when I heard rustling noises inside, and the door opened — but only as far as the chain would allow.

"Yes?" came a voice from inside. Mrs. Diamandis's voice — I recognized it from our

66

phone conversation.

At first I thought she was hiding behind the door. Then I glanced down and saw her. She was tiny. And ancient.

I doubted she'd hit the five-foot mark even if she were standing up straight instead of bent almost double over one of those walkers equipped with wheels.

I stooped a little to get closer to her ears, in case she was hard of hearing.

"Mrs. Diamandis? It's Meg Langslow and Caroline Willner from the Helping Hands project. We've come about the manure."

The tiny wizened face brightened.

"Lovely," she said. "Hang on, dearie, till I can undo this blasted chain."

She left the door open an inch or so — enough for me to see that undoing the chain required her to fetch a stepping stool. I almost held my breath until she was safely on the ground again and opened the door the rest of the way.

"Come in," she said.

She shooed us into the living room and apologized that the place was a mess — which it wasn't at all. I wouldn't have been all that worried if I had to eat off her spotless floor, and not just because it was such a contrast with Harvey the Hoarder's hovel. We had a little difficulty persuading her that we didn't need tea. Or coffee. Or hot chocolate. As soon as I could, I brought the conversation around to our reason for being there.

"So I guess I see why you need the manure," I said. "Best thing for roses, I hear."

"I don't know whether I qualify for your program." Her voice was curiously strong and vibrant — over the phone, I'd had no idea she was — how old? Eighty? Ninety? "I don't belong to any of your churches, and I'm not broke, and I'm pretty spry for my age."

"None of that matters," I said. "You just have to be a neighbor with something you're having trouble getting done."

"Well, I certainly meet that qualification." She sighed. "Ever since my husband died, the garden's gone to H-E-double hockey sticks. When he could get around, he'd go off to some farm or other every fall and bring me a nice load of well-aged manure. Even after he stopped being able to drive, he'd arrange to have some delivered. I have no idea how. I made some calls a few years ago. I found places that would be happy to give me as much as I want if I come and shovel it myself — no way that's possible. I couldn't even get there, not having a car. I gave up driving twelve years ago, when I

68

turned eight-five. And there's places that will deliver, but what they charge — highway robbery! I hope Clyde wasn't paying that much for it. And they keep asking me how many yards of manure I need, and I don't even know what that means — do you?"

"I have no idea either," I said. "But my dad will. If I tell him how big your yard is, he can do the calculations. And he can supervise the spreading if you like."

"Well, I can probably manage to do that myself if I take it slowly."

"But unless you really want to, why wear yourself out?" Caroline said.

"We can get it done in an afternoon," I said. "And Dad will love it."

I wasn't kidding. I'd grown up hearing Dad preach about the wonders of manure. Nothing made him happier than manuring someone's garden — well, with the possible exception of manuring his own, which he did every winter. His own, and ours, and anyone else within hauling range.

"That would be lovely," she said. "If it's really not too much trouble."

"Dad will have a blast. All you have to do is invite him back when the blooms come in, so he can see the results."

"He'd be very welcome." She looked pleased. "I confess, I don't get as many visitors as I used to. I'd enjoy the company."

I felt a little guilty about refusing her refreshments. I made a mental note to suggest to Dad that while he was here, he should recruit her to the Garden Club. And for that matter . . .

"May I suggest one more thing?"

She tilted her head slightly and her brow furrowed, as if expecting there to be a catch.

"While the crew's here to spread the manure, I could have one of them lower that door chain for you," I suggested. "It would be a lot safer if you didn't have to climb up on a stool every time you answered the door."

She blinked.

"I never thought of that," she said. "Yes, it would be more convenient."

"I'll make sure one of the manure spreaders is handy at stuff like that, then."

I'd brought an industrial-sized tape measure with me to get the dimensions of her rose beds, but since the whole yard was pretty much a rose bed, I just paced out the width and length of her property and subtracted out the estimated size of her house. Then I texted Dad the dimensions and asked if he could locate some sources of nice organic manure — adding that our llama pen could probably supply at least some of what was needed.

As I could have predicted, he reacted with delirious joy.

"Is there any time that would be inconvenient to have the mulching done?" I asked.

"No," she said. "I don't go out much. The only day I have something on is Wednesday — that's when the Caerphilly Market delivers my groceries. And that only takes half an hour."

"Great," I said. "I'll let you know when we've got it scheduled."

We said our good-byes, and Caroline and I went back to the car.

"Nice lady," she said.

"And amazingly spry for ninety-seven," I said. "I hope I'm half that lively if I live that long."

"So — where to now?"

CHAPTER 6

I glanced at my phone. I had several other errands I could do, but none of them was mission critical. Maybe now was a good time to take Caroline back to the house so she could put on her work clothes and we could get back to Mr. Dunlop's. But before I could suggest it, Caroline spoke up.

"We're not that far from the zoo, are we?" she asked. "Why don't we drop by and see your grandfather?"

I made a quick mental calculation. Yes, we could squeeze in a visit. As a matter of fact, since presumably he wouldn't expect me to build a ramp for the buffalo, declutter the primate habitat, or haul around the manure his many herd animals produced, visiting Grandfather might actually be almost restful.

Although I did find myself wondering if Mrs. Diamandis would be impressed by an exotic manure like the ones Caroline had suggested bringing from her sanctuary. And Grandfather's zoo would be an even more convenient source. Giraffe manure. Zebra manure. Gazelle manure. That had a certain ring to it. I should scribble a reminder in my notebook when I had the chance.

"Sure, we can drop in on him for a little while if you like," I said aloud.

"Lovely." She settled back contentedly in her seat. "I'm looking forward to seeing what he's up to."

"Up to?" The phrase triggered my instinct for danger — or at least extreme annoyance. "Why — is he up to something? Scratch that — he's always up to something. Just what is he up to now?"

"I'm looking forward to finding out myself."

She looked so innocent that I knew she was stonewalling me.

Ah, well. Probably a good idea to find out what Grandfather was up to before he added any more complications to my already crazy holiday schedule.

The zoo's parking lot was nearly full, and if I'd been a tourist, my loathing for crowds would have sent me scurrying for some less popular destination. But thanks to the fact that I often served as Grandfather's chauffeur and general dogsbody, I now possessed a card key that gave me entry to both the staff door and the staff parking lot. Although it was still slow going, making my way through the overflowing lot.

"He's only advertising the Animals of the Bible exhibit," Caroline said. "That's disappointing."

"Disappointing? Why?" Had Caroline suddenly taken against the zoo's popular holiday feature? I'd rather enjoyed doing it with the boys when they were young enough to appreciate it. In addition to informative signs at each animal's habitat, he'd created a zoo-wide scavenger hunt. When you came in, you could pick up a checklist, and if you succeeded in collecting the stickers to show that you'd found all fifty animals on the list, you could turn it in at the gift shop for a small prize. "The Animals of the Bible is wildly popular," I added aloud.

"Oh, I know," Caroline said. "But I was looking forward to the primate nativity."

"Primate nativity?" Maybe I'd heard wrong. "You're kidding, right?"

"No, he's been working on it for some weeks now. At first it seemed to be going quite well, but then one of the wise men decided that posing on a painted wooden camel was a lot less interesting than flinging poo at the onlookers. And there's a reason for the phrase 'monkey see, monkey do.' I suppose he's given up the idea of having it ready for this year's holiday season."

"Let's hope he's given up the idea altogether," I said. "Training human children to perform a nativity scene is hard enough — I should know; I've been doing it for the past several years now."

"Don't bring it up if he doesn't," Caroline said. "You know how it distresses him when his little projects don't go as planned. In fact, let's try to avoid mentioning monkeys at all, if he doesn't."

"Fine by me." Maybe if we didn't bring it up, he'd forget about it by next Christmas. Or pretend he had, which would achieve the same good results.

I snagged a parking spot as close as possible to the staff door and led the way inside.

We found ourselves in a small enclosed courtyard that lay between the Education/Administration Building — or Ed/Ad Building, as the staff called it — and the equipment warehouse. At the far side of the courtyard a gate led out to the public part of the zoo, where we could hear the shrieks and giggles of a lot of children enjoying themselves, plus the strains of "Good King Wenceslas" being played by the half-dozen musicians Grandfather had hired for the holiday season as a more civilized alternative to blasting carols over the zoo's loudspeaker system.

"If people want to hear carols, then fine," he'd said. "They can follow the musicians around the grounds if they like. And those of us who don't want to hear carols every single second of the blasted day can give them a wide berth."

I wished more retail establishments would adopt this point of view.

We turned toward the Ed/Ad Building, which was a major part of what I thought of as the backstage area of the zoo — and sometimes infinitely more fascinating than parts that were open to the public. Of course, since this was Grandfather's zoo, he cared a lot less about amusing the public than about educating them about animals and turning them into responsible citizens of the planet. I suspected that if the public ever got tired of the Caerphilly Zoo and stopped coming, Grandfather's dismay would be considerably diminished by the realization that he no longer had to worry about providing food, beverages, and bathroom facilities to a lot of wayward *Homo sapiens,* not to mention keeping them from getting scratched, bitten, peed on, or eaten. The absence of human visitors might even leave him free to focus on what he considered the zoo's real missions: Studying the animals. Breeding populations of endangered species that could be reintroduced to the wild to bring them back from extinction. And spending time with the creatures whose company he sometimes seemed to prefer to that of humans. With the possible exception of humans like Caroline, who shared his interest and expertise in zoology and was a longtime friend and collaborator.

After all, they might try to bite, claw, or dismember him, but none of his charges ever contradicted him.

In the reception area of the Ed/Ad Building we found a knot of people, some in khaki staff uniforms and some in white lab coats. They seemed agitated. Alarmed.

"Poor Fred!" someone was saying.

"I wouldn't be Fred for a million dollars!" another exclaimed.

Just then they noticed our arrival and grew quiet.

"Hey, Meg," a few of them called, or "Hi, Caroline." But most just looked stricken. And maybe a little guilty?

Apparently Caroline thought it better to ignore their agitation.

"Is Dr. Blake in his office?" she asked.

Some of the employees exchanged glances

before one spoke up.

"No, he's in the aviary."

For some reason the word "aviary" seemed to cause several of them to flinch. Caroline simply thanked them and led the way back out into the courtyard before reacting.

"What in the world is wrong now?" she muttered as we headed through the gate to the public area.

"And who is this Fred they're so worried about?" I asked.

"Who knows?" She shrugged. "No doubt we'll find out when we find your grandfather."

In spite of the serious cold — today was one of the sunny arctic days, with temperatures in the twenties — the zoo was crowded. The gift shop was overflowing with customers. All the food concessions had long lines — well, all except the ice-cream vendor, who really should have been given the day off.

Good to see that the zoo was prospering. Not that Grandfather needed the revenue that much, but he tended to sulk when attendance was down, and utter dire threats about the fate of a civilization that had lost its interest in nature.

He wasn't in the public portion of the aviary. It was filled with people peering into the habitats, hoping to spot their occupants. Since Grandfather cared more about keeping the zoo's occupants content than pleasing the tourists, he favored very large habitats that made observing some of the creatures a real challenge. Fortunately the Animals of the Bible scavenger hunt didn't actually require you to lay eyes on an animal to collect its sticker. Children were happily running up and down and squealing with excitement when they spotted the little baskets of stickers for the buzzard, the turtledove, the ostrich, the great horned owl, the raven —

"He must be behind the scenes," Caroline said.

I deployed my key card again and led the way through a STAFF ONLY door.

We traveled down a long corridor whose walls were lined with doors leading into the habitats and great floor-to-ceiling windows that the keepers could use to see into the habitats when needed — although at the moment, at least along this corridor, all the windows were concealed by curtains, to preserve the birds' peace of mind. Each door was surrounded by a variety of signs and bulletin boards giving instructions about the occupants' care and feeding, bulletins about any medical conditions they were experiencing, and repeated warnings to make sure the doors were closed and locked when you left the habitat. Some of the warning signs looked relatively new — had the zoo recently experienced the ornithological equivalent of a jail break?

At the end of the long corridor was a big open work area. There we found Grandfather. He seemed to be alternating between staring through an uncurtained window into one of the habitats and glowering at a young man in a staff uniform who was standing nearby.

The name tag pinned over the young man's breast pocket said Frederick Entwhistle. Presumably he was the Fred who was in such hot water with Grandfather.

I was pretty sure Grandfather heard us come in. We weren't trying to be quiet, and as he was fond of boasting, he had the predator's highly developed ability to sense relevant changes in his surroundings. But he just kept staring into the habitat.

"What's up?" I asked.

He ignored me.

I glanced over at the young staff member. Frederick Entwhistle didn't say anything either, but he'd clearly noticed us. His face had taken on a slightly hopeful look, and he was glancing around, as if trying to figure out how to use our arrival to engineer his own escape.

Caroline and I waited for a minute or so. Grandfather continued staring into the habitat. Frederick Entwhistle began shuffling almost imperceptibly away from him.

"Knock it off, Monty," Caroline said at last. "We get it. You're doing your best to bear up under some unspeakable blow from fate. Stop posing and tell us what's going on."

Caroline was one of the few people in the known universe who could get away with speaking that way to Dr. J. Montgomery Blake, world-famous naturalist and gadfly environmentalist. Or, for that matter, calling him Monty.

Grandfather just growled. Which was better than having him erupt, but still not exactly enlightening.

"I'm sure he doesn't want to talk about it," I said.

"About what?" Caroline asked.

"Whatever's bothering him."

"There's nothing bothering me!" Grandfather snapped.

"You see?" I said. "He's fine. Just a little cranky. Let's give him some peace and quiet."

We turned as if to go.

"It's my Corvidae," Grandfather announced.

"Corvidae?" I echoed — unfortunately, loudly enough for Grandfather to hear it.

"The Corvidae," he intoned, "are a worldwide family of oscine passerine birds."

"I know *what* they are," I said. "I just don't understand why you're in such a temper about them."

"The most common members are crows and ravens," he went on. "But of course there are also the rooks, jackdaws, jays, magpies, nutcrackers, treepies, and choughs."

"Treepies and choughs?" I muttered.

"Asian species," he said "You wouldn't know them. Highly intelligent creatures, the Corvidae. We've only begun to learn just how intelligent. That's the purpose of my latest series of experiments. I've been conducting a wide variety of tests to gauge the intelligence of the various species. And it was all going quite well until Fred here misplaced my magpies." He turned to glare at Fred.

"It wasn't my fault," Fred protested. "I followed all the instructions. I'm sure I locked the door to the habitat every time I left it."

"Then why aren't my magpies here?"

"Someone else must have made a mistake," he said. "It wasn't me."

"Maybe they let themselves out," I said. "Highly intelligent creatures, the Corvidae. You said so yourself. Didn't I read something about crows picking locks? Or was it ravens?"

"That was orangutans." Grandfather's tone was dismissive, but his scowl had been replaced by the slight puzzled frown that suggested he was seriously considering the notion. Had I accidentally said something both intelligent and apt?

"And you know very well that there's a great deal of debate going on about the relative intelligence of birds and apes," Caroline said. "Don't discount Meg's theory just because it's a lot more fun to yell at the staff."

Grandfather scowled briefly at her, and then returned to his pondering look.

"Apes have opposable thumbs," he said finally. "Some of them even have opposable big toes. No matter how clever the magpies are, I have a hard time imagining they can use their beaks and claws to open a door, much less pick a lock."

"Good," I said. "That's what they want you to think."

"Staff incompetence is a lot more likely." Grandfather returned to glaring at Fred.

"I'll give you a scenario that doesn't require opposable thumbs," Caroline said. "They've found a foolproof hiding place somewhere in the habitat. One morning, when they know it's almost time for someone to come in and feed them, they all hide there. Panic! Consternation! Whoever was supposed to feed them runs off to report the problem, leaving the door hanging wide open."

"And the magpies fly out, wearing the magpie equivalent of a triumphant smirk on their smug little faces," I said. "Sounds plausible to me."

"And to me." Grandfather was glowering at Fred again. "But any staff member who runs off and leaves the door to a habitat open — even one that appears to be empty —"

"You know," Caroline said. "I may know where your magpies are."

Grandfather stopped glaring at Fred and turned to her.

"Then why didn't you tell me?"

"Because until I got here, I didn't know you were missing any magpies." Caroline didn't actually say "so there," but you could hear it. "Of course, when I saw them I did find it odd because I thought I remembered that the American magpie's range was in

84

the Pacific Northwest and parts of the upper Midwest. But then I thought I might be remembering it wrong, and besides, climate change is affecting the ranges of so many species. I was going to ask you if you'd heard of magpies in Virginia, and of course since I knew you had magpies here at the zoo, the thought did occur to me that perhaps you'd been a little careless with yours. I was going to give you a hard time about that. And —"

"Blast it, woman, just tell me where you saw them!"

Caroline drew herself up to her full height and for a moment I thought she was going to give him what for. But all she said was:

"At Meg's."

My turn to feel Grandfather's wrath.

"What are *you* doing with *my* magpies?"

"Nothing," I said. "If your magpies are at our house, it's the first I've heard of it. I wouldn't know a magpie from a mud lark."

"There's no such bird as a mud lark," he said.

"From a meadowlark, then." I turned to Caroline. "Are you sure you saw them at our house?" I felt a sudden flash of worry — what if the missing magpies turned out to be one of Rob's crazy pranks?

"Yes," she said. "It was when I went out

to see Rose Noire. She took me to see her herb-drying shed. She feeds the birds back there on a pretty ambitious scale. That's where I spotted them."

"At a bird feeder?" Grandfather sounded skeptical. "They'd be a bit large for most bird feeders."

"A platform feeder," Caroline said. "And that's why I noticed them — they were chasing away the other birds and gobbling up all the birdseed."

"Birdseed? No!" From his tone you'd think Rose Noire was offering the birds arsenic or cyanide. "She shouldn't be feeding them birdseed. They're omnivores — birdseed should only be a small part of their diets. I'd recommend mealworms or —"

"She didn't set out to feed the magpies," Caroline said. "She was aiming for songbirds."

Grandfather harrumphed.

"You need to take me over there so I can check out these magpies." And with that he strode off toward the nearest exit, leaving the hapless Fred to breathe a sigh of relief.

"Sorry," Caroline said to me. "But if you can drop me off at your house, I'll ride herd on him and you can get back to your hoarder."

When we arrived at the house, Grandfather barely waited for me to stop the car before he was off, bounding along until he reached the middle of the backyard. There he stood with his hands on his hips, slowly turning in a circle and scowling at the magpie-free landscape around him.

The llamas hurried over to the fence where they could watch him more easily. They were endlessly curious about human behavior, the odder the better, and had long ago learned that Grandfather was a lot more fun to watch than most of his species.

"I suppose I should show him where I spotted the magpies," Caroline said. "And unless you're really desperate for people to deal with your hoarder guy, I should probably stay here and help him."

"Help him do what?" I hoped I didn't sound as suspicious as I felt.

"Heaven only knows," she said. "Something magpie-related. When I said I was going to help him, I assumed you'd understand that what I really meant was something more like 'keep him from doing anything destructive, or anything Meg would find more than usually annoying.' Could just as easily mean thwarting him completely, if that seems the sensible thing to do."

"Ah," I said. "I should have known. Carry on!"

I'd intended to head back over to Mr. Dunlop's as soon as I'd dropped them off. But I noticed that parked next to my car was the Twinmobile, as Michael and I called the minivan we'd bought for hauling around the boys and their friends. So I headed inside to see what he and the boys were up to.

Chapter 7

"There you are," Michael said, when I walked into the kitchen. "I was just about to call and see if we should come and join one of your Helping Hands projects."

They all looked considerably less contented than I'd have expected of people who were munching on freshly baked gingerbread persons.

"I thought you guys were going Christmas shopping," I said.

"We just spent two hours trying," Michael said. "And we bought exactly one present."

"Yeah, but I think we're going to have to return it," Josh said. "I just figured out that Mason already has that game."

"His grandparents get him every new game as soon as it comes out," Jamie said, with a sigh. "It's really exasperating."

"Not for Mason, I expect." Although I knew from conversations with their good friend's mother that it frustrated her as well.

"And I bet you guys enjoy it, as long as you're not trying to buy him a present."

"So I've suggested that we do what you always do at a time like this," Michael went on.

"Buy gift cards?" I was only partly kidding.

"No — we're going to do something else with our conscious minds," he said. "And see if our subconscious minds can come up with some good present ideas. So, you got any Helping Hands projects that the boys and I could pitch in on today?"

"You could ask Dad when he's going to manure Mrs. Diamandis's rose garden," I suggested.

"Ick," Josh said. "If we really have to."

"It's kind of cold today," Jamie said. "It might be better if we could help Grandpa do something indoors."

"Or you could come over and help us clear out Mr. Dunlop's house," I suggested. "It's mostly indoors, and we need a lot of volunteers."

"Mr. Dunlop?" Michael echoed. "You mean Harvey the Hoarder?"

"A real live hoarder?" Jamie asked. "Like on TV?"

"That would be gross," Josh said — but his tone reminded me that at their age, gross might not be a deal-killer.

"Just like on TV," I said. "But if you go, there are two rules you have to follow."

"I knew there was a catch," Josh grumbled.

"First, no matter what, you do not make fun of Mr. Dunlop or his stuff."

They nodded.

"And the second is that you don't throw anything away unless Mr. Dunlop says you can."

"Then what are we going to do with his stuff?" Jamie sounded puzzled. For that matter, Josh and Michael looked puzzled.

"We're packing it in boxes and taking them over to the Furniture World building," I said. "So he can take his time sorting it over there while a Helping Hands team fixes up his house so it doesn't fall down."

"Sounds weird," Josh said.

"But we can do it," Jamie said.

So as soon as they'd all changed into the oldest clothes we could find, Michael and I headed over to Mr. Dunlop's house with the twins in tow.

Back at Harvey the Hoarder's things were . . . well, not exactly hopping. But at least I could see some signs of progress. There were rather a lot of cars and pickups parked on both sides of the street, so presumably there were volunteers at work inside. Either that or more Haverhills had arrived to glower at him from afar.

Actually, I could see three of them now. Morris and Ernest were leaning against the middle of their three cars, with their arms crossed, looking straight ahead as if ignoring each other. In between and facing them was a woman, not quite as tall but just as thin and angular. She seemed to be lecturing them. Or perhaps that was merely the Haverhill style of conversation.

Michael dropped me in front of the house and the boys rode off with him to find the nearest parking space. Very near the front walk I spotted a familiar sight — Rose Noire's van with its faded lavender paint job and the HERBAL vanity plate. Given how close she was to the door, I decided that she must have been one of the first volunteers Mother recruited.

An enormous truck from the Shiffley Moving Company was parked directly in front of the house and a small squad of athletic-looking teenagers — two girls and five boys — were lounging in or near it, all either staring at their cell phones or showing their cell phones to each other. They looked up when I arrived, several of the boys scrambled to their feet, and they all greeted me with either "Hey, Ms. Lang-slow," or "Hey, Ms. Waterston," depending on which name they'd met me under.

"We're on call," one of the girls said, as if to explain why they weren't inside working.

"As soon as they have something packed and ready to load, they text me and we go in to get it," one of the boys explained, a little self-importantly. "But we're not supposed to hover around inside, 'cause it might make him nervous."

"Is stuff coming out steadily?" I asked.

"It's pretty d—. . . . um, darned slow," the girl said. "But yeah. Slow but steady."

"This is our second load," said the boy who seemed to be — or at least thought himself — the boss.

"First load was barely half full," another of the boys pointed out.

"Yeah, but Ms. Cordelia thought it was important to get some things over to the furniture store as soon as possible," the first boy said. "She thinks as more and more of his stuff goes over there he'll start being drawn there, and it'll get progressively easier to pack and move the rest. We'll probably take this load over pretty soon."

I glanced inside the truck. About half full. I could spot several small items of furniture — an easy chair almost completely concealed by quilted mover's pads, a small chest of drawers in a similar state — but most of the load consisted of Shiffley Moving Company boxes, in two sizes (medium and large), neatly stacked, all bearing labels with four digit numbers on them. I spotted one box labeled Box 0123. Did that mean they'd already packed over a hundred boxes? That was a good sign, surely.

"All *right,*" I heard one of the kids say. "Here comes the Not Just Tacos Truck!"

Several of the other kids cheered.

I turned to see the flamboyant maroon-and-gold food truck coming down the street toward us. Deacon Washington, who was at the wheel, seemed to be eyeing the available parking dubiously. The volunteers' vehicles filled most of the space on both sides of the street and nearly to both ends of the block.

"Can we move a few vehicles to make room for him close to the house?" I asked. "Because the sooner he gets settled —"

I didn't have to finish the thought. While the teenagers sprang into action, I strolled over to welcome the deacon. The food truck was his new pet project. It had started life as a taco truck, but once Abner Washington bought it he'd expanded its menu to include ham biscuits, pulled pork sandwiches, French fries, onion rings, coleslaw, chili, split pea soup, fried chicken, fried catfish, ribs, black-eyed peas, collards, candied yams, cornbread, hush puppies, egg drop soup, and sweet-and-sour chicken. It was painted to match the robes worn by the New Life Baptist Church's world-famous choir. Most of the time the deacon operated it at public events to raise funds to support the choir's activities, but lately he'd taken to showing up at Helping Hands projects and feeding the volunteers for free. Well, technically for free; he had a donation box somewhere on the truck, and once told me the donations — all of which went to support the choir — usually came to more than he'd have made selling his food, without all the trouble of making change.

My mouth had started watering at the mere sight of his truck.

"Morning," he said. "Once I get parked we'll be ready to serve in about half an hour. Can you take a menu card in for the volunteers to see?"

"Gladly," I said. "Although most of the old hands have probably memorized it and already know what they want. Save me a few of those ham biscuits."

He laughed and saluted. I took the menu card and went inside.

The living room was — well, not transformed yet. But clearly a transformation was underway. Two women were slowly packing things in boxes. Slowly, because they were using their cell phones to take a picture of every single object before they wrapped it in paper and put it into a box. One of them looked up and I recognized Joyce Grossman, wife of the rabbi of Temple Beth-El.

"How's it going?" I asked.

"Slowly but surely." She sat back on her heels and held up her phone. "We're making a kind of visual inventory. So if he suddenly decides he needs something, we can track down which box it's in."

I tried to imagine the circumstances under which Mr. Dunlop might feel the sudden need for a gilt-trimmed Victorian mustache cup, an Art Deco smoking stand, or a pair of bronze bookends shaped like peacocks. My imagination wasn't quite up to the job. Joyce laughed at my expression.

"If it keeps him happy," she said. "And keeps us moving forward."

"Amen," I said. "Carry on."

In the kitchen, several more workers were emptying Mr. Dunlop's pantry and putting most of the foodstuffs into black plastic garbage bags. As I watched, one of them picked up a box of cake mix, turned it around until she found the expiration date, rolled her eyes, and stuffed it into the bag. Had Mr. Dunlop noticed this? If he was coping this well with trashing food — even food that the eye roll suggested was laughably past its expiration date — maybe this was going to be easier than I thought.

I glanced over at the kitchen table. It was clear now, except for what appeared to be an ornately carved box in the center. Mr. Dunlop was sitting in his usual place. Cordelia and Rose Noire, sitting opposite him, looked absorbed in whatever he was saying.

"— it's actually strips of intricately tooled wood layered on top of a cigar box." He lifted up the box's lid, and turned it so they could see that the inside of the lid said, in ornate gold-accented lettering, "Hirschl & Bendheim's Prime Strictly Long Havana Filler."

"Tramp art," Cordelia said. "One of my great uncles was fond of doing something rather like this."

Mr. Dunlop seemed cheerful. In fact, he looked up and waved when he saw me.

"They've found my Christmas tree," he announced. "The artificial one. I thought of buying a new one, but I knew the other one must be around here somewhere."

"And we're going to set it up in the front window of the furniture store where everyone can enjoy it," Cordelia announced. "Harvey's got a lot of nice antique ornaments that we should come across sooner or later."

"Wonderful," I said. "Hey — we could throw a little party and help you decorate it."

"What would I serve?" He glanced over at the pantry crew and his expression looked less happy.

"We'll make it a potluck party," I said. "Much more fun. Speaking of food, the Not Just Tacos Truck is here — put your orders in."

I handed Mr. Dunlop the menu card — Cordelia and Rose Noire, as regular volunteers, probably didn't need to look at it by now. I left them discussing the options.

"Oh, I do wish I knew whether the collards are truly vegetarian," Rose Noire sighed.

"Probably not," Cordelia said. "Go for the pulled pork, Harvey. It's to die for. Or the ribs."

I left them to it and went out into the living room. Joyce was shaking her russet curls over the object she was about to photograph — a set of six pink china elephants in graduated sizes, from over a foot tall to barely an inch.

I went down the hall to see what was happening in the bedrooms. Only two, thank goodness, and both small.

In the first bedroom — the one that actually appeared to be used as a bedroom — Randall Shiffley and my cousin Horace were practicing some kind of odd dance step. They slowly circled the room, taking a short step forward and then bouncing slightly on the forward foot. Then another step and more bouncing. I watched in puzzlement.

"I think that's the only bad place," Randall said finally.

"So far," Horace answered. "We've only cleared about half the floor."

"Oh, I get it," I said. "Testing for rotten boards?"

"My foot went clear through the floor over there," Horace said, pointing toward one corner of the room.

"Once we get it emptied out we can tell whether it's worth patching, or whether we should just put down a whole new floor," Randall said. "And that ceiling's gotta go. Place will be a whole lot less claustrophobic when that's back to a normal eight-foot height."

He scowled up at the ceiling — which was only a few inches from the top of his head. Of course, Randall was at least six three and wearing cowboy boots that probably added another two inches to his height, but still.

"Are you seriously planning to raise the ceiling?" I asked. "Won't that be a big project?"

"We don't actually have to raise the ceiling," he said. "Just expose the real one. What you see is a drop ceiling."

"Why would anyone deliberately make their ceiling lower?" I asked.

"Well, the house dates from around 1900, maybe 1910," Randall said. "Long before air-conditioning was invented. Most people in that situation just use window units, but if you really want central air, you can have it as long as you can retrofit your house with some kind of duct system. Which is what they did — probably in the eighties, by the look of it. And did a pretty half-baked job of it. They ran all the ductwork across the ceiling, then covered the whole thing over with that false ceiling." He frowned and shook his head.

"I gather you disapprove," I said. "What would you have done — run the ductwork through the crawl space?"

"That would work," he said. "Though they'd have had to cut openings through these nice oak floors —"

"Formerly nice oak floors," Horace muttered.

"And they might not have wanted to do that. Looks as if there'd also be room to run the ductwork up in the attic space — that would be my preference. Either one would be preferable to this nonsense." He reached up and slapped the ceiling dismissively. "Even if they had to go with the drop ceiling option, they could have taken a little more trouble and kept it to a few inches instead of more than a foot. Not sure if whoever did this was lazy or stupid or both. But never mind. Once we get this place emptied out we'll figure out the best way."

He looked around with an almost proprietary expression and just a touch of impatience, as if he couldn't wait to get his hands on poor Mr. Dunlop's much-abused house.

Just then we heard thumping coming from below.

"I hope that's not rats." Horace looked anxious.

"Only someone in the crawl space," Randall said. "Can you call out the window and ask what they're doing?"

"Not at the moment," Horace said. "Give me an hour and I can work my way over to it."

"I have a better idea." Randall went over

to the corner where Horace had put his foot through the floor and put his face down near the hole. "What's going on down there?"

"Whole crawl space is full of lumber and cinder blocks and other junk," Michael called back. "I'm going to start pulling it out."

"I'll come and help," Randall said. He stood and turned to us. "Probably a good idea to check out the crawl space," he added. "Might give me an idea of where else the floor's gone bad." With that he strode out.

"At least we're cleaning this place out now," Horace said. "It's a total death trap. What if he had a fire here? Or fell and broke something? And can you imagine what it would be like if he died in here?"

"No," I said. "And I'd rather not try."

"Actually, you don't want to." He shook his head. "But take it from me — it's a darn good thing we're straightening him out."

With that he went back to packing.

I left him to it and went back out into the hall. From the bathroom I could hear someone humming "Go Tell It on the Mountain," in a soft contralto. I stuck my head in and saw my friend Aida stuffing towels in white plastic garbage bags.

102

"We're throwing the towels away?" I asked.

"No — trash goes in the black plastic bags." She had to pull down a dust mask to speak. "So he can't see in and change his mind. White plastic's for laundry. Because everything in his linen closet's covered with dust."

"Good plan." I glanced across the hall at the closed door to the back bedroom.

"No one working in there yet?" I asked.

"Check it out," she said.

I took a step closer and opened the door. A small avalanche of paper landed on me. And I was lucky it was only a small avalanche. The opening was full of paper, up to within a few inches of the top of the opening.

"I guess he uses this bedroom as an office," I said.

"Not sure the word 'uses' is exactly accurate — he does his computer work on a laptop at the kitchen table. But yeah, he calls that his office. Here —" Aida handed me several flattened moving boxes and a roll of packing tape. "You knock it down, you pack it."

So I assembled a couple of small boxes and began filling them with paper. At first I thought I'd try to do a little rough sorting

103

and pack like papers together, but the piles were so random that I soon gave up. I was unearthing bills, newspaper clippings, magazines, envelopes of photographs, promotional calendars, appliance manuals, coupons, letters, and who knew what else — all mixed together in what seemed like no particular order.

I gave up trying to sort — that could come later. I concentrated on filling boxes. And wondering why no one had ever taught Harvey the proper use of file folders.

Half a dozen boxes later, I started when someone came up behind me.

"Wow, this is awesome!"

CHAPTER 8

I turned to see Josh and Jamie standing in the hallway. Josh, who had spoken, was looking around as if Mr. Dunlop's hoarder house was a fascinating tourist attraction, or possibly a special event organized just for his entertainment. Jamie, who was eating the last few bites of one of Deacon Washington's tacos, looked more troubled.

"I guess this is why you keep telling us to clean our rooms," he said.

"Definitely," I said. "Are you guys up for helping?" I suspected they would be, since someone had equipped them both with dust masks like the one Aida was wearing.

They both nodded.

"Okay — see that door?"

I pointed to the door of the office. The half-dozen or so boxes I'd packed had made a barely visible dent in the mountains of paper.

"Is that room completely full of paper?"

Jamie asked.

"Maybe," I said. "I have no idea. It's a mystery. And the only way to solve it is to dig in. Start filling boxes with paper. If you come across something that's not paper, call me or your great-grandmother to look at it."

"Okay."

Normally the boys tried their best to do everything as differently as possible. But I had to suppress a chuckle when I saw them both square their shoulders, pull up their dust masks, pick up a box, and approach the door in an unconscious but perfect imitation of what Mother would do when approaching a difficult task.

I went back to the kitchen to see how that was going.

Mr. Dunlop was enthusiastically making inroads on a plate piled high with some of Deacon Washington's mouthwatering food. Cordelia and Rose Noire were working on more modest plates.

"Amazing," he said through a bit of pulled pork sandwich.

I decided he was mellow enough to bring up a possibly sticky subject.

"By the way," I said. "When I first arrived a man came up to me claiming to be your cousin. He seemed to assume I'd let him

106

come in with us, but I didn't know if you wanted him here — and for that matter, I didn't even know if he really was your cousin, so I shooed him away. And now there are three of them."

Mr. Dunlop was nodding.

"I saw them. The Haverhills; Morris, Ernest, and Josephine. And yes, they're cousins, but I don't want them here. Only second cousins. And their father quarreled with mine before I was born — I barely even met them. It's not like we have fond childhood memories of playing together or anything. I don't even know what they're doing here — they all live in Farmville."

"So we should keep them out of the house."

"And off my property. Please."

I realized his tone wasn't so much hostile as anxious.

"That's so sad," Rose Noire said. "Not to get along with your family."

"If you knew them, you'd understand," Mr. Dunlop said. "And I wasn't the one who started it."

"Do you have any family members you would want to see?" Rose Noire could be persistent.

"No." Now he just looked sad. "They're the only family I've got left. And if it's a choice between them and nothing . . . I pick nothing."

Probably a good time to change the subject.

"You know," I said. "Maybe we should knock off in time to go to the concert — it's the night when the New Life Baptist Church does its Christmas program for all the non-Baptists."

"Fabulous," Cordelia said. "Wouldn't miss it for the world — have you heard them, Harvey?"

"No, I've never managed to make their concert." He sounded wistful.

"Let's go, then," I said. "I can get Minerva Burke to save us good seats. And then after the concert, we can go over to the furniture store, inspect what's there, and have that potluck party."

Cordelia and Rose Noire immediately seized upon the idea and began embroidering it. I realized what they were doing — they were getting him to buy into the idea of leaving his house. Getting him downright excited about it. Good. And —

My phone rang. Not a familiar number, but few were these days, between calls from people for whom Helping Hands was doing projects and people volunteering for projects. I pulled it out and answered it with what I hoped was a businesslike but welcoming "hello."

"The Drunkard's Path," said a pleasant but unfamiliar female voice.

I waited for more information. In vain.

"I beg your pardon — who is this, and what was that again?"

"It's Grace Dinwiddie." The voice sounded disappointed, and a little hurt. "I was supposed to call you to give you more information about my grandmother's quilt? The one Reverend Smith thought the Helping Hands project could help me finish?"

"Oh, right." I flipped my notebook open to the section where I was keeping information on the Helping Hands projects. Yes, I had a page for Grace Dinwiddie, with her address and phone number. "What was that you said?" I asked. "I must have misheard you."

"If it sounded as if I said 'The Drunkard's Path,' then you didn't mishear me," she said, with a throaty chuckle. "That's what I've been told is the name of the quilt pattern Gran was using — at least according to my downstairs neighbor, who knows about these things. And she says to warn you that this is a particularly difficult version of The Drunkard's Path because the pieces are so small."

I stifled the impulse to mutter, "Oh, great," and settled for writing down "Drunkard's path with very tiny pieces."

"And how big a quilt is it — do you have any idea?"

"At least queen sized. Gran was always saying she wanted people to use her quilts, not just hang them on the wall for pretty. And she was savvy enough to figure out that wasn't going to happen unless the quilt was big enough to cover a modern queen or even king bed. That's the other thing — Robyn did tell you about the whole space problem, right?"

"Er . . . not really."

"I'm in one of those junior efficiencies at the Belvedere Arms," she said. "You know, the ones that make cells in the county jail look like mansions."

I did know. Thanks to the laissez-faire attitude of its absentee owner, we'd already done several Helping Hands projects at that particularly run-down apartment building. And if she had a junior efficiency, her whole living space was probably smaller than the walk-in closet Michael and I shared.

"There's barely room for me to turn around in my space," she went on. "I don't see that there's any way someone could work on the quilt in here."

"We'll figure something out," I said. "Why don't I send someone over to collect all the pieces — say, sometime tomorrow?"

"Anytime would be fine," she said. "Just give me a few minutes heads-up."

We exchanged seasonal good wishes and hung up.

"So is there a quilting bee in our future?" Cordelia asked.

"Apparently," I said.

"But not until we finish taking care of Harvey," Rose Noire said, frowning with anxiety.

"Of course not."

They both turned to beam at Harvey, who did appear to have grown slightly anxious during my conversation with Mrs. Dinwiddie.

"So tell us about this." Cordelia was holding up a rather large piece of jewelry.

"That's a Victorian mourning brooch," he said. "My grandmother wore it all the time."

"What's that inside?" Rose Noire asked. "It looks like . . . braided hair."

"Yes — one lock each from two little girls she lost as babies."

"How sad." Rose Noire looked quite ready to put on full mourning for the long-lost infants.

"It was." Harvey looked less sad than

sentimental. "My father was the only one to survive."

I left them to it and went back to the living room. A glance down the hall showed that Jamie and Josh were still hard at work, piling up boxes of paper. And making impressive progress, but so far there wasn't really enough room for anyone else to help them.

"Got a corner for me?" I asked Joyce.

"Try over there." She stood and eased her back. "What in the world do you suppose this is?" She was holding up an object. I took a few steps closer and peered at it: it was about a foot tall and made of white china painted with flowers and heavily decorated with various odd-shaped and vaguely repulsive knobs and bulges that you might have managed to overlook if they hadn't been daubed with gold paint. The knobs and bulges grew more numerous on the object's sides, forming two rather awkward handles. Joyce tilted it and I could see that it was hollow and open at the top.

"Presumably a vase," I said.

"A superlatively ugly vase," she said, in a low tone, after a glance toward the door to the kitchen. "I don't think I've ever seen anything quite like it, and I've put in my time in scouting who knows how many antique stores and junk shops."

"Show it to Mother," I said. "With any luck, it will turn out to be something rare and valuable that Mr. Dunlop can sell for a small fortune."

"I'm not holding my breath." She turned the presumed vase to study it from another angle. "You know, it doesn't look like him."

"Do you think it's supposed to? Some kind of portrait vase?" I squinted, but it didn't make the vase look any more like Mr. Dunlop.

"No, I mean it doesn't look like something he'd like or care about. The same for nine-tenths of the stuff in here. I'm not at all sure he collected all this dreck. I think maybe he inherited it and just doesn't know what to do with it."

"Or can't bring himself to part with it," I suggested, "because it used to belong to his parents, or his grandparents, or his great-aunt Sophie."

"Exactly." She shuddered, and enveloped the ghastly vase in a large sheet of packing paper. "So will that make it easier or harder for him to declutter?"

"I guess we'll soon find out," I said.

She picked up another item — one of a pair of gaily painted but insipid-looking figurines. If we were in one of those melodramas in which Mr. Dunlop was in danger of having his house repossessed by a suave, mustache-twirling villain, Mother would walk in and recognize the gaudy little figurines as priceless Dresden or Meissen or whatever — something that could be sold for a fortune and make living happily after possible. But since we were in real life, they'd probably turn out to be cheap dime-store junk. From Joyce's expression as she wrapped them, I'd put my money on junk.

I stopped worrying and settled into the slow steady routine: grab an object. Untangle it, if necessary, from all the surrounding objects. Take its picture. Contemplate, just for a moment, how satisfying it would be to throw it in a black plastic trash bag or a box marked "donations." Then sigh, wrap it neatly, and tuck it in a moving box.

I was wondering if it was possible to doze off while packing — and if so, whether I'd keep on packing in my sleep or keel over and snore — when we heard shouting outside. Joyce and I both abandoned our packing and hurried over to peer out of the front door, since the front windows weren't yet reachable.

Morris and Ernest Haverhill had squared off and were shouting insults and shaking their fists at each other.

CHAPTER 9

"Ooh," Joyce said. "It's the whooping crane people, fighting amongst themselves."

"Whooping cranes are elegant," I said. "I think of them as the praying mantis people."

"You're right," she said. "Much more apt. You know, I think if either one of them were actually going to deck the other, he'd have done it by now."

They were continuing to bellow, though it seemed to be taking them longer to think up another insult, and they were, if anything, farther apart than when they started.

"Yes," I said. "I suspect they're desperately hoping someone will step in to break up their fight before they actually have to go through with it."

Just then their sister strode over, placed herself between them, and said something. Her words didn't carry, but whatever she said interrupted their scene. To their ill-concealed relief.

115

Now she shook her fist at Morris and pointed to his car. He folded his arms and shook his head. She turned to Ernest and repeated the process. Evidently Morris and Ernest, like Josh and Jamie, liked to do everything differently. Although in my sons it wasn't because they loathed each other — clearly the Haverhill brothers did. Ernest said something — not, from his facial expression, something I was sorry to miss — before stomping over to his car. He jerked the car door open, slammed it shut after getting in, and drove off with a screech of his tires.

Josephine said something else to Morris before getting into her car and driving off in a noticeably more sedate and sensible manner. Once she was out of sight, Morris got back into his car. I was hoping he'd follow his siblings' example, but he just settled in to watch what was happening outside Mr. Dunlop's house.

"Poor Harvey," Joyce said. "With a family like that, who needs enemies?"

"Yeah," I said. "No wonder he's a hermit."

Around four I got a text from Caroline, asking if I could pick her up at the zoo in an hour or so. The zoo? Well, she'd probably gone back there with Grandfather after searching our yard for the magpies. Since

I'd been trying for some time to think of an excuse to take a break from packing, I texted back "of course!" If I stopped work now, I'd have time to check on what was happening elsewhere in Harvey's house before heading for the zoo. And we should probably stop anyway when the light went, given the perilous state of his front walk.

I let Rose Noire and Cordelia know where I was going. Along with Harvey, they had relocated into the bedroom, and were ostensibly helping him figure out what he would wear to the concert and party this evening. Actually, they were gently but firmly talking him out of the better part of the mountains of clothes that filled every corner of his room — the socks with holes in the toes, the pants with rips in the knees, the unflattering or ludicrously out-of-style shirts. A dozen boxes marked "donate" were packed and ready for pickup. The lone "keep" box was only half full.

"It's just so much easier to get rid of almost anything if you know someone else can use it, isn't that so?" Cordelia said.

"Yes." Harvey smiled and looked a little less tense. I had the feeling this wasn't the first time they'd had this exchange.

"We're making real progress," Rose Noire said. "Harvey, do you think you're ready to tackle the closet?"

Ready to tackle the closet? They'd filled a dozen boxes without even starting on the closet? But yes, she opened the door and we could see that the closet was full to bursting.

"The closet?" Just for a second, his face wore a surprised expression, as if he'd forgotten there was a closet somewhere behind all the stuff. Then his expression grew . . . sad? Anxious? "Oh, yeah. That was all my father's stuff. It can all go."

Curious. He seemed almost overly sentimental about everything else that had a family connection. There had to be a story there, and probably not a cheerful one. I could see from Cordelia's face that she shared my sense of puzzlement. I'd leave it to her find out what was up between father and son.

Rose Noire was holding up a black suit so long and narrow that it clearly wouldn't fit someone of Harvey's average height and plump frame. It would probably fit either of the Haverhills quite nicely, though.

"Good decision," Cordelia said. "Let's take a look at everything while we pack it, to make sure there's nothing valuable in the pockets." She picked up a roll of packing tape and began assembling another box.

"I'll see you later," I said.

"At New Life Baptist," Cordelia said. "And your mother said don't worry about refreshments for the party. She's on it."

When I walked outside I felt, just for a moment, as if I'd gone out on stage. The high school kids looked up from where they were loading boxes onto the truck. Josh and Jamie turned around from where they were standing by the Not Just Tacos Truck, evidently about to refuel. Mr. Brimley was sitting on his porch, wearing a down jacket and with his legs tucked into a sleeping bag, unabashedly keeping an eye on what was happening. Mrs. Gudgeon's binoculars were visible. Morris Haverhill was still there. I fought the impulse to take a bow.

"What's up?"

I started slightly, and then relaxed. It was only Randall, carrying the front end of a small stack of half-rotten boards. I moved aside to make way for Michael, who was carrying the other end.

"Harvey okayed our hauling off all the junk from under the house," he said in passing. "We're going to load it now, before we lose the light. Can you recruit a few more people to help us?"

I could indeed. Soon Josh, Jamie, and all but one of the high school kids were trudging back and forth carrying boards, bricks, and cinder blocks and loading them onto a large Shiffley Construction Company truck.

"We'll sort out what can be reused from what's pure trash when we get it down to the dump," Randall said as he surveyed the load. "The important thing is to get it away from here before he changes his mind."

"I doubt if he will," I said. "I'm beginning to wonder if Harvey's dad was the real hoarder and he just never learned any better."

"That would be a good thing," Randall said. "Still, maybe we should take anything else that's actual trash to the dump while we're at it. Unless you think he's going to freak when he sees it all leaving."

"I think he's going to be okay with it," I said.

"We can put all the bags right inside the gate until we're sure of that," Randall suggested. "That way if he has second thoughts, we can just bring those bags along to the furniture store."

Clearly Randall was a kinder person than I was. If Mr. Dunlop suddenly decided he couldn't live without several bags of expired dry foods — which included a dozen boxes of Nut & Honey Crunch, a cereal I was pretty sure hadn't been manufactured since the nineties — I'd be inclined to say we'd taken them to the dump and had no idea where to find them.

"Let's load your pickup, then," Michael suggested. "But quietly."

Between the food from the kitchen and the miscellaneous trash from the rest of the house — empty pizza boxes, used paper towels, water-ruined cardboard boxes, and other things that had been so obviously useless that Harvey hadn't had much trouble letting go of them, the black plastic garbage bags filled the bed of Randall's large pickup truck. Randall and Michael recruited a few of the high school kids to help out at the dump, and then the construction truck and the pickup drove away.

I was standing by the side of the road, watching the trucks disappear into the distance and taking a small breather before heading for my car, when I noticed someone nearby. Mrs. Gudgeon, the binocular lady. She appeared to have been lurking behind one of the more robust sections of boxwood hedge, and I was pretty sure she'd been there for a while. But when she realized I'd spotted her she pretended she had just arrived at the curbside. She lifted the lid of her trash can and deposited a small plastic bag.

121

Then she looked over at me and glared.

"How come the town's doing all this work for Harvey?" she demanded. "What's so special about him?"

"It's not the town doing the work," I explained. "It's the Helping Hands for the Holidays."

"Charity!" She snorted in disgust. "He doesn't deserve charity. He's not broke — not if he can afford to sit there in his house all day, not doing a lick of work. He's not the least bit needy."

"It's not charity," I said. "It's a project of neighbors helping neighbors. Organized by the Ladies' Interfaith Council."

"Harvey hasn't been to church in years, you know."

"That's okay." Staying cheerful and polite was becoming harder. "You don't have to be needy, or a churchgoer. Just a neighbor who could use some help. You can put in a request if you have any projects you haven't managed to get done. We do plumbing, electrical work, carpentry, yard work —"

"I'm perfectly able to take care of my own affairs, thank you very much!"

"And of course anyone who wants to volunteer their skills is more than welcome."

"I have better things to do than to help a bunch of no-count, lazy freeloaders."

She stormed back up her driveway and disappeared into her house, slamming the door behind her.

I breathed a sigh of relief. Having a next-door neighbor like that on top of the relatives? I no longer wondered why Harvey had become a hermit.

I spotted her binoculars at the front window. I waved at her.

The binoculars disappeared and her venetian blinds snapped shut.

I'd give it fifteen minutes before she eased them open and started spying again. Not that I was planning to stay around. It was time I left to pick up Caroline.

I texted her when I was nearing the zoo, and by the time I pulled up at the staff gate she was waiting for me just outside it.

"You're leaving Grandfather to his own devices?" I asked.

"Clarence Rutledge dropped by to check on the pregnant zebra," she said. "And your dad came along to help out. Does he actually know anything about equine obstetrics?"

"Oh, yes," I said. "A lot about animal obstetrics generally. He and Clarence attend all the zoo births. Haven't lost a mother or an offspring in years."

"Good to know. By the way, Clarence has

a project for the Helping Hands group."

"Great." I suspected my effort to sound enthusiastic wasn't working.

"Don't worry," Caroline said. "Your mother and I are taking point on this one. Seems the animal shelter's getting over-crowded."

"It often is," I said. "Especially since Clarence took over running it. If you put out the word to every shelter and rescue organization within five hundred miles that you'll take any animals they can't find room for, some of them are going to take you up on it, and yeah, it's going to get over-crowded." Of course, Caroline probably already knew that, since her sanctuary performed much the same function for injured wild animals and rescued exotics.

"It's worse than usual," she said. "Even Clarence is getting a little concerned. But don't worry — your mother and I have some good ideas to perk up his adoption campaign. We'll soon have him back in good shape."

"I will leave it in your capable hands," I said

"I've been meaning to ask — if the animal shelter's inadequate, why doesn't Clarence lobby the town for a bigger building? There's plenty of room for some expansion. Caerphilly isn't broke. And there are certainly enough animal lovers here."

"The problem is that the animal shelter isn't a public facility anymore," I said. "Back when the Pruitts were running things, they kept trying to cut the shelter's budget or turn it into a kill shelter. And then when we found out the Pruitts had mortgaged all the town buildings and the lender repossessed them all — including the old, totally inadequate shelter — Clarence ended up with all the animals at his veterinary practice. He decided enough was enough and started a private nonprofit, the Caerphilly Animal Welfare Foundation — CAWF for short. He even managed to buy the old shelter when it went on the market — not that much competition for a secondhand animal shelter — and enlarge it to the size it is now."

"But why not go back to having a public shelter, now that both town and county government are united and in friendly hands?" Caroline sounded on the verge of another diatribe on the crazy ways we locals did things.

"Ask Clarence." I shrugged. "I think he worries about what would happen if the Pruitts or someone like them got control again. I can't imagine it happening, myself, but the very idea keeps Clarence up at night. Besides, being a private foundation, he can run it any way he likes."

"Good point," she said. "If it were government funded, he might not be able to keep up that policy of taking in other shelters' overflow. The taxpayers might object to him spending their money on animals from all over the state."

"The taxpayers might be unpleasantly surprised if we reminded them how much it cost to take in just Caerphilly's strays and run the old completely inadequate shelter," I said. "Anyway, the CAWF board of directors thinks it's time to have a big fundraising drive for the building expansion — maybe even a new purpose-built building — but so far we haven't talked Clarence into it."

"We? So you're on the board?"

"Along with Dad, Grandfather, Minerva Burke, and a retired zoology professor from the college," I said. "But Professor Pedersen is thinking of moving back to Norway, so we may have an opening coming up. I'm supposed to sound you out to see if you'd be interested."

"Consider me sounded, then," she said with a laugh. "And I'll spend some time while I'm here in town digging into this CAWF thing to see if I can add value."

126

"Perfect." I was pulling into the driveway. "And while you're — wait. What's going on in our backyard?"

"Now that's a very interesting question," Caroline said.

CHAPTER 10

An interesting question? Clearly Caroline was trying to avoid answering me. I got out of the car and strode closer to get a better look.

The entire backyard was swarming with birds. And not in the sense that our entire flock of two dozen or so Welsummer chickens were holding a forbidden convocation with an equal number of the Sumatrans — who were supposed to stay in their own pen across the fence on Mother and Dad's land, to avoid the kind of fraternization that would result in Welmatrans or Sumsummers instead of purebred heritage chickens. What was going on right now took "swarming with birds" to a whole new previously unimagined level. It was a vast flock — almost a living carpet — of songbirds.

Robins. Blue jays. Bluebirds. Chickadees. Doves. Depressingly vast numbers of starlings and pigeons. Evening grosbeaks.

Goldfinches. Woodpeckers. And who knows how many birds that, to the despair of my ornithologically savvy father and grandfather, I could only think of as random nondescript brown-and-white birds.

I did see a few copper-brown Welsummer heads and black Sumatran heads — they kind of stood out above the crowd of much smaller birds, as did the dozen or so crows. I even spotted one enormous turkey vulture, sitting patiently by himself near the edge of the crowd, as if hoping that sooner or later, at least one of the hundreds of frantic birds would overeat to the point that it shuffled off this mortal coil, so the vulture could join in the feasting.

And I could see the dogs in the nearest windows. Tink was merely watching with interest. Spike was barking hysterically at this monstrous avian invasion of the yard he considered his domain.

"It's just your grandfather's latest project," Caroline said.

"What is he doing? Filming a remake of *The Birds*?"

"Trying to recapture his magpies."

"And just how's this circus going to help him do that?"

"Just between you and me . . . I don't think he thought this through very carefully," Caroline said. "In fact, while I generally make it a rule never to say 'I told you so' to your grandfather — well, the temptation's getting more irresistible by the hour."

"Have you even spotted any magpies in the crowd?" I asked.

"Well, I have," she said. "But only in passing a couple of times. And only because I've been patient enough to sit here and observe them. Your grandfather stormed off a couple of hours ago to sulk and think of a better plan."

"So he's wasting all that birdseed?" I asked. "Well, I don't suppose the birds feel that way, but rather a waste from his point of view, since he's no closer to recapturing his magpies than he was to begin with. What's he planning to do next?"

"I'm open to suggestions," Caroline said. "I expect he is, too."

"Magpies are on the big side, aren't they?" I asked. "What about putting out some kind of trap — one that lets any size bird in, but only lets the little ones out. Our poor hens would be the first ones to charge inside, of course, and you'd probably also catch the crows, but you could pen all of those somewhere else temporarily until the magpies take the bait."

"Not a bad idea." Caroline looked

thoughtful. "Wouldn't be too hard to design a trap like that. Of course, I doubt if we could design and build it before the birdseed supply runs out. Actually, I'm hoping when Rose Noire gets back from her volunteer work she can help us recapture them."

"You'll have to convince her that they're better off in the zoo," I said. "And that will take some doing."

"Yes." Caroline shook her head. "She seems quite taken with them. And she's convinced they're happier here. They bring her little presents."

"Presents?"

"She's got a regular collection of things they've left on the doorstep of her herb-drying shed. I'll show you."

She led the way through one side of the yard, scattering the nearby birds as we passed, but only briefly. Greed had made them careless and unwary. I hoped someone had locked up Skulker and Lurker, our barn cats, before Grandfather had spread out the birdseed. If not, odds were they had stuffed themselves silly with a few of the slowest early arrivals and then crawled off into some quiet corner to sleep off their feast.

We went through the gate that separated our yard from Mother and Dad's farm. They'd allowed Rose Noire to begin her organic herb garden here some years ago, and then, this past spring, she'd erected the herb-drying shed — which also provided storage for all the supplies she needed for her business and included a small but useful greenhouse on one end.

We went inside, and I closed my eyes while I took a few deep breaths. Before Rose Noire set up the herb-drying shed, I'd have assumed that if you put a hundred different herbs and spices in a small room they'd fight each other and produce a chaotic mess, but instead they all blended into a pleasing if slightly overwhelming whole. If I worked at it, I could tease out individual scents: a lot of evergreen, cinnamon, and clove, since she was busily making seasonal potpourris and teas. Dried apples and lemons to remind me of the harvest season, along with rose and lavender to keep alive the hope of spring. After the second or third time I'd walked in here, I'd gone back to the kitchen, thrown out most of the contents of my spice rack, and adopted a policy of buying only tiny quantities from the organic sources Rose Noire recommended. I knew my kitchen — and everyone it fed — was the happier for it.

"Here's where she keeps them." Caroline pointed to Rose Noire's worktable. In addition to a few tools — a mortar and pestle, a small grinding mill, and a stack of empty muslin bags waiting to be filled with pot-pourri — the table held a shallow square bowl — or was it a gently curved plate? — on which rested a small collection of items.

An inch-long fir twig. A bit of pink beach glass slightly smaller than a marble. Two tiny feathers, one red and one blue. An old-fashioned crinkled foil Christmas icicle. A small bit of quartz. And a delicate silver hoop earring.

"The magpies brought all this?" I asked.

"So she says."

"Has she seen them do it? What if she's giving the magpies credit for things that are actually coming from some shy admirer who happens to have the same ideas as a magpie about what makes a proper gift?"

"Another good question," Caroline said. "I didn't think to ask. It's definitely behavior that's been seen in crows and ravens."

"But if she knows that, she might jump to a conclusion," I suggested.

Caroline pondered for a moment.

"We could put up a little camera right over the door." She pointed up into the eaves of the shed. "That way, not only could we confirm if the magpies are actually bringing Rose Noire presents, we could also learn more about their habits. Could help your grandfather recapture them."

"Make sure Rose Noire's cool with it," I said, as I turned to head back to the house. "Or she'll do her best to aid and abet the birds, and Grandfather might never see them again."

"Yes, she could do that." Caroline fell into step beside me. "And she would, too."

Back at the house, things were hopping, especially in the kitchen. I worried briefly that we might be having a repeat of last summer's communications breakdown, when both Mother and Dad had thought they were in charge of parceling out our spare bedrooms to relatives coming for a big family gathering. Michael and the boys had thought sleeping in tents in our own backyard for a week had been great fun, but I doubted even they would enjoy it at this time of year.

But to my relief it turned out that Mother had recruited a large crew to prepare the food for Harvey's party in the furniture store.

"Don't you worry about a thing," Mother said when I offered to help. "You run along to the concert."

That probably meant she had some other, bigger project to spring on me later. But I'd worry about that when the time came

"Your grandmother's taking Harvey and Rose Noire over," Mother said. "So you don't need to worry about them. But you and Caroline should hurry if you want to catch the start."

So we took off — in Caroline's car, so both mine and the Twinmobile would be available to ferry things over to the furniture store for the party.

When we got to the New Life Baptist Church, I dropped Caroline at the front door and went off to see if I could find a parking space somewhere this side of the county line. By the time I got back to the church, it was standing-room-only in the sanctuary. Apparently Minerva Burke was looking out for Harvey — I spotted him sitting in a place of honor in the front pew on the right, with Cordelia, Caroline, and Rose Noire on one side and Deacon Washington on the other. The enormous organ was playing "O Come, O Come, Emmanuel" softly enough that people could still converse if they really tried. When Cordelia spotted me, I waved, and shook my head to turn down her pantomimed offer for them to scrunch together and make room.

I went out into the vestibule and found a likely-looking patch of floor where I could lean against a wall and wasn't in much danger of being stepped on. Then I closed my eyes and focused on enjoying the music.

Okay, I nodded off for a few minutes and missed the end of "Silent Night," but the first glorious chords of "Joy to the World" woke me with a start.

"About time you woke up." I glanced over to see my friend Aida Butler sitting on the floor beside me.

"Why aren't you inside?" I asked. Aida's daughter, Kayla, was a soloist with the choir.

"With luck, I'll get to hear the program at services on Christmas Day," she said. "But just in case half the force is still out sick and I have to patrol then — well, I figured I could spend my dinner break here tonight."

As we listened to "Go Tell It on the Mountain," she opened a carryout bag from Muriel's Diner, unwrapped a gigantic sandwich, took a hearty bite, and sighed with contentment.

She was nice enough to share her potato chips, which were the diner's own made-on-the-premises kind, and still warm. We munched contentedly throughout the rest of the concert.

"Are you patrolling Harvey's neighborhood tonight?" I asked when she stood up to go.

"Me and Vern," she said.

"Good," I said. "I bet that will make him feel better — not only that someone is patrolling the neighborhood, but that it's someone he knows."

"He's a nice guy," she said. "Never says an unkind word about those nasty neighbors of his — not even when they'd called in a complaint about him." She smiled and strode off.

When the choir started its final number, I decided to begin my hike to where I'd parked Caroline's car. Maybe we could beat the crowd leaving — or at least arrive at the furniture store a little sooner than Harvey. I pulled up in front of the church just as Caroline dashed out the front door, and watched as she shook hands with Reverend Wilson.

"Put the pedal to the metal," Caroline said as she hopped in the car. "Minerva Burke's giving Harvey a tour of the church, so we have time to get there and make sure everything's ready."

"Call Mother and warn her that the concert's over," I said. "And she'll make sure everything's ready."

And indeed, Mother was there to welcome us.

"Isn't this nice!" She held out her arms as

if to call attention to our surroundings, beaming as if presenting an elegantly decorated room in a designer show house.

Actually, it wasn't looking that bad. Along with all the boxes, Randall had rounded up at least a dozen sturdy metal utility shelves, and the crew had arranged them along the walls in the front of the store, ready for the sorting to come. Meanwhile the boxes were stacked three or four high and arranged in neat rows — and to my delight, someone had done at least some rough labeling. A lot of MISCELLANEOUS DECORATIVE boxes probably contained things like the ghastly vase and the pink elephants. Quite a lot of smallish boxes were labeled BOOKS. And an impressive number of boxes were labeled, in Josh and Jamie's neat printing, PAPERS.

While we'd been at the concert, someone had brought over Harvey's kitchen table — the slab of marble on its wooden base — and his customary chair. They were arranged in the very back of the store, near the door that led into the back room. The back room held a rough kitchenette — no more than a hotplate, a sink, and an under-the-counter refrigerator, but it would make it much nicer for everyone to work here as we helped Harvey with the sorting. There was even a small closet-like bathroom in one back corner of the main room — not a very satisfactory bathroom by Randall's standards, since it was partitioned off from the main room with wallboard so thin and cheap that it was barely a step above cardboard. But it was there. Harvey could actually live here in the short term, if he insisted on staying with his stuff, although I was hoping we could convince him to move into a bed-and-breakfast a few blocks away where, wonder of wonders, the owner had gotten a cancellation and could put Harvey up at Helping Hands' expense starting tomorrow night.

But for tonight, we'd christen the new space with the party before hauling him back home — to what I considered a much improved space. Mother and the visiting relatives were finishing the work of turning the furniture store into a festive Christmas party venue.

Some had set up folding tables — borrowed, as I noted from the labels on the underside, from Trinity — and were flinging red and green tablecloths over them. Others were ferrying great quantities of food in from their vehicles, and I could hear the beeping of several borrowed microwaves from the back room. Still others were teetering on the top steps of ladders to hang the last few garlands of tinsel, evergreen, and red ribbons as high as possible along the double-height walls of the furniture store. One cousin was even going around flinging large red or green drop cloths over the stacks of boxes and sticking on enormous bows, so it began to look as if the entire room was filled with oversized Christmas presents.

A lively guitar riff that I recognized as the opening of Chuck Berry's "Run Rudolph Run" suddenly blasted through the store at a volume that made most of us jump and grab our ears. But the cousin in charge of the stereo dialed it back immediately, and began reassuring us that he had plenty of more sedate Christmas music to play during the actual party.

"I just thought this would pump everyone up while we get the place ready," he explained.

Mother gave her approval; and "Run Rudolph Run" was followed by "Rockin' Around the Christmas Tree," "Jingle Bell Rock," and Run-D.M.C.'s "Christmas in Hollis."

Harvey's Christmas tree was standing in the front of the store, visible from the display window. The decorating crew had put lights on it, but Mother discouraged any other attempts to decorate it.

"It's Harvey's tree," she said. "Let's give him the chance."

"I assume someone found his Christmas ornaments," I said to Mother in an undertone.

"What there was of them," she said. "He has some very nice antique blown glass ornaments — obviously family heirlooms — but not nearly enough for a tree this size. So I brought over a few more, to make sure it looked festive." Following her glance I spotted six boxes neatly labeled CHRISTMAS ORNAMENTS.

We were running out of things to do, and the people who had been working so hard on the decorations were eyeing the plates of food with intent, when my brother, Rob, ran in, closely followed by Delaney, his fiancée. "They're coming! They're coming! Let's surprise them!"

CHAPTER 11

We hadn't actually rehearsed anything in particular for Harvey's arrival, but someone turned out the store lights, and we all crouched where we were until we heard fumbling at the door.

"Well, at least the door's open," Cordelia was saying. "But I'd have thought there would be someone here to —"

Just then the lights went on, and everyone yelled either "Surprise!" or "Merry Christmas!" Harvey stood for a few moments, obviously startled, before smiling broadly.

"Merry Christmas everyone!" he said.

Mother led Harvey to a seat of honor in a shabby armchair by the Christmas tree. I recognized the armchair as one a well-meaning parishioner had donated to Trinity several years ago, to the consternation of Mother and Robyn, who thought it spoiled the whole look of the parish hall and had been conspiring to get rid of it ever since.

Rose Noire hurried up with a plate of food, and she and Cordelia arranged their folding chairs around Harvey, keeping up a cheerful conversation with him while Mother took charge of seeing that people who wanted to talk to him arrived singly or in small groups that wouldn't overwhelm him.

I was pleased to see that the meal Mother had organized avoided some of the holiday staples. So no turkey or stuffing and no cranberry sauce. Ham, but also roast beef. Big vats of several different kinds of salads. A lot of casseroles that were the specialties of the best Trinity and New Life church cooks. And tons of finger foods — ham biscuits, samosas, quesadillas, dumplings, and spring rolls.

"So that's your hoarder," Grandfather said through a mouthful of samosa. "It's common in the animal world, you know. Though most of them only do it with food. Very common with rodents and certain bird species."

"I think humans are most likely to hoard paper," I said, the sight of Harvey's office springing to my mind unbidden.

"In fact, in German the verb for hoarding is *hamstern* — after the hamster," Grandfather went on. "And there are similar connections in Dutch, Swedish, and Polish."

143

I had a mouth full of spring roll, so I merely made a noise intended to convey polite interest.

"In birds it's usually referred to as caching rather than hoarding," he added. "And several of the species I'm studying practice it. Crows, magpies —"

"I knew magpies would come into it sooner or later," I said. "Hold that thought — I should see what Josh and Jamie are up to."

In fact, what they were up to was introducing Harvey to Spike and Tinkerbell. Tink was no problem — she never met a human — or for that matter, a living creature — that she didn't like. But Josh seemed to be holding out Spike for Harvey to pat, which was sheer madness. Didn't he realize — ?

But evidently being in the company of the only two humans he was fond of had a beneficial effect on Spike's behavior. He only growled faintly when introduced to Harvey, and allowed himself to be scratched behind the ears without retaliating.

A pre-Christmas miracle.

Mother had begun helping Harvey decorate his tree with the ornaments they'd brought over from his house — most of them vintage if not antique glass ornaments that, according to Harvey, had belonged to his Dunlop grandmother. He was visibly excited, telling anyone what little he remembered of her and his long-ago Christmas visits to her house.

I had the depressing feeling that it had been many years since he'd decorated a tree. And then I banished the feeling. We were engineering a fresh start for Harvey. This was going to be the best Christmas he'd had in years — maybe decades. And the start of a brand-new life for him.

Others seemed to have the same thought.

"Poor Harvey," Rose Noire said. "Do you suppose he usually spends Christmases alone?"

"If the choice is solitude or the Haverhills, I know what I'd choose," I said.

"Not the Haverhills." She bit her lip, and I could tell her devotion to seeing the best in everyone was warring with the reality of Harvey's cousins. "They have a very negative aura," she said finally. "And those neighbors of his aren't much better. I think it would be a very good idea to do a cleansing of that house — of his whole property. I'll check my sage supply tonight."

At one point Spike suddenly froze, growled, and walked stiff-legged toward the front door. I followed him and peered out into the night.

No one.

I opened the door and glanced up and down the street. Still no one, although that didn't mean there hadn't been. I thought, uneasily, of all those reports of prowlers around Harvey's house.

I closed the door and went back to where I'd been listening to Michael telling Grandfather about some interesting behavior he'd observed in our llamas.

"Who was it?" Michael asked.

"No one there," I said.

"Maybe they ran away?"

"Maybe," I said. "I hope it wasn't one of the Haverhills. That seems like the sort of thing they'd do."

"Haverhills?" Michael echoed

"The praying mantis people." I did a quick imitation of the Haverhills, hunching my shoulders and rubbing my hands together.

"Ah," Michael said. "I only saw the one. There are more?"

"Three," I said. "Two of them are —"

"By praying mantis people, I assume you mean entomologists?" Grandfather sounded interested. While vertebrate predators were his favorites, he didn't look down his nose at invertebrates, and he was always alert for the possibility of a meaningful discussion

146

with fellow natural scientists.

"No," I said. "Merely three people whose physical appearance happens to remind me of praying mantises. I'm not trying to make fun of them, which would be politically incorrect as well as downright unkind, but they give me the creeps in much the same way praying mantises do. And don't remind me that praying mantises are a natural part of the ecosystem and a valuable biological pest control —"

"Actually they're not," Grandfather frowned. "Not a valuable biological pest control, that is."

"They're not?"

"No." He struck a pose as if recording a bit for one of his television shows. "What you want in a biological pest control is a predator that specializes mainly if not entirely in a specific pest species, and multiplies rapidly when there's an increase in its prey. Mantises are general predators. They eat whatever they can catch, including beneficial insects as well as harmful ones. So, an interesting species, and very effective predators, but of negligible use for pest control."

"Well, damn," I said. "So all this time I've been apologizing to the wretched things for calling them creepy and thanking them for their service to our yard, and they're nothing but self-centered imposters? Just eating what they damn well please? Hmph!"

"The value of a species does not lie in its utility to mankind," Grandfather said sonorously.

"Humanity," I corrected. "And I never said it did. But I intend to stop apologizing to them."

"You said there were three of them," Michael said. "Haverhills, that is."

"Two brothers and a sister," I said. "All praying mantises in human shape. And Harvey doesn't like any of them. For that matter, I don't either. It didn't occur to me until afterward, but he said they all lived near Farmville — that's the other side of Richmond. It must be at least two hours from here. Maybe more if you ran into traffic, which would be pretty likely, since you'd almost certainly have to go through at least the outskirts of Richmond to get here from there."

"So they drove a couple of hours to help their cousin?" Michael asked. "What's not to like?"

"More like they drove a couple of hours to park across the street and glare at him," I said. "Because that's all they did. Well, except for possibly trying to make in-person visits to the building inspector and Adult Protective Services. But this is the weird part — they drove in three separate cars."

"Why would they do that?" Michael mused.

"No concern for the environment," Grandfather grumbled. "Taking three cars when one would do."

"Well, maybe they just dislike each other so much that they couldn't stand being cooped up in the same car for a couple of hours," I said. "But I'm wondering if they had some kind of plan to haul away a lot of his stuff. And I don't mean hauling junk to the dump — if that was the plan, they could use one car to ferry it back and forth. I think they were planning to help themselves to whatever they decided was worth hauling away. Three cars meant more than three times the cargo space."

"Wow," Michael said. "They clearly didn't make a good first impression on you, did they?"

"I wouldn't trust them an inch," I said. "And Cordelia agrees with me, and Rose Noire says they have very negative auras."

"I was ready to dislike them on your word alone," Michael said with a laugh.

"When we go over in force tomorrow, we'll have to warn all our volunteers not to let them in," I said.

"Do you have a lot of them?" Grandfather asked.

"If everyone who signed up shows up, maybe three dozen." I wondered why he'd asked — was he actually thinking of helping out?

"Signed up?" He looked puzzled. "What are you talking about — I wanted to know if you have that many praying mantises in your yard."

Okay, so he wasn't going to help out.

"Sorry," I said aloud. "I thought you were asking if we had a lot of people coming tomorrow to participate in one of the Helping Hands projects. I should have realized you were talking about insects. At the moment we don't have any praying mantises that I know of, which I assume is because they all died out when the weather got cold."

"Obviously." His impatience was showing. "But in season, did you have an unusual number of them?"

"Not that I noticed," I said. "Just what is the usual number?"

He made a growling noise.

"Sorry," I said. "My mind wasn't on mantises this summer."

"We should keep an eye on the situation," he said. "Lately I've been seeing some fascinating studies about the incidence of mantid predation on birds."

It took a second for that to register.

"Wait — do you mean praying mantises are eating birds?"

"Mostly Trochilidae," Grandfather said. And then, seeing our blank looks, he clarified. "Trochilidae — hummingbirds. Although there are cases on record of them bagging birds as large as twenty grams. Five or six times the size of a hummingbird. But I doubt if that was done by native mantises. Ever since people got the wrongheaded idea that mantises are good for pest control they've brought in a lot of non-native mantises. Some of them huge."

"And they're going after the hummingbirds?" For all I knew Grandfather might disapprove, but I much preferred hummingbirds to almost any insect.

"Not in any significant numbers," he said. "Free-range cats are a much bigger threat. But still, there have been dozens of reported cases. Many from people with backyard hummingbird feeders. They're partial to the brains."

"Who's partial to brains?" Josh had joined the conversation. "Are we talking about zombies?"

"He's not talking about eating brains,"

Jamie said, with a dismissive wave.

"Yes, I am," Grandfather said. "If you go on the Internet you can find any number of pictures of praying mantises feeding on hummingbird brains."

"Gross," Jamie exclaimed.

"Gross," Josh agreed. "Mom, can we borrow your phone?"

I refused to surrender my phone for the purpose of letting them view pictures of mantid predation on Trochilidae. Michael proved to be less squeamish, so before long the boys were off in a corner, wincing and exclaiming "gross!" at intervals.

"Should they really be watching that?" Michael asked.

"It's never too early to learn about nature, red in tooth and claw," Grandfather said.

"It will motivate them," I said. "I plan to assign them the task of keeping our hummingbird feeders mantis-free this summer."

"The other interesting thing about them," Grandfather said, "is the controversy over the degree to which they practice sexual cannibalism."

"Sexual what?" Michael asked.

"Cannibalism," Grandfather repeated.

"That's what I thought you said." Michael raised an eyebrow. "I assume we're back to talking about praying mantises again, not the Haverhills."

"I hope so," I said. "I'm not sure I want to think about sexual anything in connection with the Haverhills."

"It's generally considered to be very common among many arachnids and a few insect orders, like the Mantodea," Grandfather went on. "The female will bite off the male's head immediately after or even during mating."

"Like black widow spiders?" Michael asked.

"Same phenomenon," Grandfather agreed. "Entomologists have developed a variety of theories. Adaptive foraging is the most interesting — that upon encountering a male of her species, a female quickly assesses his value as a mate against his nutritional value — the hungrier she is, the more dangerous for him. But lately there's been some work that suggests the high rate of sexual cannibalism is actually caused by intrusive laboratory observation."

"Wait — the female mantises resent having their love life spied on, so they bite off their mates' heads?" Michael asked.

"They're very visually oriented, mantises," Grandfather said. "Easily distracted by bright laboratory lighting, or the presence of observers. Also, if you're doing a study like this and you don't want mantises hopping all over your laboratory, you have to keep them confined, and that may increase male mortality by making it harder for them to escape. Ah — there's Rose Noire. I need to talk to her about my magpies."

He strode off.

"Does he really think he's ever going to get those magpies back?" Michael asked.

"He might, if he can convince her it's for their own good," I said. "If I were him, the first thing I'd do would be to stop calling them 'my magpies.' Because I'm sure by now she thinks of them as her magpies."

"I think I'll wander over and see if I can guide the conversation into a productive channel," Michael said. "If I can think of one."

"The fact that they're not native to this part of the country," I suggested. "And that we don't know whether conditions here are suitable for them to have a long healthy life. Plus the fact that we have no idea what harm they're doing to the local ecosystem."

"Excellent." He drifted off in Grandfather's wake.

I went back to the buffet for another helping.

The party flowed on. From time to time I heard Grandfather holding forth on some

154

natural history topic or other. I wasn't sure why he was telling one brace of cousins how to hypnotize a frog, and I suspect Aunt Verity would have been happier not knowing that three percent of the ice in Antarctica was composed of penguin urine. Or that fields and forests generally contained an average of fifty thousand spiders per acre. But at least Grandfather seemed to have lost interest in brain-eating praying mantises.

I saw Mrs. Diamandis chatting animatedly with Dad and several other garden club members. Apparently they'd all been admiring her roses from afar for years, but for some reason had never gotten around to introducing themselves to her, much less inviting her to share her obvious expertise and love of roses with the club. Well, now that would change. Another victory for the Helping Hands.

Eventually the crowd began thinning out. Everyone seemed to have had a great time — well, with the possible exception of Aunt Verity. Everyone stopped to say goodnight to Harvey and wish him a merry Christmas. Harvey had had a glass or so of wine, and seemed slightly tipsy and utterly happy. It occurred to me that I should pitch in to clean up, but then I realized that everything

I could think of doing had already been done. The leftovers that hadn't already been taken away were neatly packed up. The trash had been taken out. The kitchen and bathroom were scrubbed clean.

Maybe I'd actually get to bed on time.

"Who's taking Mr. Dunlop home?" Jamie asked.

CHAPTER 12

Drat. Yes, someone had to take him home. And it should probably be us, which was unfortunate, because the route to his house led in almost exactly the opposite direction from the one that would take us home. Dropping him off would add at least half an hour to our trip.

But when I glanced around at the people still here, I realized that only a few of them were people Harvey knew well enough that I'd feel comfortable suggesting he ride with them, and those were all family and friends who'd be taking the same direction out of town.

"We can take him," I said. "I'd actually like having a chance to see what you all got done after I left."

"It's out of your way, isn't it?" Harvey said. "I hate to be a bother."

"I have a better idea," Cordelia said to me. "Meg, why don't you take my car and drop him off? I can take your spot in the Twinmobile."

"You don't mind?"

"I was thinking of asking if someone could drive me home anyway," she said. "You know how I hate driving after dark with my terrible night vision — especially since they're predicting rain any time now. I'll feel much safer riding with Michael."

I didn't recall her ever complaining about her night vision, and while Michael was certainly a very reliable driver, I also couldn't recall any previous occasions when she'd preferred being driven by anyone to getting someplace under her own steam — was this a new sensible aging thing or was she just trying to avoid making Harvey feel he was a burden?

I'd figure that out later.

"Perfect," I said aloud, and caught the keys she tossed me.

I had to wait until Harvey said good-bye to various new-made friends, and expressed his eagerness to accept all their invitations and suggestions. Yes, he would love to see Rose Noire's greenhouse and herb-drying shed. And he'd always wanted to see the Caerphilly Zoo — the idea of getting a behind-the-scenes tour was wonderful. And yes, he would like nothing better than to meet the Waterston family llama flock. And he would love to see Michael's performance of *A Christmas Carol*. And yes, maybe he would come to the next meeting of the library's book discussion group — what was this month's selection again?

This was what the Helping Hands project was really about, I decided. Maybe we weren't just making a small improvement in someone's physical surroundings. Okay, in Harvey's case a pretty big improvement. But we just might be making an even larger positive change in his whole life.

He chattered happily — and a little tipsily — all the way to his house. About how beautiful the New Life Baptist Choir's concert had been. How nice all the Helping Hands people were. How much he was looking forward to his new decluttered life.

I parked right beside his front walk and decided it would probably be a good thing to wait until I'd seen him safely inside. Better still, I should go in with him — make sure he didn't trip on the cracked and broken walkway. If he questioned it, I could say that I wanted to remind myself how much there was left to do.

I was pretty sure Randall already had a new walkway on his list of repairs the house needed. We should add a nice bright porch light to the list. And maybe a second light here at the street end of his walk. I'd jot the idea down in my notebook once I'd seen Harvey safely inside.

He was standing just outside the car with the door still open, and he had fallen silent. I glanced over and saw him staring into the darkness, his face turned anxious.

"Something wrong?" I asked.

"There's someone out there," he whispered, pointing.

He wasn't turning paranoid, was he? No, I spotted it, too. Just a hint of movement, a shadow barely seen against the not-quite blackness of the moonless night.

I motioned him to get back in the car while I pulled out my phone and called 911.

"What's your emergency, Meg?" Debbie Ann, the dispatcher said.

"I think there's a prowler at Mr. Harvey Dunlop's house." I climbed into the car myself and clicked the button to lock the doors. "I just pulled up to drop him off, and we spotted someone in his yard."

"Hang on a sec," she said.

Harvey and I waited in tense silence for a few moments. Any second, I told myself, Debbie Ann would tell me that one of the deputies was only a few minutes away. But it seemed to be taking forever.

"Meg," Debbie Ann said. "Is the prowler waving at you?"

I peered through the window. A shadowy figure had detached itself from the larger shadow of the house and was waving both arms overhead, as if trying to attract our attention.

"Yes, the prowler is waving," I said. "So I guess I should deduce that it's not really a prowler."

"It's Aida," she said. "And she says the coast is clear, so meet her at the front door."

"It's Aida," I told Harvey. "Deputy Butler. She was here helping earlier."

"That's all right, then." A little of his good cheer returned. "But I wonder why she's here."

"Let's go find out."

Aida was waiting for us on the front porch. The almost completely decluttered front porch — apart from two wicker rockers flanking a small weathered wooden table, it was empty. Under any other circumstances I'd have found it a little stark. But compared with what it looked like when we'd arrived this morning — okay, stark probably still applied. But starkly beautiful.

"Sorry," Aida said. "Didn't mean to spook you. Mrs. Gudgeon next door called in a prowler report. Didn't see anybody, but I

161

was checking the backyard when you drove up. And I didn't recognize the car, so I slipped behind the house to see what you were up to."

"Glad it was a false alarm," I said.

"But what if there really was a prowler?" Harvey asked. He was fumbling with the key to his front door.

"If there was, they were long gone by the time I got here," she said. "And if you ask me, Mrs. Gudgeon is . . . well, I just wish I had a nickel for every time she's called in to report prowlers. Or bears. She's real big on the bear sightings, too. Still, if you like, I'll check the premises before you settle in."

So Harvey and I waited just inside the front door while Aida methodically went room to room, inspecting every place large enough for even a stray cat to hide, and checking that all the windows and doors were secure.

"All clear," she said. "And if it'll make you feel better, I can ask for extra patrols on your street tonight."

"It would," he said. "Thank you."

"You want to look around yourself?" Aida asked. "See if everything looks okay?"

He nodded, and made his own tour of inspection. While he did, Aida radioed in the request for extra patrols. Harvey finally returned to the living room, looking slightly uneasy.

"I think everything's okay," he said. "It's kind of hard to tell."

"Did you notice anything missing?" I asked.

"Yeah — about half my stuff." He gave us a surprisingly goofy grin. "But I'm pretty sure it's all in boxes over at the furniture store." His grin faded. "It just looks so different."

I wanted to point out that a lot of people had been working very hard to achieve that difference, but I wasn't sure how he'd take it.

"Is that a bad thing?" I asked instead.

A look of surprise crossed his face.

"No," he said. "I guess maybe it's a good thing. Just really different, you know. It'll take some getting used to. But . . . well, I guess I can get used to it."

He flashed us the grin again.

"Starting to look pretty nice to me," Aida said,

"You know, it's a little less cozy," he said. "And I feel . . . I don't know . . . disloyal, maybe? Or wasteful?" He took a deep breath and exhaled slowly. "But you know, I think maybe I can breathe better in here now."

Maybe he was just reacting to the fact that

all the dust we'd raised during our packing efforts had settled while we were at the concert and the party. Or maybe his reaction was emotional rather than physical.

"You know, I'm glad I know the Helping Hands can also fix the place up after it's empty," he went on. "Without the stuff in the way you kind of focus on everything that's wrong with it. Dents and scrapes and broken parts."

"It'll be like new when you move back in again," I said.

He smiled at that. And that made me suddenly very happy, in spite of my tiredness.

"Do you think we'll finish tomorrow?" he asked. "Moving the stuff out, I mean."

"We might," I said. "If not tomorrow, then certainly the day after. It'll help if we get an early start. Would it work for us to come by at eight a.m.?"

"That will be great."

"Oh — I almost forgot something." I fished into my purse and drew out one of the keys Randall had given me. "Your key to the furniture store. So you can go over and look at your possessions any time you want to."

"Thank you." Harvey got a little choked up. I did too, actually. So we all watched in solemn silence as he added the key to his own key ring.

Then Aida and I wished him goodnight and filed out. We paused on the front porch and listened until we heard him lock both of his doors and put on the security chain.

"He should be okay," Aida said as we picked our way carefully down the uneven surface of his front walk.

"Do you really think there's some kind of danger?"

"Probably not, but why take chances?" She stopped just outside the hedge and surveyed not only Harvey's house but the neighboring ones. "You want to know what I think? I'm not even sure there was a prowler tonight — I'm guessing maybe all the activity over here has unsettled Mrs. Gudgeon. Got her jumpy. Doesn't take much with her. But some of the other prowler calls were real. And I bet it's someone in the neighborhood who's trying to scare him. Get him upset enough that he moves out."

"I doubt if it would work that way," I said. "I don't think he'd be capable of organizing a move, and the more scared he got the more he'd freeze."

"Could be — but they wouldn't know that." Aida had given up glaring at Harvey's two next-door neighbors and had turned to glance at the neighbors across the street. Directly in front of us was a small playground. The houses to either side were both dark. For that matter, so were most of the houses up and down the street. Even Harvey's now. "Most of the neighbors aren't thrilled with how his house looks, but they're not being jerks about it that I've heard. Just Mr. Brimley and Mrs. Gudgeon. I'm betting if there is a prowler it's one of them. Or maybe the two of them are in it together."

"Don't forget his cousins," I said. "Especially the one who showed up here."

"A good point. We won't." Aida turned her gaze back to Harvey's house. "You know, as long as the Helping Hands project is fixing up his house, let's install a good security system. One with cameras and motion-activated lights. The whole shebang. Maybe he won't need it — maybe once he's no longer the neighborhood eyesore the prowlers will stop bothering him. But just in case they don't, it would be nice to get the goods on them."

"I'll add it to my list," I said. "Along with a light for that damned front walk."

"Now you're thinking," she said. "See you tomorrow."

I climbed into my car and headed home.

When I got home, things were quiet. The relatives had gone to bed, except for a few hardcore gamers playing either Dungeons & Dragons or Settlers of Catan in the library. Michael was pacing in his office, doing a little bit of last-minute rehearsal for his annual one-man performance of *A Christmas Carol,* since the first show was tomorrow.

I pulled out my laptop so I could check my email, and sat in the living room in front of the fire. The group email I'd sent out to the Helping Hands list, asking for volunteers for tomorrow, had received several dozen answers and I wanted to acknowledge them all, if only with a quick "Thanks! See you there!" As soon as I finished that I was going to hit the hay. And —

"Mom?" I looked up to see Josh hovering in the doorway. He looked unhappy. "Can I ask you something?"

"What's up?" I pushed away my laptop and sat back, stifling the impulse to ask why he was up so much past his bedtime. And braced myself for what I expected would be another frustrating attempt to think of the perfect gift for everyone on his Christmas list. I hoped I could convince him to put off the search till morning. What I wouldn't give for them to still feel last year's blithe confidence that they knew exactly what all of us wanted.

He perched on the arm of the sofa and kicked its leg a couple of times before remembering how much it annoyed me and making a visible effort to hold his foot still. I couldn't help thinking that one abrupt move would send him fleeing away, like the birds that had been flocking in our yard that afternoon, easily startled yet lured back by the birdseed.

"It's about Mr. Dunlop," he said. "And his house."

He paused there.

"Pretty unusual," I said eventually, just to get the conversation moving again.

"Yeah." Suddenly the dam opened. "I was making fun of him. I know I shouldn't have, but the whole thing was just so . . ." His hands gestured as he hunted for the right word.

"Weird?" I suggested.

He nodded.

"You're not alone," I said. "Seems pretty weird to me, too. Did you make fun of him to his face?"

"No. Just to Jamie. And there's no way Mr. Dunlop could have heard me — I waited till we were outside. I still feel bad."

"I understand," I said. "I've been having a

hard time with it myself."

"Wanting to make fun of him?" He looked surprised.

"A little bit, but mostly wanting to shake him and say 'Wake up! Look at what you're doing to yourself!' And resenting how hard it is to be patient and move at the speed he can handle — that's tough. Luckily Rose Noire and Gran-gran are better at it than I am."

"Rose Noire is," Josh said. "I think Grangran feels a lot like you do. Whenever she couldn't take it anymore she'd go out and walk in circles around the house till she felt better."

"She's a good example to all of us," I said, not trying to hide my smile. "I get that you feel bad. I think you should do what I'm going to do."

"Apologize to Mr. Dunlop?" He looked glum at the idea.

"No, if you're sure he never heard you, apologizing wouldn't help. You could apologize to Jamie — tell him you're sorry you said those things in front of him."

Heavy sigh, and then a nod.

"But mostly what I'm going to do is try to figure out why Mr. Dunlop can't get rid of things," I said. "And then see if there's anything we can do to fix that. For example, maybe he's sad because he's lost all his family and doesn't have many friends."

"He was telling Rose Noire and Grangran all these stories about his things, and the family members who used to own them," Josh said. "I can kind of get that. Some of his stuff is cool. But most of it's just . . . old. And all that paper."

"Well, maybe he's afraid to get rid of the paper," I said. "What if he throws it away and then he needs some of the information?"

Josh was silent for a bit.

"Mason still has every video game he's ever owned," he said. "Even the ones that only work on the PS3 that broke when he was, like, seven. Drives his mom crazy. But he's only really like that with games. He doesn't get upset if she gives away his old clothes or anything. Just games. I guess Mr. Dunlop is like that with everything. You think once we get his house clean he can keep it that way?"

"I hope so," I said. "But even if he doesn't, he'll be better off for a while. And maybe if it starts getting messy again he'll let us help him."

"Yeah." he stood up, and then paused again in the doorway. "You know those old bicycles that are too small for us that you

170

wanted us to donate? The ones we put up in the barn loft for the time being?"

I nodded.

"Maybe it's time to unload those," he said. "Mine, anyway. I'll check with Jamie, but I expect he'll be fine with it, too."

"Good idea," I said. "If you're both sure, let's take them down to the women's shelter. The kids who are staying there can use them, and you can see them occasionally and know they went to a good home."

"Yeah. That'd work okay."

With that he disappeared and I heard his quick footsteps going up the stairway.

I made a few entries in my notebook, to remind myself to talk to Jamie about his outgrown bike. To schedule a trip to the women's shelter. And to do some online reading about hoarding. I didn't get it. And that bothered me.

And I scribbled another item — to ask Dad about Harvey. He might have some insights that would make this whole thing easier on all of us. He might even know a therapist who could work with Harvey.

But all of that could wait. I needed to be up before seven to make it to Harvey's by eight. And it was already past midnight.

I shut my notebook and headed upstairs.

CHAPTER 13

Tuesday, December 22

When my alarm rang I suppressed the impulse to toss it out the window. Harvey's party had gone on longer than I'd expected, and I'd gone to bed later than was quite consistent with waking up cheerfully a little before dawn. And then I remembered that the day would be a decluttering marathon.

"Rise and —" Michael began, reaching over to wake me.

"Don't finish that," I said. "I am rising, but I have no intention of shining before noon. Why did I tell everybody we were starting at eight?"

"Because you checked the weather report and heard that the rain will be moving into the area by noon?" Michael looked up from his phone. "Intermittent thundershowers all afternoon followed by heavy rain tonight."

"Ick," I said. "I picked eight because I wanted to get it over with as soon as possible. Rain won't help."

"Should I go fix breakfast?"

"Deacon Washington said he'd have the Not Just Tacos Truck there at dawn," I said through a yawn. "And Muriel at the diner's sending fresh bagels."

"Then I'll just whip up some smoothies to tide us over." He leaped out of bed, doing a very convincing impression of a morning person, and dashed downstairs.

When we got to Beau Street, my jaw dropped. Cars and pickups were parked all up and down the street, starting two blocks away from Harvey's house.

"Whoa," Josh said. "Half the town must be here."

"See, Mom?" Jamie said. "We should have no problem finishing it all today, so you can go back to doing more fun things."

More likely, so I could go back to managing other, less massive Helping Hands projects. But still, my heart lifted at the sight.

Near the end of Harvey's front walk, a group of about a dozen people were singing "Joy to the World." Most likely members of the New Life Baptist Choir, to judge from the power and beauty of their voices. And Deacon Washington was there in the Not Just Tacos Truck, dishing out breakfast burritos, breakfast croissants, and, at least in theory, hot oatmeal — although he rarely got many takers for that.

"I'll drop you off at the door and find a parking space," Michael said.

The boys immediately hopped into the breakfast line. Dad was there, putting in his order and chatting to Chief Burke, who was already nibbling on his burrito. I saw Cordelia standing on Harvey's front walk, just in front of the porch talking to —

Yikes! She was talking to Mother. Did she not realize how very hard I had been trying to keep Mother from seeing what Harvey's house looked like inside? I quickened my step.

"Meg, dear," Mother said. "I can't stay long — I just came to pick up the keys to the furniture store."

"Your mother's going to supervise arranging things as they arrive at the furniture store," Cordelia said. "Your dad's going to take her over now."

"Well, right after James gets us both a little bite of breakfast," Mother said. "So kind of Deacon Washington to come out this early."

I fished out my key ring, handed over the furniture store key, and breathed a sigh of relief as they strolled down the sidewalk and joined the boys in the breakfast line.

Then I glanced at my watch. Eight o'clock. Well, seven fifty-nine. Close enough. I squared my shoulders and mounted the wooden steps to the porch. Was it just my imagination, or were they more wobbly than before? Had all the foot traffic yesterday done a number on them?

I'd sic a Shiffley on it as soon as I spotted one in the crowd. First things first.

I knocked on Harvey's door and waited for an answer.

And waited. And waited.

I knocked again.

Still no answer.

"Bother," I muttered under my breath. Had he gotten cold feet? That would be a pretty pickle, with what looked like half the town here to help him.

And all of them staring at me, even the carolers and the many people munching on their breakfasts.

"Harvey?" I called. "It's Meg."

Now people were coming up the walk. Only a few — Cordelia, Rose Noire, and Minerva Burke. But they could be the start of a general migration.

"Something wrong?" Cordelia asked.

"He's not answering," I said. "I'm worried that he might have gotten cold feet."

"Drat the man," Minerva muttered.

I could see a few more people drifting our way.

"Minerva, can you keep everyone back on the sidewalk until we sort this out?" I asked.

"Can do." She strode down the walkway and began shooing the venturesome ones back to the sidewalk. I looked at Rose Noire and Cordelia.

"You two spent more time with him than anyone yesterday," I said. "Can you keep trying to get him to answer — Cordelia, why don't you try from here, and Rose Noire, you can call to him from the kitchen door, or maybe at the bedroom window."

Rose Noire nodded and scurried off toward the back of the house.

"What are you going to do?" Cordelia asked.

I took a few steps away from the door — in fact, I went back down to the front walk.

"I'm going to call Randall and see if he can send his cousin the locksmith down here to get us inside." I kept my voice low, in case Harvey was ignoring us from just inside his front door. "And then — is Chief Burke still here?"

"Chatting with your dad."

"Great — I'll ask if he can do an official welfare check, which might keep us from getting sued if Harvey has changed his mind and doesn't want us helping him."

"Good plan." She went back to the front door and knocked.

"Harvey? It's Cordelia. May I come in?"

I decided to put some distance between me and the house before making my calls. And then —

"Joy to the World!"

I started slightly at how loud the carol was. Had Minerva brought the entire choir? No — apparently she was keeping everyone from coming near Mr. Dunlop's house by recruiting them into the caroling. Except for a few people still munching their croissants or burritos, everyone who'd come to help was now singing vigorously.

"Well, that should help rouse him," I said to myself.

But it wasn't going to help me make phone calls.

I moved a little farther from the house. And for that matter, a little farther from the caroling.

At least with Randall I could text. I opened up my phone and typed.

"Harvey not opening door. Might have cold feet. Send locksmith!"

Only a few seconds later, Randall replied: "On it!"

But I didn't think texting would work as

well with Chief Burke.

Should I maybe go back to the van? Of course, Michael might have parked it blocks away.

The garage. I'd probably be able to hear if I put it between me and the singers.

Better yet, I noticed that the side door was open a crack. I could call from inside. Of course, the open garage door could be a problem, if Harvey had noticed it. He'd probably be upset — maybe that was why he wasn't answering our knocks. Or worse, what if his relatives and neighbors had gotten in again and hauled off more stuff? In which case, he might be sulking inside, lumping the Helping Hands crew in with the predatory Haverhills.

But when I stepped inside, the garage looked just as it had the last time I'd seen it. Only slightly cluttered. And his car was here, so he couldn't have gone anywhere. And —

What was that on the floor in front of the car? It looked like a hand.

I took a few steps forward.

Yes, it was a hand. Attached to a body. Harvey's body. There was a pool of blood around his head. A really big pool.

But it wasn't spreading

I was pretty sure that meant he was dead.

CHAPTER 14

I pulled out my phone and called 911. Debbie Ann, the dispatcher, picked up on the first ring.

"Meg, what's wrong? Neighbors causing trouble again at Mr. Dunlop's?"

"It's Harvey," I said. "He's hurt — maybe dead. In the garage."

"Oh, my."

I heard the quick rattle of a keyboard. Without hanging up, I sent a quick text to Dad: "Need you in the garage now. Bring your medical bag."

"Chief's already here somewhere," I said into the phone. "If you could tell him —"

"He's on his way over," Debbie Ann said. "What happened to Mr. Dunlop — do you know? Are you sure he's dead?"

I sidled forward again until I could get a better look at him.

"I haven't checked his pulse," I said. "But there's a really big pool of blood around his head. Maybe he tripped and hit his head on the concrete floor. Or maybe —" I was inching a little closer and spotted something. "Oh, my. It looks as if he was hit on the head with a brass spittoon."

"Lord have mercy," Debbie Ann said. "I hope they can keep that part out of the obituary. I'll let you tell the chief. I can try to get hold of your dad."

"He's already here." I could see Dad trotting toward me. I suspected Harvey was beyond help, even from Dad's medical skills. But since Dad was also the local medical examiner, they'd probably need him to make the death official. And the chief was walking behind him, and a little more slowly, since he was talking on his phone. "I'll get back to making sure no one barges in."

"He's in there?" Dad asked when he reached me.

I nodded, and stood aside so he could run in. Then I closed the door behind him and looked around. Cordelia was still knocking on Harvey's door, and from this angle I could see Rose Noire, standing on her tiptoes beneath the middle of the three windows in the side of the house, shouting for Harvey. I should call them off.

The chief strode up, and I stood aside so

he could follow Dad.

Should I go over and notify Cordelia and Rose Noire?

Just then Rose Noire glanced over at me. I beckoned for her to come near.

"I think the window might be unlocked," she said as she drew near. "If we had a ladder, we could try to get in through there."

"No need," I said.

"But what if something has happened to him?" she asked.

"Something has," I said. "He's out here in the garage. And I'm pretty sure he's dead. Dad and Chief Burke are in there checking."

"Oh, my." Her hands flew to her mouth, she closed her eyes, and her face took on an expression of pain. "That must be what the magpies were trying to tell me this morning."

"They talk?" I asked. "Or were you talking to them in . . . magpie-ese, or whatever you call it."

"They don't actually talk," she said. "At least not yet. Though I've heard of talking magpies, and I was thinking of trying to teach them. But they bring me things. Little gifts to thank me for feeding them."

"Yes, so Caroline was telling me." I wondered if the magpies ever did this to their keepers at the zoo. I suspected they hadn't. Maybe what they were thanking her for was not so much for feeding them as for letting them fly away freely afterward. Still, what did it have to do with Harvey?

"But I should have known this was a bad omen."

"So what was this ominous gift?"

"A black butterfly wing." She shuddered slightly. "I should have known."

"Okay, that does sound a little creepy," I said. "But how could you have known it was foretelling death for Harvey? The universe's department in charge of omens needs to up its game a bit. Look, can you watch the door here for a minute — I want to break the news to Cordelia so she can stop knocking and calling."

"And the rest of the crowd?"

"We'll let Chief Burke decide," I said. "Who else to tell, and how, and when."

"The chief." Her face grew solemn. "You think someone killed Harvey?"

"Let's hope not," I said. "Maybe Dad can save him. And it could be just a horrible accident. Sheer luck that it didn't happen years ago, and the only weird and ironic thing is that it happened just when we were about to clear all the dangerous clutter out of his house. But even if it was an accident, if he dies it will still be an unattended death, so we still need the police. Anyway — stay here."

I walked back to the front porch. Cordelia turned away from the door and came down to meet me.

"What if something's happened to him?" she asked. "Should we break the door down?"

"He's in the garage," I said.

"Well, that's a relief," she said. Then she must have picked up on my expression. "Or is it?"

I explained what I'd found. It didn't take more than a few sentences, but before I was finished, a police cruiser with the lights flashing had pulled into Harvey's driveway. Aida Butler hopped out.

The ad hoc choir's rendition of "O Little Town of Bethlehem," started sounding a little ragged, as most of the singers craned their necks to see what was happening. But Minerva Burke managed to keep them singing away — and more important, out from underfoot.

The chief met Aida at the door, and the two of them were talking to Rose Noire.

"I should go," I said.

As I approached the garage, I heard Rose Noire explaining.

183

"I don't know — Meg is the one who found him."

The chief nodded, and stepped back inside.

"Oh, dear," Rose Noire muttered. "What a terrible thing to happen — and just when the Helping Hands program was creating so much good energy in the town."

I was about to protest that what had happened to Harvey probably had nothing to do with the program. But what if it did? What if the reason he'd been out in his garage had something to do with our being here?

The chief came out again.

"Send someone to the street to steer the ambulance in when it gets here," he said.

"I'll go," Rose Noire said.

"Harvey's not dead?" My face probably wore the same sudden, hopeful look I'd seen on Rose Noire's.

"Your dad's a stubborn man." The chief's bleak expression snuffed out my momentary surge of hope. "Horace should be here soon to work the scene."

I was momentarily surprised — working the scene already? It probably meant that the chief didn't have much hope. And as I'd already reminded Rose Noire, an accidental death was still an unattended death. Or was

Dad being his usual suspicious self? His addiction to reading mystery books probably made him — well, not exactly more eager than the average medical examiner to come across a murder, but certainly slower to give up on the possibility. And while the chief didn't share Dad's enthusiasm over homicides — he'd seen plenty during his years as a Baltimore homicide detective — he appreciated Dad's thoroughness. If nothing else, it could help fend off problems with the Haverhills.

In fact, that was probably the reason for the ambulance that was already pulling into the driveway. The Haverhills would know we'd done everything we could.

"What should we do about them?" I nodded toward where the assembled volunteers were still singing away. A good thing Minerva was choosing old standard carols whose words everybody already knew, because hardly a single person was actually looking down at the carol books she'd passed out. "I'm assuming you don't want us moving ahead with the decluttering."

"Not today," he said. "I might need to talk to some of your volunteers, but not right now. Can you send them all home?"

"Or off to other projects," I said. "Can do."

Just then I stood aside to let the EMTs run past. The chief followed them in. I headed over to address the carolers.

Minerva saw me approaching, so she cut off "The Twelve Days of Christmas" at the end of the seven swans a-swimming.

"Thank you all for coming out so early," I said to the crowd. "I'm afraid Mr. Dunlop has had an unfortunate accident."

My expression probably signaled how bad it was. Murmurs ran through the crowd, and various people crossed themselves, took off their hats, or shook their heads sadly.

"We can't really go forward with the de-cluttering without him," I went on. "So we're postponing that. But if you'd like to help out with another project, stand by while I pull together a list of what else is going on today."

I took a few steps away, pulled out my notebook, and began scanning all the projects I'd planned for us to start tomorrow. A few people headed for their cars, but most were waiting patiently. Randall Shiffley had appeared and Cordelia seemed to be briefing him.

Minerva came over to join me.

"I bet Henry was hinting that he'd be happier if there were fewer people hanging around lollygagging here," Minerva said.

"Hinting?" I chuckled. "I'm not sure he knows the meaning of the word."

"True enough. So I'm going to take my choir members over to the hospital to do some caroling. Unless you need us for any other Helping Hands projects."

"I can probably find work for everyone here if I have to," I said. "But I won't complain if you whisk a few of them off for another good deed."

Minerva strode off, calling the names of various choir members as she went. The rest of the volunteers seemed to be gathering around me.

Including Josh, Jamie, and Michael. I was touched at how disappointed the boys looked.

"So I guess we don't get to pack any more boxes for Mr. Dunlop," Josh said.

"Not today," I said.

"Won't he still want his stuff packed up when he gets better?" Jamie asked.

"I'm sure he will," I said, trying to project an optimism I didn't feel. "But we can't go ahead without him. So in the meantime, anyone who wants to can help with other Helping Hands projects."

Although I was speaking to the boys, I said it loudly enough that the rest of the waiting volunteers could hear us. I turned back to the crowd.

"Okay, who here knows how to sew?" I asked. Most of the women and two of the men raised their hands. "How would you like to help with a quilting project?"

I spun out the tale of Mrs. Dinwiddie, whose grandmother, a legendary local quilter, had died leaving one last ambitious project unfinished. And the fact that even if Mrs. Dinwiddie had been a quilter, she was living in an efficiency apartment so small she didn't have room to spread out a bath towel, much less a queen-sized quilt. As I talked, I texted Robyn to ask if we could use the parish hall for the quilting project. Luckily she was by her phone and quickly texted back that it would be fine, and she could meet the volunteers there within the half hour.

"So, does anyone know Mrs. Dinwiddie?" Two women raised their hands. "Great! You two can go over to her apartment and fetch all the quilt pieces. Actually, you might want to take another person or two with you to carry everything. And the rest of you, go fetch your sewing baskets and assemble in the Trinity Episcopal parish hall for a big quilting bee!"

Amid a buzz of excited chatter, about half the crowd streamed off in the direction of their cars — except for half a dozen who were already forming an ad hoc refreshments committee. Their faces showed that for most, their new assignment was arguably an improvement over clutter busting. The rest of the volunteers, about three-fourths of them men, crowded closer. I glanced up at Randall.

"Can you use a work crew for that handicapped ramp?" I asked.

"Sure can," he said. "We were thinking that might have to wait till poor Harvey's situation was sorted."

"Next project," I said to the crowd. "Anyone with carpentry skills — Randall could use you on a crew to build a wheelchair ramp." I rattled off the address. "If you're nearby, go home and fetch your toolboxes. If you're not, just meet Randall there."

"Roger," Randall said, and strode off. Most of the men and at least half of the remaining women followed.

We were down to a scant dozen volunteers. Including Michael — who was probably a better carpenter than many of the men, thanks to years of building sets. For that matter, he'd probably spent enough time on costume crews that he could have done just fine helping with the quilts. But I suspected he was planning to volunteer on whatever the boys would be working on.

"The rest of you are probably going to want to take lessons in sewing or carpentry sometime soon," I said. "At least you will once you hear the project I have for you. We're going to fertilize Mrs. Diamandis's rose garden."

Expressions of relief crossed a few faces, and even a few chuckles.

"Michael, why don't you start them off with that nice pile of well-aged llama manure behind our barn? And when that runs out, Dad's been collecting a list of the local organic farmers who'd be glad to let us haul away a few truckloads of the stuff."

Much laughter. A few people winced. But they all copied down Mrs. Diamandis's address, and most of them dashed off to their cars.

"Here, you're going to need this." Michael handed me a foil-wrapped breakfast burrito. "Seth's giving me a ride." He nodded at where our neighbor from across the street was pulling up in his pickup truck. "So I can leave you the Twinmobile. I'll just move it a little closer before we take off."

"Thanks," I said. "The way the sky looks, you might not get more than one load of manure in before the rain starts. And I'm not sure anyone will want to shovel manure in the middle of a rainstorm."

"We'll at least make a start," he said. "After that I'll see if they can use a few more hands on the wheelchair ramp."

And then everything stopped for a few minutes as the EMTs came dashing out with Harvey. Their rolling cart was hung with medical gadgets — an IV bag and other things I couldn't name. Dad was running along behind. Remembering that huge pool of blood on the garage floor, I avoided trying to get a better look.

The grim look on Dad's face told me all I needed to know.

Once the ambulance had raced off, Beau Street saw what was probably the first traffic jam in its existence. Then the road cleared and police vehicles outnumbered civilian ones, and something that looked deceptively like peace and quiet settled over the neighborhood.

A few people had stayed to rubberneck, which I knew the chief would find annoying. Cordelia and Rose Noire had seated themselves on the front steps of Harvey's house and seemed to be keeping an eye on the stragglers. And at least enough people had taken off that there was a clear space for Horace to park when he drove up.

He stepped out of his car and stood, looking at Mr. Dunlop's house with a stricken look on his face.

"Oh, God," he muttered. "Please tell me it's not so."

"I'm sorry," I said. "I didn't know you were that close to Harvey. Should we call in someone else to work the crime scene?"

"What? No, I barely knew him. It's this house. It's my recurring nightmare, having to work a crime scene in a place like this. Do you know how hard this is going to be? How long it's going to take? How impossible it will be to do it well?"

"Oh, right," I said. "Would it make you feel better if I told you that we don't even know for sure that it is a crime scene? Could be just an accident. And whatever happened didn't happen in the house anyway."

"It didn't?" A condemned man getting a reprieve on the steps of the gallows would have worn the kind of expression that was now spreading over his face. "Then where did it happen?"

"In the garage."

"So smaller, at least," he said.

"And a lot less cluttered. Almost normal, in fact. Follow me."

I led him over to where Aida was standing, talking to Chief Burke as she guarded the garage doors.

"Hey, Horace," she said. "They took Harvey away, but I got some photos while the EMTs were working on him."

"What does it look like?" Horace asked.

"The garage's not nearly as cluttered as the house," Aida said. "But there was a lot of random stuff stored up on the joists. Looks as if a honking big brass vase fell down and hit him on the head."

"Ouch." Horace winced.

"A spittoon, actually," I said.

"Ick," Aida said. "And here I was, thinking if there's an estate — er, a yard sale later, how nice the thing would look holding flowers on the altar if only folks could get past the fact that it had almost taken Harvey out of this world."

"I think even if they didn't know its bloodthirsty history they'd have a hard time getting past the fact that it was a spittoon," I said.

"Would anyone even know that?" Aida asked. "I didn't."

"Old folks would," the chief said. "And according to Dr. Langslow, the spittoon didn't fall on him."

"Oh, no," I muttered. I had a feeling I knew what he was about to say.

"Someone tried to murder Mr. Dunlop."

CHAPTER 15

"Murder him?" Aida winced slightly. "You're sure? I mean, it sure looked like an accident — like the vase — er, spittoon — fell down from the rafters and hit his head."

"He was hit over the head by the spittoon," the chief said. "And yes, it could have fallen on him from above. But only once. No way it could jump back up into the rafters and tumble down to whack him again."

"Ah," Aida said.

"It couldn't have . . . um . . . rebounded?" I asked. I'd have said "bounced," but it sounded too frivolous.

"Three blows of roughly equal force," the chief said. "So no. It's attempted homicide. And with all due respect to Dr. Langslow, I'll be astonished if poor Mr. Dunlop pulls through. So let's get Horace in to start working the crime scene. Meg, can you find someone reliable to guard the door while he's working? I'd like for Aida to start interviewing some of those blasted volunteers to see if anyone saw anything suspicious."

"I could stand guard," I said. "Assuming I qualify as reliable."

"Maybe later," the chief said. "Right now, we're going to find a quiet place, and you're going to tell me exactly how you found Mr. Dunlop, and then after that, everything else you can think of about him and what went on here yesterday. Maybe your grandmother could stand guard for a bit."

Horace hoisted the heavy bag containing his crime scene kit. I heard him utter an audible sigh of relief when he saw the relatively uncluttered garage interior.

I went to fetch Cordelia. She and Rose Noire were on the porch, talking to a Shiffley carrying a tool bag. I didn't recognize him, but I spotted the Shiffley Lock & Key truck parked by the front walk. They turned to me.

"You still need the door opened?" he said.

"You should probably ask the chief." I pointed toward the garage.

He nodded and strode over.

I turned to Cordelia. "The chief would like you to keep an eye on the garage door, if you're willing."

She nodded, and dragged over a chair from Harvey's porch so she had a place to sit.

When I got back to the garage, the chief and the locksmith were both standing, gazing at the door.

"If it's not on him he didn't drop it in here," Horace called back.

"Blast," the chief said. "Yes, we'll need you to unlock the house. Can we wait until Horace has had a chance to examine the locks? And then, if we don't locate those keys, I may need you to change the locks on the doors. I don't like the idea that whoever tried to kill Mr. Dunlop may be running around with access to my crime scene."

"Front and back doors?" the locksmith asked.

"Yes," the chief said. "And the garage."

"And the furniture store," I said. Seeing their surprised looks, I went on. "We've been moving all of Harvey's stuff into the old Furniture World building on Scott Street. I gave him a key last night so he could feel . . . I don't know. More in control of his stuff."

"The furniture store, too, then," the chief said. "Too early yet to tell what's relevant. But not till after Horace has seen them."

"I'll do a visual inspection now, figure out

what kind of locks I'll need, and then fetch them," the locksmith said.

The chief and I paced back and forth in Mr. Dunlop's backyard while I told him everything I could remember that seemed at all relevant. The morning visit yesterday, when Cordelia and Caroline and I had seen the inside of the garage — which yes, had looked very much then as it did now. What we'd accomplished in the decluttering. The various interactions I'd had with his neighbors and his cousins. Our trip to the concert and the party at the furniture store. How I'd dropped him off just before midnight, full of ham and scalloped potatoes and chocolate cake, just a little merry from the wine, and guardedly optimistic about the next day's work.

When he'd finished asking me what felt like several million questions, he thanked me.

"One more thing," he said.

Just then his phone rang.

"It's your father." He turned slightly aside as he answered. "How is he?"

His face hardened slightly, and I knew it wasn't good news.

"You did what you could," he said. "I'll notify the family. And see if you can get the autopsy scheduled as soon as possible."

He hung up and stared into space for a moment or two.

"So now we have a murder investigation." He turned and went back to the garage. He said a few words to Aida, then went inside to see what Horace was doing.

Poor Harvey. I looked around for something to do — anything to distract myself. There were still a few gawkers lurking nearby, but none of them were my volunteers. Which meant they were the chief's problem, not mine. Or, more immediately, Aida's problem, since he'd put her in charge of keeping people away from the crime scene. The locksmith had scoped out all the doors and departed. Cordelia and Rose Noire, relieved of guard duty, had gone off to one of the other Helping Hands projects in progress. Probably about time I did the same thing myself.

I was about to get into the Twinmobile and make good my escape when a battered van drove up and parked crookedly just opposite Harvey's house. Not a car I recognized. In fact, definitely not from around here — it had North Carolina license plates.

I've never denied being curious. I paused, car keys in hand, to see what this new arrival was up to.

A young woman got out of the van, pulled

a key ring out of her pocket to lock the door, then stood up and looked around as if to get her bearings. She wore a baggy black men's overcoat, black leggings, and clunky black ankle boots. The only note of color was a blood-red scarf wrapped several times around her neck with the ends trailing down her back — presumably for decorative purposes rather than warmth, since it was made of some kind of delicate open lace-work. Her eyes were hidden behind enormous sunglasses, in spite of the fact that the day was becoming increasingly overcast, and there was something lost and waiflike about her.

She started down the walkway to Harvey's house, and then froze in place, like a rabbit who has spotted a hawk overhead. I suspected once she passed the boxwoods that flanked the opening she'd spotted the bright yellow crime scene tape.

I strolled over.

"Can I help you?" I asked.

She started, uttered a small yelp, and stared at me, as frozen as if I'd said, "Stick 'em up!"

My first impression had been off — she wasn't young. In her mid-thirties, probably. I could tell better if I saw her eyes. And not all that waiflike — that was a fleeting impression created by the oversized coat. She was maybe a hair on the plump side of average. And also on the short side, about five two without the thick-soled boots.

"Are you looking for someone?" I asked.

"Is this Mr. Harvey Dunlop's residence?" Her voice was high, almost squeaky, with a faint almost lisp. And curiously mannered. I suddenly wondered if she'd cultivated that voice in her teens, in an attempt to seem arch and sophisticated, and never realized that she'd outgrown any charm it had ever had.

"Yes, it is," I said. "Are you a friend of his?"

"Yes, I — Who are you, anyway?" I liked her the better for this tiny burst of spirit. And when she took off her sunglasses to give me the benefit of her indignant gaze, I revised my estimate of her age upward. At least forty.

"My name is Meg Langslow." I held out my hand. She reluctantly pulled hers out of her coat pocket and barely touched mine by way of a handshake before shoving it back in her pocket.

"Oh!" She suddenly looked alarmed. "You're the one who's making Harvey clear out his stuff!"

Okay, she probably did know Harvey.

"Actually, it was the county building inspector making him declutter," I said. "I only came to help him get through it as painlessly as possible."

Just then Aida, who'd been patrolling the perimeter, came around from the back of the house and spotted us. She strode over in our direction.

The woman in black froze. Was it merely shyness, or had Aida's uniform spooked her?

"Let me introduce you to Deputy Aida Butler," I said to the woman. "Aida, this is a friend of Mr. Dunlop's. Ms. — Sorry, I don't know your name."

"Tabitha," she whispered. "Tabitha Fillmore. Why can't I just go in to see Harvey?"

"I'm sorry, Ms. Fillmore," Aida said. "Mr. Dunlop passed over this morning."

I winced slightly. To Mother's despair, I deliberately avoided euphemisms, and I thought "passed over" was a particularly odd one to use if you were talking about someone who'd been bashed over the head three times with brass spittoon. I'd have just said "he's dead." But maybe it was a good thing I wasn't the one breaking the news to anyone. Even "passed over" hit Tabitha hard. She gasped and staggered slightly, as if about to faint under the shock of the news.

"Are you all right, Ms. Fillmore?" Aida

had slipped a protective hand under Tabitha's arm. I was braced to catch her in case she keeled over completely — she was already listing in my direction.

"If I could just sit down for a minute," Tabitha said.

"Of course," Aida said. "Meg, maybe we could use your car?"

I unlocked the Twinmobile and opened the back door, and then we helped Tabitha into the seat. From her glance at the house and the slightly peeved expression on her face, I suspected she had been expecting — even hoping — to do her sitting down in the house. I rummaged in the back of the car, found the water jug and plastic cups I kept there, and poured her a glass.

"It's such a shock," she said as she took the proffered water. "How did it happen? Was it the hoard? Ever since he told me how bad it had gotten, I've been expecting him to go like the Collyer brothers."

"Collyer brothers?" Aida looked puzzled.

"Famous hoarders," I explained. "Lived in a brownstone in New York City. One of them died when some of their stuff fell down and crushed him, and after that happened the other one was trapped inside and died of starvation."

"A horrible story." Tabitha shuddered. "A

lot of people on the forum have nightmares about it — at least the ones who aren't in denial."

"What forum would that be?" Aida asked.

"An online forum called A Perfectly Good Place." Talking seemed to be reviving her. "That's where I first met Harvey. It's for people who have issues around clutter."

Yeah, that would be Harvey, all right.

"A Perfectly Good Place?" Aida seemed to find the name as peculiar as I did.

"It's named after something we all say a lot," Tabitha explained. "As in 'I can't throw it away — it's a perfectly good whatever.' "

"You say you first met there," Aida asked. "Had you also met him in person?"

"Not yet — I mean no." Tabitha took a gulp of water and a deep breath. "We started private messaging each other, and then eventually calling and texting each other. We . . . we found we were soul mates. We even hoarded some of the same things. We were making this plan, you know? We were going to meet in person, and help each other declutter our houses, and while we were doing that we could figure out if we had a future together. We were hoping — I mean, like I said, we were soul mates, but we needed to figure out how to make room in our lives for each other. But I guess that's not going to happen now."

She looked as if she were about to burst into tears, and I glanced around to make sure the box of tissues I kept in the car was within reach. But instead of opening the floodgates, she just snuffled in very loudly and took another gulp of water.

"Anyway," she went on. "When this whole thing about forcing him to clean up happened, I told him if he wanted me to, I could drive up and help. Or at least provide moral support — I knew people who didn't have clutter issues wouldn't understand how hard it was for him. So when he called last night and sounded so stressed, I packed my bag and set my alarm to get up really early, and, well, here I am."

Odd. I'd have sworn Harvey was feeling rather cheerful when I'd dropped him off at his house. Had going back into the still-cluttered house destroyed his good mood?

Or had it been talking to Tabitha that brought him down?

Or maybe he'd been fine, and she was the one who'd felt stressed. Worried, perhaps, that someone else was coming in to do the decluttering that she'd expected to serve as a bonding experience for them?

What if she was the one who'd killed him? In which case pretending that he'd been stressed and she'd driven up to provide moral support would be a good cover story.

Why was I so suspicious of her? Just because her reaction struck me as overly theatrical didn't mean it was fake. And for that matter, even if she was faking — or at least exaggerating — her grief, that only made her self-centered — it didn't make her a killer.

"But I was too late," Tabitha was saying. "Too late to do any good. So what happened?" Suddenly her mouth and eyes both flew open. "He didn't kill himself, did he? I know he was under tremendous stress, but surely he didn't. . . ."

Her voice trailed off and she looked from Aida to me, clearly dreading the answer.

"No," Aida said. "He didn't kill himself. I'm afraid someone else killed him."

Tabitha was speechless for at least thirty seconds. Then her face hardened into a mask of anger. "It must have been those hateful neighbors of his!" she spat out. "Or his cousins. They never left him alone, and one of them must have sicced the county on him. I guess they couldn't wait to get rid of him!"

CHAPTER 16

While Tabitha briefly succumbed to noisy but curiously dry sobbing, Aida and I exchanged a look. I wondered if she was thinking the same thing I was — that just because Harvey's relatives and neighbors had reported him to the county didn't mean they had murderous intentions toward him. In fact, I'd have assumed that having the county — or at least the Helping Hands program — show up to help him clean up his act would have calmed the worst of their rage rather than inciting them to murder.

"I don't suppose you could let me see inside," Tabitha asked, making a show of drying her eyes. "I'll never be able to meet Harvey in person, but if I could see where he lived . . . it would make me feel closer to him somehow. And give me some kind of closure."

"I'm sure that can be arranged later," Aida said. "But right now — well, it's possible that you know Mr. Dunlop better than most of the people here in town. And the more we know about him, the better chance we'll have of catching whoever killed him. May I ask you to come down to the police station so our chief can interview you? It could be a big help."

"Well . . ." Tabitha sniffled some more, and cast a few longing gazes at the house. "I suppose that would be okay."

"I'll drive you over to the station," Aida said. "It's not far, but the directions can be a little confusing. And then afterward, I can bring you back here to your car and see about arranging that look inside the house."

"Okay." She sounded more interested now. "Let me get my purse."

She hopped out of my car and clomped over to her van.

"Interesting how eager everyone is to get inside that house," I said in a low voice, once Tabitha was too far away to hear me.

"Isn't it?" Aida was keeping her eye on Tabitha. Did she have some reason, or was she only feeling the same instinctive, groundless dislike and suspicion I'd noticed in myself? And what would she do if the woman made a break for it — would she just call it in and let the other deputies intercept her? Probably, since her cruiser was — well, not completely blocked in by Horace's cruiser, but it would take a little maneuvering to get it out. Or would she snatch my keys and give chase in the Twin-mobile?

"Maybe this isn't the first time Tabitha has driven up here," I suggested. "Maybe it was her sneaking around that made Harvey think he had prowlers."

"No." Aida shook her head. "At least not all of the incidents. The first time I got called out it was that Mrs. Gudgeon next door, trying to take pictures of the inside of his house so she could report him to the county. But it wasn't all Mrs. Gudgeon, either. The other time I came out here on a ten-seventy, I could see Mrs. Gudgeon in her window with her binoculars, watching me chase the prowler. But yeah — we should check Tabitha's story. For starters, I bet the chief has already requested his phone records, so we'll see about this late night phone conversation. And there's another even more puzzling question — no matter who the prowlers were, what were they after? What could they possibly think he had in there that was so all-fired interesting?"

"Beats me." I shook my head. "Incidentally, since the chief's still in the garage, I assume you're taking her downtown to avoid letting her know that's the murder scene."

"Partly," she said. "She does seem to be pretty focused on the house, doesn't she?"

"You mean, if she were the killer, she'd be at least a little interested in the garage?"

"Yeah." Aida nodded. "Of course, maybe she's smart enough to figure that out and is doing a great job of pretending to be fixated on the house. And maybe I'm a bad person for suspecting her. Maybe she's just a poor lonely soul who thinks she's just lost her last chance at romance and happy ever after, and I'm doing her an injustice."

"Maybe," I said. "And maybe there's a reason she keeps darting looks back here, as if she's hoping you'll turn your back."

"Yeah," Aida said. "Squirrelly, if you ask me. But some people are just like that."

Tabitha appeared to have found her purse — a large shapeless lump of black suede. But now she was rummaging through the floor of her van, picking up things and stuffing them into the purse.

"Would you call her a Goth?" Aida asked.

I studied Tabitha for a moment.

"No," I said. "I think you need a little more . . . flair to be a Goth."

"Trying to be a Goth, but not really succeeding?"

"That's more like it."

"Why is this taking so long?" Aida was visibly fretting. "How hard can it be to find your damned purse?"

"She's a hoarder, remember?" I said. "Maybe she's got a hoard-infested car."

"Good heavens." Aida shuddered. "I had a great aunt who was at least halfway to being a hoarder. But with Great-Aunt Minnie you could kind of understand why — she went through the Great Depression. That left a mark on people. But Ms. Tabitha isn't old enough to have that particular excuse. What could possibly bring on this hoarder thing in someone her age?"

"No idea," I said. "Do we have any idea what brought it on in Harvey?"

She shook her head.

Tabitha finally hoisted her refilled purse over her shoulder and began slowly walking our way.

"Vern's on his way to take over guarding the place," Aida said. "Any chance you could hang around for a few minutes till he gets here? Chase away any nosy onlookers?"

"Can do," I said.

Aida escorted Tabitha to her cruiser and, after some careful maneuvering, escaped from the driveway and headed for the station.

I locked up the Twinmobile and set out to patrol the yard.

Although I stopped by Tabitha's car long enough to glance inside. Yes, if there was such a thing as a car hoarder, she was one. The front seat was merely bad — about as bad as the Twinmobile had looked after I'd returned from taking the boys and five of their friends on a field trip to Williamsburg and Jamestown. The back seat was completely filled with stuff up to the window level, and the cargo area was just solid junk. A quick inspection showed that while McDonald's was Tabitha's fast-food venue of choice, she did not entirely neglect Burger King, Taco Bell, Popeyes, Wendy's, Pizza Hut, and KFC. Given her North Carolina license plate it probably wasn't a surprise that she read *The Raleigh News & Observer*. And — wait. Were those letters strewn along the top of the hoard in the back seat?

I moved to a window on the opposite side of the van and confirmed that yes, they were letters. And one of them — from Duke Energy — was right-side up, and close enough for me to read the address. I jotted it down — you never know when a bit of information like that will come in handy.

Then, remembering that the neighbors might be watching, I ostentatiously tried all the van's doors, nodded officiously when I'd confirmed that they were all locked, and strode on to continue my patrol.

Harvey's backyard — and most of the backyards on the block — bordered the now-empty parking lot of a large, nondescript three-story building that belonged to Caerphilly College. It was a building to which the college's Building and Grounds Department exiled the unloved. Junior faculty members of departments that were not on good terms with B&G could find themselves housed in overflow offices there. Adjuncts were almost guaranteed a berth there. Faculty committees and work groups that had outlived their usefulness went there to die lingering deaths. Even when college was in session, the people who ostensibly had offices there seemed to avoid it, and I sometimes made use of Michael's faculty sticker to park there when some big event filled all the closer-in and more convenient lots.

But the winter break had begun some days ago. The lot was empty now, and probably had been overnight. A pity. If there had been anyone in the building, they'd have had the best view of Harvey's backyard — especially from the second and third floors, where they could have easily seen over his scraggly hedge.

Of course, there were still Mr. Brimley and the lady of the binoculars, who might have seen something, Although I wasn't sure I trusted them — and not just because they were probably suspects, although there was that. They were also so hostile to Harvey that I wasn't sure they were trustworthy on anything that involved him.

Thank goodness all this was the chief's problem, not mine. And besides —

I had come around the back of the house and was in the front yard now. A good thing, since I spotted Mr. Haverhill as soon as he parked.

I pulled out my phone and called the chief.

"Yes." His voice held that "this had better be important" note.

"Morris Haverhill, Mr. Dunlop's cousin, just drove up."

"I was expecting him," the chief said. "Notified him this morning, since he and his siblings would appear to be the closest relatives. Thank you." He hung up.

I hoped he was coming right out. Mr. Haverhill had popped the trunk of his car and took out three brightly colored boxes. I recognized the packaging of the same industrial-strength black plastic garbage bags we'd been using for Harvey's trash.

I planted myself in the middle of the front walk.

"Out of my way," Mr. Haverhill said when he saw me.

"Sorry," I said. "No one's allowed in."

"It's my house now," Mr. Haverhill said. "And I'm finally going to do what should have been done years ago."

He tried to sidestep me, but I stepped with him.

"I said out of my way!" He barged ahead, evidently trying to knock me down, but I stood so firm that he actually bounced back.

"Get out of my way!" He drew back his arm as if about to throw a punch, and I braced myself to dodge. "Or I swear I'll —"

"Police! Don't move!"

Mr. Haverhill and I both started, and turned to find Horace in the approved stance, pointing his weapon at us.

Correction: at Mr. Haverhill. I snuck in a couple of backward steps, and Horace's gun remained steadily pointing at him. And make that just plain Haverhill. I wasn't going to keep mentally giving him the polite "Mr."

"Thank you, Horace." The chief had been a few steps behind Horace. "I think we have

Mr. Haverhill's attention now."

"Who the hell are you?" Haverhill snarled. Considering that both Horace and the chief were in uniform, that struck me as a singularly stupid question.

If the chief thought so, he didn't let it show.

"Chief Henry Burke of the Caerphilly Police Department," he said. "I'm afraid I can't let you go in there right now."

"But it belongs to me," Haverhill said.

"We don't know that, Mr. Haverhill."

"I'm next of kin," Haverhill protested. "Harvey doesn't have any relatives other than me and my two siblings."

"And if he died intestate, or executed a will leaving his estate to you, then the house will be yours in good time," the chief said. "But we don't yet know who owns it. And even if we did, the house is presently part of my crime scene. Anything in the house or on the property could be evidence in a murder investigation."

"But he was killed in the garage," Haverhill said. "At least that's what you told me."

"His body was found in the garage," the chief said. "We don't yet know for sure where he was killed."

Haverhill muttered something under his breath. I caught the phrase "damned hick

215

cops." If the chief or Horace heard, they didn't show it.

"Mr. Haverhill, allow me to express my sympathy on the death of your cousin," the chief said.

Haverhill nodded as if grudgingly accepting something he was owed.

"I'm sure you're as eager as I am to find whoever did it," the chief went on. "And the more we know about him, the better chance we have of doing that. I'd like to ask you to accompany me to the police station. I have a few questions I'd like to ask you."

Evidently Haverhill wasn't completely clueless. He recognized that the chief had just issued a command rather than an invitation.

"If you tell me where it is, I can drive over there myself."

"I don't want to put you to any trouble," the chief said. "Ah! Here comes Vern. He can drive you."

He strolled over to talk to Vern. Horace stayed where he was, keeping a wary eye on Haverhill. I went over to stand by Horace.

"Chief must be pleased," I said, too low for Haverhill to hear. "Useful witnesses piling up down at the station."

He nodded, visibly suppressing a grin, and went back to staring fixedly at Haverhill, with his hand hovering near his service weapon.

The chief returned from his conversation with Vern.

"Deputy Shiffley will take you down to the station," the chief said. "Your car will be safe here, and we can bring you back after we've had that little talk."

We watched as Haverhill popped his trunk, flung the boxes of trash bags inside with obvious temper, and got into Vern's cruiser, his every move telegraphing resentment.

"Meg, Aida's on her way back from dropping Ms. Fillmore at the station," the chief said. "And we're a little shorthanded. If you could just keep an eye out for trespassers here until she arrives, I'd appreciate it. That would let Horace get back to his work."

"No problem," I said. "This is a lot less strenuous than most of the Helping Hands jobs I could be working on."

And a lot more interesting, I added silently, as he strode off.

CHAPTER 17

Once the chief was safely back in his car and couldn't hear me, I turned to Horace.

"So is there some doubt about where he was killed? I'd have thought from the size of the pool of blood —"

"No doubt at all," Horace said. "The chief was probably just saying that to shake up Haverhill. But that doesn't mean Harvey's house isn't part of the crime scene. What if he was killed for something in his house?"

"Then why didn't whoever killed him go inside and take it?"

"Maybe they couldn't get in," he suggested. "Place was locked up tight when you arrived, right?"

"Yes, we tried all the doors, and any of the windows we could reach. But someone could have used his keys to search the house and locked up afterward. Or tried to break in."

"With Mrs. Gudgeon and her surgically

attached binoculars on one side and Mr. 'I pay your salary' Brimley on the other?" Horace shook his head.

"Let me guess," I said. "You've responded to one of Harvey's prowler reports."

"Three times. If there really was a prowler, he's lucky no one on this part of the street owns a gun."

"As far as we know," I said. "Of course, it's always possible Harvey did, but he'd never have found it in time to do any damage with it."

"Good point." Horace shook his head sadly. "Poor sap. Why did someone have to bump him off just as we were going to help him turn his life around?"

"Yeah," I said. "I should let you get back to whatever you're doing."

Horace nodded. But instead of disappearing immediately into the garage, he stood for a few moments gazing back and forth between Mrs. Gudgeon's house and Mr. Brimley's.

"If you ask me, we need to interview those two ASAP," he said. "What are the odds that someone snuck in without either of them seeing?"

"When you put it that way, wouldn't one of them be the most likely killer?" I asked. "Mrs. Gudgeon would only have to elude

Mr. Brimley's observation, and vice versa. And as neighbors, they probably know the best way to do that. What time the other one's likely to be out or sleeping. A third party would have to avoid them both."

"I like the way you think," he said. "Of course, maybe that's only because I know what total pains in the . . . neck both of them are. Well, that crime scene won't work itself. Just yell if there's any trouble."

With that, he went back into the garage. I stood by the open door for a few moments, listening. Before too long he began a sort of not-very-tuneless humming that I knew was a sign he was absorbed in his work.

I stepped away from the door far enough that I could keep an eye on the rest of the yard and almost bumped into Mr. Brimley. "You shouldn't be here." Being startled probably made me sound more fierce than usual.

"I hear he got beaned with some of his own junk." Brimley had that tense, eager look people sometimes get when they're gossiping about some choice bit of scandal.

"I'll have to ask you to stay on your side of the property line," I said.

"Nonsense. What's the harm in — ?"

"This whole yard is a crime scene," I said. "Leave now! You could be trampling critical evidence."

"I just want a peek."

He took a step forward, and so did I, making us toe to toe. I braced myself in case he tried to shove past me. He wasn't quite as tall as I was, and his body was round-shouldered and pudgy, like the before picture for a diet and exercise program.

"Dammit, what's your problem?" he whined. "All I want —"

"The little lady already told you to leave three times since I got here."

Mr. Brimley and I both started — we hadn't heard Vern Shiffley arrive. He loomed over us, in the sort of relaxed yet alert pose that almost shouted "just try it!"

"And I don't intend to say it more than once," Vern went on. "Move your sorry self back into your own yard and stop interfering with our investigation."

Mr. Brimley reluctantly backed away for a few steps before turning and walking rather quickly back to his own yard. In fact, all the way back to his own porch. I suspected if the weather had been fine he'd have sat down there and glared at us from the safety of his rocking chair, but the temperature had dropped into the thirties and it was starting to rain.

"Just my luck to draw guard duty in this

mess." Vern looked up and sighed.

"Unless you need my help, I'm going to head out," I said. "With luck I can find an indoor Helping Hands project to join."

He laughed and waved as I dashed toward the Twinmobile. When I looked back, I saw that he'd settled on Harvey's porch.

I buckled myself in, but instead of starting the car I pulled out my notebook and looked at my list of Helping Hands projects. No way I was joining the manure project. In fact — I pulled out my phone to text Michael.

"You still doing manure?" I asked.

"Did one load. Heading over to help your grandfather with something."

Probably the magpie project.

"Have fun," I texted back.

I'd drop by later to see if the wheelchair ramp crew were persevering in spite of the rain.

"I should go help out with the quilting project," I said aloud. With any luck I'd show up and find they had more quilters than they needed, and I could praise their efforts and move on to some other project.

But as I was starting up the Twinmobile I realized what I really wanted to do: go home, boot up my laptop, and take a look at that hoarder website where Tabitha had met Harvey.

Where Tabitha claimed to have met Harvey. I still wasn't sure I trusted her.

Then, on a sudden impulse, I turned right instead of left, and headed in the direction of the Caerphilly Public Library. Not only was it several miles closer than home — I wasn't keen on doing any more driving than I had to in this rain — but I could be reasonably sure the library wasn't currently infested with several dozen visiting relatives who might want to make claims on my time.

But when I had squelched into the library, deposited my umbrella in the trash can that served as a makeshift umbrella stand, and strolled over to the line of public computers, I found that all three were occupied. I inched closer, pulled out my notebook, and pretended to be looking something up, which gave me the chance to observe the computer users and see if any of them looked close to finishing whatever they were doing. The first computer was occupied by an elderly man who I knew had recently discovered the joys of online genealogical research. Two middle-school kids were using the second, apparently to get a head start on a school science fair project involving cockroaches and earthworms. On the third, a high school student was reading

Julius Caesar — and she was only in Act 1, scene 2.

I sighed and closed my notebook. Should I go home to use my laptop? Or get back to checking on Helping Hands projects?

"Merry Christmas, Meg." I turned to see Ms. Ellie Draper, the head librarian. "Come on back to my office," she added, in that soft yet penetrating voice librarians cultivate to set a good example to the patrons.

I followed her through the STAFF ONLY door. Once it shut behind us, she turned and spoke in a normal tone.

"I saw you coveting the computers," she said. "And technically, at least two of those folks have already been there long enough that I could ask them to let someone else take a turn, but they're none of them wasting time, so how about if I let you use my computer?"

"I would love it," I said.

She led me into her office, cleared a stack of *Library Journals* off her desk chair, and left me to it.

I called up a search engine and typed in "Perfectly Good Place." And then, after a moment of thought, I added "Hoarding" and hit the enter key.

Bingo! There it was. A cheerful red-and-blue graphic at the top of the page showed a cartoon person trying to peek over a towering pile of stuff. There were links to books about hoarding and decluttering, services to help you with your cleanup, and yes — message boards.

My initial thought was that I would just poke around the message boards a bit until I found some of Harvey's posts and could see what he was telling people about himself. Maybe he had a good idea who his prowlers were and just hadn't told the police. For that matter, maybe something he'd said in the forum had inspired the prowlers. If he'd implied that there was something valuable beneath the clutter, for example, and been indiscreet enough to mention where he lived.

But I soon realized it wasn't going to be that easy. There were dozens of topics on the message boards and thousands of messages, and none of the users went by their full names. Some used first names, others had nicknames like "JunkLady" or "Lost in Clutter." I tried to look for topics that would seem to relate to Harvey's situation, but the more I searched, the more I realized how little I knew about his situation. And I found myself getting distracted by reading some of the stories people had posted about their problems. Heartbreaking stories about people losing their houses to clutter. Broken marriages. Clutter-induced physical illnesses. Worse, clutter-causing mental illnesses.

I looked up and realized half an hour had passed, and I was no closer to finding any traces of Harvey on the site. Was this even worth doing?

Especially since the whole subject was making me impatient and antsy. The collected misery was depressing me, and although I was trying very hard to empathize with their struggles, I just didn't get it. Part of me just wanted to swoop down and fix things for them. Organize them! Even though I knew that it was more complicated than that, and my organizing efforts would probably just make things worse.

I glanced down at the long list of bulletin board topics again, and one caught my eye.

"Do I need professional help?"

I had no idea whether or not the forum-dwellers did, but I sure did.

I pulled out my phone and called my nephew Kevin, the cyber wizard.

"Don't worry, I talked them out of it," he said when he answered the phone.

"And a Merry Christmas to you, too," I said. "Who did you talk out of what?"

"Just pretend you didn't hear that, then,"

Kevin said. "Michael had me talk Josh and Jamie out of a pretty crazy idea they had for a Christmas present for you. You'd have hated it."

"Then thank you," I said. "I don't suppose you're going to tell me what I'm not getting for Christmas."

"Nope. You'll sleep better not knowing."

"Probably something involving reptiles. If you're not going to spill, can I maybe talk you into doing a little cyber sleuthing for me?" I asked. "Because in case you haven't heard, we had a murder in town?"

"Awesome. Granddad must be over the moon. Who bought it this time?"

I explained about Harvey the Hoarder and the arrival of Tabitha, who claimed to be his friend from A Perfectly Good Place.

"So what do you want me to find out about this site?"

"Anything you can."

Silence on the other end.

"Okay — is Harvey Dunlop on the site? That's D-U-N-L-O-P, although he probably uses a screen name and I want to know what it is. And the same for a Tabitha Fillmore. And did they interact on the site — either publicly or in private messages? And did he say anything on the site that would give anyone a motive for murdering him?"

"You don't want much, do you? I'm looking at the site now. Some of these people are whining about how hard it is to throw away orphaned Tupperware lids — what could he possibly say that would make someone want to kill him?"

"What if he complained that if he could just clean up his house he could find that two million dollars he saved up from his youthful career as a bank robber?"

"Okay, that'd work. I'll see what I can do. I'll probably need to hack in so I can match the message board names to their real emails. I'm assuming you're okay with that. You know his email?"

"Yes." I pulled out my phone and opened up the contact app. "From when we did his yard cleanup. Although eventually I figured out he had a much harder time ignoring us if we just showed up on his doorstep." I found the email and rattled it off to him. "And I don't have Tabitha's email, but I've got her snail mail address. I'll text it to you."

"Cool. I'll let you know when I find something." With that, Kevin hung up.

When, not if. I liked his confidence.

I stopped by to thank Ms. Ellie on the way out.

"Did you find out what you needed?" she asked.

"I found out it was smarter to get my techie nephew Kevin to do my online searching," I said. "So after a fashion, yes."

"Is this something for the Helping Hands program, or something you think Chief Burke needs to know to solve poor Harvey Dunlop's murder?"

"Maybe both."

"Harvey was a big reader, you know. At one time he used to come into the library regularly. Almost the only place he went after a while — I think he was an agoraphobe, on top of being a hoarder. Then once we started carrying ebooks, he mostly checked those out. I know it's more convenient for some people, but in his case, I think they took away his last link to the outside world. Kind of sad."

She fell silent and looked thoughtful. I waited, because Ms. Ellie's thoughts were usually worth hearing.

"You know, I think his father was the real hoarder," she said finally. "I think Harvey just inherited the hoard and didn't really know any other way to live."

I thought back over the few hours I'd spent with him.

"Makes sense," I said. "Except for the

paper, I didn't see a whole lot of new stuff. Most everything I saw was old. And some of it's nice, but most of it's just . . . old."

"Like what you'd find if you cleared out some sweet little old lady's overstuffed house and just took home everything that didn't sell at the yard sale?" Ms. Ellie said. "Because I think that's what happened after old Mrs. Dunlop died — Harvey's grandmother. The way I heard it, his father thought he was going to make a mint selling the old lady's things, but he didn't like the prices any of the local antique dealers would give him, so he turned down their offers. I figure he just kept it all out of spite."

"That makes a lot of sense," I said. "I confess, I was surprised how quickly Harvey got over his reluctance about the decluttering. Surprised and even a little worried that he'd have a reaction. But as the place started clearing out a little, he began getting really cheerful."

"And maybe he wasn't even really agoraphobic," she said. "Just painfully shy."

"Yeah," I said. "We took him to the New Life Baptist concert and then had a little tree decorating party over at the furniture store. As far as I can tell, he had a blast. And then someone killed him, just as he was really starting to live."

"You made his last night happy, all of you," Ms. Ellie said. "Take some comfort in that."

"I'll take a whole lot more comfort if I can help the chief catch his killer and put them away for life."

"Let me know if there's anything I can do to help," she said.

"Will do."

It was still drizzling. I checked my phone's weather app, hoping to find that the rain was nearly over, but I saw nothing but little rain clouds filling not only today but the rest of the week. Drat.

But at least after tomorrow I could stop worrying about Helping Hands projects for a couple of days. I wasn't about to send anyone out in the rain to do volunteer work on Christmas Eve or Christmas Day.

But the chief's murder investigation wouldn't stop for the rain, and it was probably too much to hope that he'd find the killer in the next few days. Maybe working on Helping Hands projects would be a good distraction.

I'd worry about that later. Time to check on some of today's projects.

CHAPTER 18

I headed over to Trinity Episcopal and managed to dash inside just as the rain was revving up again. As I was shedding my raincoat and finding a place for my umbrella in one of the metal trash cans in the vestibule I ran into Robyn.

She looked worried.

"Meg, I heard about poor Harvey Dunlop. Have his relatives been contacted? Should I go over and call on them, in case they want us to handle the funeral?"

"Was he a parishioner?" I asked. "Or even Episcopalian? Not that he would have to be, of course —"

"No, of course he wouldn't have to be, but actually he might be. I told you he has family buried here, didn't I? So I assume they attended at some point."

Or perhaps had taken advantage of the welcoming policies of Robyn's predecessors.

"Yes, you mentioned it," I said. "Where

are they? We don't know much about his family, and I'm curious."

"Over by the big camellia, on the west side of the graveyard," she said. "Come down to the parish hall when you're done — you should see this quilt."

With that she dashed toward the corridor that led to the parish hall. I retrieved my umbrella and trudged out into the graveyard.

There were eight Dunlops buried by the big camellia, in what would be a pleasant, shady spot in the spring, when the surrounding oaks got their leaves back. And the burials probably covered four generations. From their birth and death dates I deduced that Wilberforce and Miriam Dunlop were probably Harvey's great-grandparents, Aristede Senior and Jane his grandparents, Aristede Junior and Alice his parents. Sad — Alice had died young, at only twenty-eight, when Harvey was nine. Aristede Junior had outlived her by decades and died fifteen years ago. There were two small headstones for little girls who'd died young, at eighteen months and not quite two years — Aristede Junior's younger sisters, the ones whose hair was in the mourning brooch. No other graves. I wondered if there were children or siblings who had been buried elsewhere or if this was all the Dunlops there ever had been.

I took pictures of all of the tombstones, the oldest replete with carvings and biblical verses, the newest very plain, with nothing carved on them but names and dates. Maybe the maiden names of the women would lead us to other relatives. It would be nice if Harvey had mourners other than the Haverhills.

I sloshed inside again, stashed my umbrella, and headed for the parish hall.

It was a beehive of activity, though I couldn't immediately figure out what some of it had to do with Mrs. Dinwiddie's quilt. There were quilters in the end where I'd entered, yes. In the middle of the room, one of Randall Shiffley's cousins appeared to be teaching a hands-on class in lamp repair. And the far end was filled with dogs. Puzzling. We'd had the annual blessing of the animals right on schedule, in October. And while I'd heard of places organizing canine nativities, I hadn't heard that Robyn was planning one at Trinity. And I definitely would have heard if she was, because I'd almost certainly be recruited to wrangle the dogs.

The quilting squad had pushed together four of the room's large tables and laid out the hundreds of quilt pieces on them, in all their intricate splendor. And yes, splendor was the word. I'd been picturing a traditional quilt, made up of quaint old-fashioned prints and pastel colors. Mrs. Dinwiddie's gran was clearly no traditionalist. The quilt's dominant colors were black, purple, and metallic gold, with small accents in jewel tones of turquoise, fuchsia, and cobalt blue. And The Drunkard's Path had just shot up there next to Tumbling Blocks in my list of cool favorite quilt patterns.

My mouth was hanging open in amazement, and I realized I coveted the quilt. It wasn't even finished, and I coveted it. I wasn't sure where I'd put it if I owned it — I'd probably ignore Gran's wishes and hang it on a wall somewhere. A highly visible wall, one where I could see it daily and everyone who came to the house could admire it. If Gran were still alive, I'd be first in line to beg her to make me one just like it. She could name her price.

I felt a brief stab of resentment at Mrs. Dinwiddie for owning the quilt. She almost certainly didn't have a queen-sized bed to use it on. Did she even have a wall big enough to display it?

Then my common sense returned. It was

Mrs. Dinwiddie's quilt. Made by her grand-mother. If she was living in one of those miserable little efficiencies, who was I to begrudge her something that would make the place more beautiful and homey? Something that reminded her of absent loved ones.

Of course, maybe the quilt wasn't to her taste — maybe she preferred the kind of more traditional quilt I'd been expecting. Maybe once it was finished she'd want to sell it. I could keep my eyes open for an opportunity to find out.

Worst case, I could take plenty of pictures of it — not only for selfish reasons, but also to document the Helping Hands project. I could — okay, not make my own quilt. I probably had the sewing chops, but I knew myself better than to imagine I'd find the time to do that much sewing anytime soon. But surely I could find a quilter who would make me one on commission? Better yet, I could ask Mother to find one.

I reluctantly tore myself away from the quilt and went to see what else was going on.

The Shiffley in charge of the lamp repair class looked up and I realized it was Beau — who would have been out driving his snowplow if we'd had any snow worth plowing. During winters like this one, with the summer's dust and cobwebs still decorating both his plow and his snowmobile, he tended to brood and utter dire threats about packing it all in and moving to Fairbanks.

But at the moment he seemed happy, putting his pupils through their paces. Six of them were high school kids, the rest in what Dad liked to call "late middle age" — which seemed to mean not yet in need of a walker. And more women than men in both age groups, which pleased me.

"Hey, Meg," Beau said, nodding. "Y'all created a monster with this helping Hands thing. You wouldn't believe how many people called in to ask for help with broken lamps and light fixtures. And a good half of the so-called broken stuff just needed someone to climb up on a ladder and put in a new bulb."

"And we're installing LED bulbs," one of the high school kids added. "Randall donated a couple of cases. Which means not only will the bulbs not need changing for, like, forever, people will save money on electricity."

"Yeah," Beau said. "Don't tell Randall, but for the seniors, if they want us to, we're putting LEDs in anything they can't easily reach."

"I doubt if he'd object." Randall was savvy enough to realize that generosity in small things — providing lumber at cost for Helping Hands projects, or donating a few cases of LED bulbs for the local seniors — defused any resentment people might have over the Shiffleys' near monopoly on construction and repairs in Caerphilly. "And if he does, just tell my mother. Or Robyn. I expect the Ladies' Interfaith Council could find enough money for a few cases of lightbulbs."

"Good deal." Beau nodded. "Anyway, we're going great guns with the lightbulb changing, but we could use a few more people to help with the repairs. So I put out a call for volunteers who want to learn, and here they are. Okay, everybody — let's get back to work."

I left them to it and went to the other far end of the hall — the part that was filled with dogs. At close range, I could also spot a few people. But mostly dogs. Dogs in crates. Dogs on leads. Dogs in portable pens. In the farthest corner a teenage girl was holding on to the collar of a large and rather shaggy dog while a woman with an elaborate head of frizzy curls brushed the dog's coat and teased it into fluffy perfection with the aid of a handheld hair dryer.

I recognized Ariel, proprietor of the Caerphilly Beauty Salon.

Just then the door from the hallway opened, and Clarence Rutledge, our local veterinarian, strode in. He was carrying a towel from which a bedraggled dog head was protruding.

"Don't let that little beast shake himself in here," Ariel warned. "I've just about got Miss Boom Boom Lady ready for her close-up."

"Don't worry — I'll keep him on this side of the room for now."

I had to smile at the curious sight of Clarence, who was almost as tall as Michael's six feet four and considerably wider, dressed in his customary biker's denim and leather, holding a dog so tiny he could almost have hidden it in one hand — all I could see was a ridge of spiky fur sticking straight up like a Mohawk. I wasn't quite sure what kind of dog it could be — was there such a thing as a punk Pomeranian?

"Something wrong with the bathing facilities down at the shelter?" I asked.

"Full of geckos," he said. "There's not a square foot down at the shelter that isn't full of something. Caroline did tell you that I asked the Helping Hands project to help me move some of these critters into good homes, didn't she?"

"She did indeed," I said. "And I said that was a great idea, although you wouldn't be in such a pickle if you learned to say no when other shelters ask you to take their overflow."

"I'm not turning down any chances to save animals from kill shelters," he said.

Okay, I could understand that. But they weren't all kill shelters. And how was bringing the animals here for baths going to help with the overcrowding? And — wait. He hadn't talked Robyn into using Trinity for his overflow, had he?

"Your mother came up with a fabulous idea," he was saying. "And she recruited Ariel to do the grooming, and your brother and Delaney are doing the glamour shots."

"Glamour shots?"

"Check it out — they're in the room next door."

I followed his directions and made my way to the room next door — a Sunday school classroom festooned with bright felt Christmas banners in blue and gold or red and green, and featuring a truly impressive Lego biblical diorama. It ranged from the serene (if somewhat knobbly) buildings of the village of Bethlehem through the green felt pastures on which the shepherds were abiding with a truly astonishing number of cotton-ball sheep, which were both fun and easy for the younger children to make, and ended with a towering re-creation of the palace of Herod.

Normally I'd have spent several minutes appreciating the diorama. But now my eyes were drawn to the other end of the room, where Rob and Delaney were, indeed, taking glamour shots of the recently groomed shelter dogs.

Technically, Delaney was doing the actual photography, which was a good thing, because Rob was notoriously inept with cameras. Give him a point-and-shoot camera and half the time he'd take a picture of his own eyeball, and we knew better than to let him get his hands on more sophisticated — and easily broken — photographic equipment.

But Delaney, his fiancée, was already proving to be an asset at family gatherings. Not only was she a good photographer, she was fierce about deleting any shot whose subject found it less than flattering.

Right now she had one of her fancier cameras mounted on a tripod and was staring through the viewfinder at a dog. Not the most prepossessing dog I'd ever seen. He started out looking a little like a beagle, but then you suddenly realized that his legs were about twice as long as any beagle legs you'd ever seen. Probably a trace of greyhound in his pedigree. Clarence had nicknamed him AT-AT, after the long-legged armored vehicles that were always lurching gracelessly across the landscape in *Star Wars* movies. The last time I'd visited Clarence at the shelter, I'd seen AT-AT cowering in his cage with a terrified expression on his face and all four legs splayed awkwardly around him. I'd felt sorry for the poor thing and wondered if he'd end up as one of the shelter's semi-permanent residents.

But now, washed and groomed, sitting on a red tufted-velvet love seat with a big gold bow around his neck, he actually looked rather handsome. It helped that he'd arranged his legs in an elegant pose. No, actually it helped that Rob had arranged his legs in an elegant pose. Rob was adjusting the angle of the hind legs slightly, and the dog simply wagged his tail and cooperated.

"Great!" Delaney said. "That's perfect! Now let's get some shots. Work it!"

Rob sprang into action.

"Who's a good boy?" he crooned. The dog's long, skinny tail thumped against the upholstery. Rob continued crooning praise and bits of baby talk to the dog, who gazed back at him with utter adoration. Rob had that effect on dogs.

Delaney clicked away like a paparazzo on speed, eventually abandoning the camera on the tripod and grabbing a smaller camera. She circled around, snapping shots from a variety of angles, while Rob coaxed and praised, and AT-AT lolled and grinned and wagged his tail with abandon.

"Okay! Cut! Print!" Delaney said at last. "Good boy!" She let the camera dangle from its neck strap and went over to pat AT-AT and scratch behind his ears.

"You think maybe AT-AT will have a better chance at getting adopted now?" Rob asked, looking up from his post by the love seat.

"I'm almost ready to take him home myself," I said. "But where are you going to put these glamour shots?"

"Your nephew Kevin's doing up a new website for the shelter," Delaney said. "And once we get a bunch of these new pictures up, we've got a whole bunch of social media gurus ready to get it out there on the Internet."

"You won't be able to turn around on the Internet without seeing some of our dogs," Rob said. "Facebook, Twitter, Instagram, stuff I haven't even heard of yet."

I worried, just for a moment, that all this virtuous animal welfare work would distract Kevin from the snooping I'd asked him to do. Then I reminded myself that Kevin was expert both at multitasking and at dragooning other people to help him with projects.

"Can you get some physical prints ready by tonight?" I asked.

"Yeah," Delaney said. "But what for?"

"Michael's one-man staged reading of *A Christmas Carol*," I said. "This year the proceeds are going to the shelter. Why not put some photos up in the lobby of the theater?"

"And donation boxes," Rob said. "So anyone who doesn't want to adopt a dog will feel guilty and throw in some cash."

"Great idea!" Delaney said. "When should I have them at the theater?"

"The house opens at six," I said.

"You've got it. And here comes our next supermodel! Who's this little lady?"

Clarence had come in with the dog I'd seen Ariel working on.

"Miss Boom Boom Lady," Clarence said. "Not my idea," he added, seeing Rob and Delaney's expressions. "She came with that."

"There's part of your problem." Rob took the lead from Clarence and squatted down so he was at eye level with the dog. "That's a terrible name. I think she should be Lady. Ye-e-e-es. La-dy!"

As he crooned the name, the dog wagged her tail with such fervor that Delaney had to grab her tripod to keep it from tipping over.

Clarence took AT-AT and led him away, tail still wagging. Rob gestured for the newly christened Lady to hop up on the love seat.

I left them to it and went back to the parish hall.

Ariel was working on yet another dog — a large brindle hound with a scarred face and a heavy jaw. I'd have described him as unappealing, but at the moment, with Ariel talking baby talk to him as she brushed his short fur to a glossy sheen, the dog had his eyes closed in what seemed like real enjoyment, and he suddenly looked quite adoptable. Just wait till Rob got hold of him.

I headed for the other end of the hall. Beau's students had made progress. Some of them had plugged in their lamps. One or two were still fiddling.

Beau glanced at the window and sighed.

"Raining again," he said. "We've had three inches of rain in the last two weeks. Do you know how much snow that would be if the temperature was right?"

245

"Um . . . a foot?" I guessed.

"A foot if we were talking heavy, wet snow," Beau said. "If it was average to light snow, more like thirty inches."

"Plenty more moisture where that came from," I said. "Don't despair."

I refrained from saying that I was just as happy we weren't getting thirty inches of snow as we had this time last year. Beau would think I was a Grinch. For that matter, so would most of the town. Everybody had forgotten how hard it was to cope with more than two feet of snow. I'd decided to keep my curmudgeonly preference for a dry winter to myself.

I went back to check on how the quilters were doing — pulling out my phone so I could get a few shots of the coveted quilt.

CHAPTER 19

"Beautiful, isn't it." I tore my eyes away from the quilt and saw that Judge Jane Shiffley, matriarch of the Shiffley clan, was among the workers. And beside her was Mrs. Diamandis.

"It's amazing," I said. "I didn't know either of you was a quilter."

"From way back," Judge Jane said. "I took it up back when I was a brand-new lawyer and had to spend so much time cooling my heels in the back of a courtroom, waiting for my cases to be called. And Ida here used to win sewing prizes at the state fair."

"My fingers are a little stiffer than they were," Mrs. Diamandis said. "But I can still make myself useful."

"I gather the crew had to quit before they finished all your mulching," I said. "Sorry about that, but they'll come back as soon as the rain lets up."

"That's fine." She waved her hand as if to

dismiss the need for any apology. "I don't want anyone to catch pneumonia on account of my roses. They've survived without manure for nearly ten years now — I think they can cope a few days longer. I just hope the weather isn't going to complicate Chief Burke's murder investigation. Any idea how that's going?"

I had to admire how smoothly she'd turned the conversation to what was clearly the town's hottest topic of conversation. Around the tables, conversations died and people feigned the kind of close attention to their stitching that would make eavesdropping easier.

"You know the chief," I said. "He keeps everything pretty close to his vest. But he's interviewing a bunch of people, and Horace is still hard at work at the crime scene."

"And have they been able to notify poor Mr. Dunlop's family?" Mrs. Diamandis asked.

"I didn't know he had any family to speak of," Judge Jane said.

"Only a few cousins that we know of," I said. "Second cousins on his father's side. And all the cousins were here yesterday, busily reporting him to Adult Protective Services and the building inspector, so I suspect the chief called one of them —

probably Morris, since he's the one who showed up here — and left it to him to notify anyone else who needs to know."

"Still, family." Judge Jane frowned. "How's he taking it, this cousin?"

"If you ask me, any tears he sheds would be crocodile tears. I expect as long as his alibi checks out and the chief's not looking at him as a suspect, he'll be relieved that Mr. Dunlop's death solves a longstanding family problem."

"Poor man," Mrs. Diamandis said. "But maybe it's no surprise someone killed him. I guess his family history came back to haunt him."

"His family history?" The idea took me by surprise — and then it occurred to me that Mrs. Diamandis, at ninety-seven, probably knew more about Caerphilly's history than most people in town. Possibly even more than Judge Jane, in spite of the legendary Shiffley family grapevine. And Mrs. Diamandis was still sharp as the proverbial tack. "What do you know about his family history?" I asked. "All I know is that his family once owned a bank."

"The Farmers and Mechanics Bank." Mrs. Diamandis nodded sagely and pursed her lips. Her disapproving tone made me wonder what could possibly be so disreputable about a bank.

"He's one of *those* Dunlops, then?" Judge Jane asked. "I didn't know any of them were still in town."

"Yes, he is," Mrs. Diamandis said. "He was the last one left."

"What Dunlops?" I asked. "Enlighten me — what's so bad about having once owned a bank? Why would that inspire anyone to kill someone else?"

"The Dunlops owned the Farmers and Mechanics Bank," Judge Jane said. "Founded in the late 1800s. Not sure exactly when — the 1870s, maybe?"

"More like the 1880s, I should think," Mrs. Diamandis said.

"But still — shortly after the Pruitts took over the town," Judge Jane said. "And definitely as a reaction against them."

Mrs. Diamandis nodded in assent.

I knew about the Pruitts, a family of carpetbaggers who'd founded a textile mill in Caerphilly during the Reconstruction and ruled the town like a private fiefdom for more than a century. I liked to think I'd played no small part in breaking their stranglehold on the town a few years back. But as far as I knew, the Pruitts were long gone. Was she suggesting that they were back, and had done in the last survivor of their former rival banking family?

"If you want to know when it opened, we'd have to look it up," Judge Jane said. "But I know when it closed — March 6, 1933."

"Mr. Roosevelt's bank holiday. I remember it." Mrs. Diamandis nodded. And then seeing my puzzled look, she added. "As soon as Mr. Roosevelt was inaugurated, which happened in March back in those days — and we're talking FDR, not Teddy; I'm not *that* old — he declared a bank holiday. Shut down every bank in the country until the government could figure out which ones were strong enough to be allowed to reopen, and how they could make sure they didn't fail after they reopened."

"And the Farmers and Mechanics Bank wasn't allowed to reopen." Judge Jane's voice was solemn. "But the First National Bank of Caerphilly — the Pruitts' bank — was." I suspected from her tone that she considered this a miscarriage of justice.

"I was only ten when it happened, but I vividly remember overhearing Mama and Daddy arguing more than once over how the Pruitts managed that," Mrs. Diamandis said. "Daddy always said the Pruitts must have bribed someone, and Mama would say don't be a fool — the Pruitts didn't have two dimes to rub together, same as everybody else, so it had to have been blackmail."

"Knowing the Pruitts, I'd have sided with your mama," Judge Jane said. "Even so, the bank failure wasn't really the Pruitts' fault — or the Dunlops'. Several thousand banks were victims of the same economic disaster. They had to reform the banking system to fix it."

"Which wasn't much comfort to the people who lost their money," Mrs. Diamandis said. "No insurance on bank accounts in those days — the FDIC was one of the things they invented to fix the system — so if you had money in the Dunlops' bank, you just plain lost it."

"Or the Pruitts' bank," Judge Jane put in.

"Yes." Mrs. Diamandis shook her head. "Terrible times. My family wasn't hit as hard as some, because Daddy had seen the problem coming. Started putting his paycheck under the mattress instead of in the bank, and taking out any money he did have in the bank — but gradually, so the bank manager wouldn't give him a hard time. He always said that if the banks had lasted six more months he wouldn't have lost a penny."

"Your daddy was a smart man," Judge Jane said. "Some people lost everything.

Their houses. Their farms. Their businesses."

"And they blamed the local bankers," Mrs. Diamandis said. "The Dunlops and the Pruitts."

"So if Mr. Dunlop's family was still hated as much as the Pruitts, I'd see where you're coming from," I said. "Definitely a possible motive for murder. But even though I'm not from around here, I've been here a good while now, and I've never heard anything about the Dunlops, much less people hating them."

"Because unlike the Pruitts, no one helped them put their bank back on its feet," Judge Jane said. "And they didn't go on to lord it over the rest of the town for seventy or eighty more years. The Dunlops just faded away into — well, genteel poverty would be an exaggeration. They weren't in any danger of starving. But they kept themselves to themselves. Mr. Dunlop's daddy was almost as much of a hermit as he was."

"And I suppose eventually any resentment against the Dunlops died off with the people who'd lost their money," I said.

Judge Jane snorted.

"If you think that made any difference, you're forgetting how people around here think," she said. "I know people who could tell you to the penny how much their great-granddaddies lost when the banks failed. But there weren't really a lot of Dunlops around to hate, I guess, so people just focused on the Pruitts. And the Pruitts' bank was bigger anyway."

"It's not just that," Mrs. Diamandis said. "The Pruitts never even tried to make things right. Aristede Dunlop — Aristede Senior, Harvey's granddaddy — tried. He kept a copy of the bank's records, and once things started getting better and he was earning some money over and above what he needed to feed his family and keep a roof over their heads, he started paying people back. With interest."

"I never knew that," Judge Jane said.

"He never made a big fuss about it," Mrs. Diamandis said. "I wouldn't have known myself if one of my close friends hadn't been the last survivor of one of the families that got repaid. And there was never much talk — I expect people were a little embarrassed when they figured out he was trying to do the right thing after they'd bad-mouthed him for so long. And then a few people were still angry, and said they could have used the money back in the Depression times, but what good was it now when times were good again, and even with the interest the money wasn't worth as much. There were even a few people who said Aristede could have started paying them back faster if he'd tightened his belt more — and believe me, that was just pure meanness. The Dunlops were not living high on the hog."

"Doesn't sound as if people were all that grateful," I said.

"No, but his trying to pay back kind of took the wind out of their sails," Mrs. Diamandis said. "Made them look a little whiny if they bad-mouthed the Dunlops too hard. So they focused on hating the Pruitts and just kind of forgot the Dunlops even existed."

"But you think there could be someone out there who still hates them enough to kill Mr. Dunlop?" I asked.

"Who knows?" She shrugged. "Maybe some family nursed the grudge instead of letting it fade."

"Or maybe someone just recently found out his family had a reason to hate the Dunlops," Judge Jane suggested. "Someone digging into the past and getting all bent out of shape about something that's been over and done with so long no one else remembers it. Puts me in mind of that time when my cousin Morford got all gung-ho about genealogy and started trying to map out his family tree. Suddenly noticed that little two-year discrepancy between when his grandfather was born and when his great-grandparents later got married."

"Found out they were human and jumped the gun before the honeymoon, did he?" Mrs. Diamandis chuckled.

"No, he found out his biological great-granddaddy was a no-account sneak thief who got himself shot while trying to rob the local ABC store." Judge Jane grinned and shook her head. "Which wouldn't have hit him quite so hard if he hadn't also found out that Sheriff Wilmer Shiffley, who he'd been brought up to think was his great-granddaddy, was the one who did the shooting."

Mrs. Diamandis burst out laughing, and I had to chuckle myself.

"Went through an identity crisis, did he?" I asked.

"Lord, yes." Judge Jane nodded. "Everyone pointed out that his great-gran waited a decent time before she remarried, and since she was also a Shiffley, it wasn't as if we weren't still kin. But he took it hard. Anyway, that makes me wonder: what if someone started digging into their own family history, found out just how much their family suffered from the failure of the Dunlops' bank, and did him in out of revenge?"

I thought about it for a moment.

"Makes about as much sense as any of the other reasons I can think of for killing him," I said.

"What other reasons?" Mrs. Diamandis asked. "I don't get out much these days, remember, so I don't know much about it."

"For one thing, that someone just got so fed up with his hoarding that they lost their temper and brained him," I said. "One of the neighbors who had to look at it, or maybe his family, who saw it getting worse every day and knew they'd have to be the ones to deal with it eventually. And with all due respect to your theory about his family history coming back to bite him, that sounds the most logical to me."

Mrs. Diamandis nodded.

"And I bet people will wonder if someone killed him so they could get their hands on something he has hidden in his house," I said. "But I can't imagine anyone who's actually been inside thinking that. So far I haven't seen a single thing I would pay a quarter for at a yard sale."

"I hear some of it's nice stuff," Judge Jane said. "Just not the sort of thing young people like you want nowadays. Antiques just don't sell well anymore, or so they say."

"Good point," I said. "I'll wait till Mother weighs in on what it's all worth."

"You never know," Mrs. Diamandis said. "There were rumors, back in the day, that the Dunlops had hidden all the money from their bank in the house. Of course it was mostly kids saying that — kids who heard their parents griping that the Dunlops had stolen everybody's money and thought that meant they had literally taken all the bills and coins out of the bank. And that was over eighty years ago."

"Rumor and gossip have a long half-life," Judge Jane said.

"What did they do for a living?" I asked. "Aristede Senior and Junior. And for that matter, Harvey."

"Aristede Senior took to farming," Mrs. Diamandis said. "On rented land. He never was much good at it, from what I heard, but he worked hard and they got by."

"But Junior looked down his nose at farming," Judge Jane said. "He took up being a traveling salesman. And I don't know that Harvey's ever done much of anything, so I figure Junior must have left him enough to live on."

"That would make sense." Mrs. Diamandis nodded thoughtfully. "Once Aristede

Senior died, the whole repayment thing stopped cold, so I heard. I always did think Junior was a lot more interested in making money than his father ever was. And he was a right old skinflint, so unless he figured out a way to take it with him — and if anyone could, it'd be him — he probably did leave Harvey something."

"You know, I bet I could find out the answers to all of these questions," I said. "I doubt if Harvey ever threw away a piece of paper in his life. The answers are all going to be right there in the house — or in the boxes we moved to the furniture store. I took a look at some of the stuff as it was going into the boxes. Harvey's got bank statements and canceled checks going back decades."

"But talk about looking for a needle in a haystack," Judge Jane said, shaking her head.

"It could be a needle we need to find," I said. More properly, a needle the chief might need to find in order to solve Harvey's murder.

Though probably not something he could spare anyone to do.

"If you're thinking of sifting through all those boxes of paper, I'd wait at least a day or two," Judge Jane said. "With luck, Henry Burke will find out who did poor Harvey in

259

without you having to wade through all that."

"Here's hoping," I said. "I should head out."

"More projects to supervise, I assume," Judge Jane said. I nodded.

More projects to supervise, yes. And I really ought to focus on that, I reminded myself, as I made my way down the hallway toward the front door.

What I really wanted to do was drop by the police station. The chief probably already knew the various things I'd learned about Harvey's family history. And I had no idea if any of them was the least bit relevant to his murder.

But what if some of them were? And what if the chief hadn't yet learned about them?

I pushed open Trinity's glossy red front door and stepped outside. Then I stopped while I was still under the small overhang that sheltered a part of the front step. It was pouring again. Puddles were forming in the parking lot, highlighting every low spot that could use a little supplemental dirt and gravel. I decided to wait under the overhang for a few minutes. Surely the rain couldn't keep on like this indefinitely.

Maybe all the snow lovers did have a point. A few inches of snow would be a lot prettier. And a lot less depressing. As long as it was inches, not feet.

And I suddenly remembered something and swore under my breath.

"Meg? Something wrong?"

CHAPTER 20

I started, and turned to find Clarence Rutledge had opened the door behind me and was peering out. He stepped out and crowded in to stand beside me under the tiny overhang.

"Nothing's wrong," I said. "At least I hope not. It suddenly occurred to me to wonder what this rain is doing to Harvey Dunlop's house."

"Good grief — you're right." Clarence glanced up at the sky. "That roof of his. More tarp than shingle. The last time I helped him add a new tarp I tried to talk him into getting it fixed, but he didn't think they could do it without coming inside. Said he wanted to get all his stuff organized and then he'd get some estimates on the roof. Typical. He was putting his whole life on hold till he got himself organized, but he never got off the starting block." He shook his head. "I was so pleased to hear he'd let the Helping Hands in."

"You knew him, then?"

"Not very well." He folded his arms and leaned against the church door — evidently he was also going to wait for the rain to ease. "But maybe better than most anyone else in town, come to think of it. He made donations to the shelter. Not very big, but probably more than he could easily afford. I visited him sometimes. Brought around puppies and kittens for him to play with. He loved that. His father never let him have a pet when he was a kid, even though he loved animals. I kept hoping he'd give in and adopt one. And he wanted to — I could tell. He just kept saying it wasn't safe to have a pet yet, he'd get one when he finished organizing his house. And see how that ended up." He looked gloomy for a few seconds. "He did have a feral cat he's been feeding the last week or two. Beautiful little gray thing — female, we think, and possibly still young enough to be socialized if we get her soon. So I was going to sneak around with a humane trap this week."

"Sneak around?"

"Well, if I waited for Harvey to give me permission, the poor thing would be way past socializing. I mean, look at the roof." He brooded for a few moments. "And yeah, the roof's not bothering him anymore, but still, someone should check to make sure there are no new leaks."

"Because if there are, the rain could be dripping into his house."

"Pouring even," Clarence agreed.

"And it wouldn't ruin useless stuff like pink china elephants or homicidal spittoons, but it could wreak havoc on all the paper that's still left in his office."

"You think he's got something valuable in his papers?" Clarence didn't look as if he bought the notion.

"No idea," I said. "But unless the chief's already got the case figured out and the culprit in handcuffs, he might need to know more about Harvey to solve the case. And those papers might be the only way to do that."

"Makes sense."

"And even if the chief doesn't need all that paper, eventually it will belong to his family," I said. "And I wouldn't put it past Morris Haverhill to pitch a fit if any of their property is damaged. Even if it's only a bunch of canceled checks from the fifties and several hundred old Radio-Shack sales flyers. And even if it's Harvey's roof, not anything we did, that causes the damage."

"Would this Morris Haverhill be a tall,

cadaver-thin character with bad posture and a whiny voice?" Clarence asked.

"Sounds like him."

"Met him once," Clarence said. "At least if grabbing someone by the scruff of the neck and hustling him out the door with orders to get out and stay out counts as meeting someone. Made Harvey's day when I did that, poor soul. He was scared of the dude."

"Of his cousin Morris?"

"Sure looked that way."

"Did you ever meet his girlfriend?" I asked. "Or hear anything about her?"

"Girlfriend? Harvey?"

"Online girlfriend," I said. "Woman named Tabitha Fillmore. Claims she met him through a forum for hoarders and was coming to see him in person and help him through the decluttering ordeal."

"He never mentioned her," Clarence said. "And I think he would have if he'd met someone. If he was excited about something — or upset — he'd talk about it. I remember him telling me one time about some online group he'd checked out, but I didn't get the impression he was that into it. More like reading their stories made him feel he wasn't that bad off."

"He seemed like a nice guy," I said.

"He was." Clarence shook his head sadly. "Needed to get out more, you know? Spend more time with people. I kept telling him to go out and look for a job, but he preferred working from home."

"Working from home?" This was a new idea. "What did he do?"

"Data entry. Companies would send him stacks of paper forms and stuff, and he'd type it all in."

"A perfect job for an agoraphobe," I said. Clarence nodded.

"You should talk to the chief," I said. "Sounds as if you knew Harvey better than most people in town."

"That'd be sad, but you could be right," he said. "I'll go over as soon as we finish with the dog glamour shots. Let the chief know while you're there."

"While I'm there?"

"You mean you're not headed over to the station to talk to the chief about Harvey's roof and the need to save his papers?" He grinned.

"You're right," I said.

"While you're at it, let him know I'm going to drop by with the cat trap. I'd put it in one of the neighbor's yards, but I don't trust them. I can't prove it, but I think one of them put out poisoned food at least once."

Yet another reason to dislike Harvey's neighbors.

Just then I heard a static-filled squawk and heard, very faintly, the chief's voice. It appeared to be coming from Clarence's pocket. He pulled out a police radio, and we both listened as the chief asked Debbie Ann to send the locksmith back to Harvey's house.

"Since when are you carrying that around?" I asked as Clarence stashed the radio back in his pocket.

"I'm a special deputy at the moment," Clarence said. "I figure the chief mainly wants me to show up and look menacing if they have any more unruly drunks who need to be intimidated. I think it's letting up a little. Think I'll make a run for it. Bring over the next batch of dogs."

I wasn't sure he was right about the rain. More like wishful thinking. But he was right — I needed to talk to the chief about Harvey's papers.

So after making a mad dash through the rain, I left Trinity and headed toward the police station.

The parking lot was mostly empty. I didn't spot any out-of-town license plates, which was probably a good thing, since if I had seen any they'd probably have belonged to reporters. Chief Burke hated having reporters trying to horn in on his investigations. For that matter, the whole town would be happier if press coverage of Harvey's demise was limited to the weekly *Caerphilly Clarion*. Christmas in Caerphilly was in full swing, and we didn't want anything to derail an annual event that had such enormous financial benefits for the local merchants and bed-and-breakfast owners. Randall, in his role as mayor, was already plenty worried about keeping up the town's quaint and cozy quotient in the absence of snow.

I was thankful to get a parking spot near the door. The rain had slowed and then stopped while I was driving over, but it looked as if it would start back up before long. Probably just when I was ready to leave.

Vern Shiffley was minding the reception desk. Which was unusual. When George, the appendicitis victim, was out the chief usually liked to replace him with someone less plainspoken than Vern. The department must really be hard up for bodies.

At least they hadn't neglected to decorate for the holidays. A six-foot artificial tree stood in one corner of the waiting room, decorated with gold and silver ornaments in the form of handcuffs, badges, and guns. In a new touch this year, it was covered with tiny blue Christmas lights and the star-shaped gold badge on top of the tree rested on what looked like a miniature version of the blue beacon that topped the department's squad cars. And someone had decorated all the walls with garlands and bows made of yellow crime-scene tape and red danger tape braided together.

"Chief in?" I asked. "I wanted to consult him about something."

Vern was already buzzing the chief on the intercom.

"Hey, Chief — Meg's here. Shall I —"

"Send her back."

Vern waved in the direction of the chief's office, although I already knew the way. I was a little worried. I wanted to talk to the chief — but I wasn't sure it was such a good thing for him to want to talk to me.

But he didn't look mad — that was a relief. Just . . . glum.

"I'd ask how the case was going," I said. "But you'd think I was trying to pry, instead of realizing it's just the polite thing to say when you're greeting a police chief."

"And I'd say 'great,' except you'd know it was a lie the minute I said it."

"Sorry to hear that." I took one of his two visitor's chairs and tried to figure out what he was up to.

"And if your ears were burning just now, it hasn't been five minutes since I told Vern that maybe I should figure out some excuse to invite you down here, so I could see if you'd remembered anything else useful. Or heard anything useful around town. Because I know darn well someone in town knows something that will help me solve this murder, but they sure as the dickens haven't shared it with me."

"And here I was trying to figure out a plausible reason for dropping by to see if you already knew some of the stuff people have been saying about Harvey," I said. "I decided I should come down and ask if any of those people had listened to me when I told them to talk to you."

"Not yet." He reached open and flipped open his trusty notebook. "Just who should I hope comes down to see me so I don't have to go looking for them?"

I did a brain dump of what I'd learned about Harvey. What Ms. Ellie had said about Harvey being a reader and his father the real hoarder. What Judge Jane and Mrs. Diamandis reported about the demise of the Dunlop family bank. About Clarence Rutledge helping Harvey with his roof and bringing him kittens and puppies to play with, and knowing what he did for a living but never hearing anything about a girlfriend.

The chief took a satisfactory number of notes. Satisfactory to me, at least, since it suggested that I was being useful rather than annoying.

"Interesting," he said.

"Oh, and you know that website where Tabitha says she met Harvey," I said. "A Perfectly Good Place."

"Yeah." He shook his head. "I checked it out. It's going to take some doing, searching that whole site to see if it has anything to do with the murder. They all use aliases, you know. Of course, I think I would, too, if I were confessing some of the really personal stuff some of them have been sharing. But it's going to make it very hard to check out her story — much less see whether there might be anyone else on there that he interacted with. And that wretched woman seems to think that telling me the aliases she and Mr. Dunlop used would be the equivalent of a priest breaking the seal of confession. I've had to turn that battle over to the town attorney. Of course, I've sent Mr. Dunlop's laptop over to the computer forensics experts at your brother's company.

With any luck that will give us something useful."

"Glad to hear the Mutant Wizards are on the case," I said. The chief winced, and I reminded myself to suggest to Rob that however catchy Mutant Wizards was as the name of a computer game developer, he might get more business from law enforcement if he came up with something else for his forensic division. Even Forensic Wizards might be an improvement.

"Would it make you feel any better to know that I set my nephew Kevin to work on that website?" I went on. "Because I was dying to find out what Harvey had said there, and I couldn't make head or tails of it when I checked it out."

"I would very much appreciate it if you could share any information young Kevin finds."

"It's been at least an hour since I briefed him," I said. "In fact, close to two. Maybe I should see what he's learned."

"Please do."

The chief leaned back and laced his hands over his belly while I put my phone on speaker and called Kevin — who, as usual, refrained from answering his phone with anything as predictable and conventional as "hello."

"What now?" he said. "I'm busy."

"Just checking to see there's anything else you need to investigate that website."

"Have you got anything else?"

"No, but the Mutant Wizards forensic guys are playing with Harvey's computer. I could have them call you if they find anything of interest."

As I could have predicted, Kevin couldn't resist the challenge of playing cyber one-upmanship.

"Tell them to look for any email exchanges between TyreGuy and BuriedinTreasure33," Kevin said, and rattled off a couple of email addresses. "So far I haven't found any signs that they interacted on the site. But I'll let you know what I find once I've figured out the private messaging system."

"Did TyreGuy ever say anything that would give away his location?" I asked. "Or anything that suggested he had anything valuable in his house?"

"He complained a few weeks ago about the Caerphilly building inspector giving him a hard time," Kevin said. "Someone who was trying to find him could have used that. But as far as valuables — half the people on that site think they've got the lost gold of the Incas hidden somewhere in their clutter. Harvey said some stuff about finding family treasures, but nothing all that different from anybody else."

"So if you were trolling the forum, looking for someone to knock off for profit, you wouldn't necessarily pick him?" I asked.

"No," he said. "Actually, if I were looking for someone to knock off for profit, I wouldn't be trolling a hoarder forum. I'd go after the rare coin freaks, and people stashing gold bars in their basements so they have something to spend in case of a zombie apocalypse."

"Good point." I glanced over at the chief and raised an eyebrow, in a silent question. He shook his head. "I owe you one," I said to Kevin.

"Big time," he agreed, and hung up.

"Very useful," the chief said. "I wonder — should I have asked you to have him liaise with the Mutant Wizards forensic people?"

"Pretty sure he will anyway," I said. "Although it won't look like anything you or I would think of as liaising. He'll almost certainly get in touch so he can taunt them with anything he figured out before them, and they'll all go into a frenzy of competitiveness to see who can find you the most information the soonest."

"That sounds even better than liaising," the chief observed. "I will await the results with great pleasure. And knowing the aliases she and Mr. Dunlop used on the site does potentially give me a lever to use on the very uncooperative Ms. Fillmore. Perhaps I should call her again."

"Good," I said. "But you probably want to use the term 'screen name' so she'll know what you're talking about. As long as I'm here, there was actually something else I wanted to talk to you about — Harvey's stuff."

"If Mr. Haverhill is badgering you about getting access to the house, refer him to me," the chief said. "And I will explain the situation to him for the tenth or eleventh time. I don't yet know if there's anything in that wretched house that will help me solve Mr. Dunlop's murder, and quite apart from that, I don't know who inherits it all, so he can just cool his jets."

"And meanwhile, there's the challenge of protecting his stuff," I said.

"I wish I had the personnel to put a guard on the house," he said. "We've stepped up patrols in the area. Of course I realize that didn't do much to protect Mr. Dunlop, but I don't think his stuff's likely to unlock the door and wander out to the garage, so maybe there's hope."

"But it's not just burglars we need to

worry about," I said. "You saw all the tarps on his roof. Clarence said something about the last time he was there helping Harvey add a new tarp. What if they didn't quite get it right? This latest rain could already be turning all those papers in his house into a sodden mess."

"Good point." He grimaced. "We should probably finish moving Mr. Dunlop's stuff into the furniture store for safekeeping. Easier to keep an eye on it there, anyway. Only one place to guard. problem is getting the work done — because no offense, but we can't just have a random collection of townspeople wandering in and out carrying stuff. Do we have any idea who packed the papers that are already down at the furniture store?"

"Yes," I said. "Josh and Jamie. Except for half a dozen boxes I packed myself. And there were only a dozen people working there yesterday — I could give you a list."

"That's something," he said. "If I wasn't so shorthanded, I'd get my deputies to do the packing, but we're already stretched thin. So —"

"Chief?" Vern's voice on the intercom. "Randall's here."

"Send him in," the chief said.

Randall Shiffley strode in, shaking the rain

out of his hair.

"Meeting of great minds, I see," he said as he folded his long, lanky torso into the chief's other guest chair. "What did you want to see me for?"

"The furniture store," the chief began. "It has a security system?"

"Not sure, but if it doesn't I can have one in by evening," Randall said. "Are you suggesting poor old Harvey might have had something worth stealing?"

"No idea," the chief said. "But I don't like the way so many people are bound and determined to get their hands on his stuff. So I want to move it all to the furniture store and get some good security on the place before some vital piece of evidence disappears. That's the other thing." He sat up a little straighter in his chair and his voice took on a more official tone. "Given the department's current personnel shortage, I'd like to put in an official request to have you assign some city or county personnel to assist us in transferring the remaining evidence from Mr. Dunlop's house to a more secure storage area."

Randall looked briefly puzzled.

"You want me to assign government employees to pick up where Meg and her crew left off?" He gave me a sidelong glance.

"Well," the chief said. "Since Meg, being your assistant, is a part-time government employee you could recruit her to run the show. And find her a couple of strong backs to help out with the hauling. It was one thing to have a mob of volunteers shoving Mr. Dunlop's stuff into bags and boxes when we thought it was just clutter. Now that there's the possibility that it could be evidence —"

"We need something a little more official." Randall chuckled. "Okay — Meg, you're hereby on temporary assignment to the police department. And I'll get Beau and Osgood — they're on the county books as part-time staff for when they do the snow-plowing, and it's not like they'll be doing any of that in the next day or so. Heck, I'll pitch in myself. I'm about as official as it gets."

"Thank you." The chief looked happier. Well, at least a little less stressed. "I'll assign at least one deputy to the project, so the whole thing can be done under police supervision."

"I'll head over as soon as I grab some lunch," I said. I'd just checked my watch and realized that it was nearly one. No wonder the breakfast burrito Michael had given me seemed so long ago.

"I'm on it," Randall said. "How soon can you get the deputy over there?"

The chief punched a button on his intercom.

"Vern. Head over to the Dunlop house, will you? You're overseeing the packing."

"Right away, Chief."

"See you there," Randall said.

"I'll drop by myself to help if I can," the chief said. "And —"

"Chief?" Vern again. "Any chance you could come out here for a sec?"

CHAPTER 21

The chief frowned and hurried out. Since I was supposed to be leaving anyway, I followed.

Two of the Haverhills were standing in the entrance area — Josephine, the sister, and one of the brothers. Probably Ernest. They were both in the same pose — leaning forward with shoulders rounded and both hands resting on the handle of an oversized black umbrella.

"Good morning," the chief said. "Thank you for coming in. Ms. Haverhill, perhaps we could start with you."

They both stared at him as if puzzled.

"What do you mean 'start with me'?" Josephine asked.

"I assumed you were responding to my request to interview you," the chief said. "Any information you can provide about your cousin could help us find his killer."

"Unfortunately, we didn't know him very

well," Josephine said. "He cut himself off from the rest of the family years ago, and was resisting our efforts to help with his hoarding problem. I'm not sure what information we could provide that would be useful."

"Any family background at all," the chief began.

"And no offense intended, but one hears so much about overzealous policing," Josephine went on. "Innocent people accused of crimes because they are too trusting. I think we'd like to have our attorney accompany us when we talk to you."

Evidently Ernest was used to letting her do the talking. He just nodded.

"That's your right, of course." The chief probably sounded calm to them. I could tell he was furious. "If you need an attorney —"

"I will contact our family attorney to find out when he's available," Josephine said.

"Thank you," the chief said.

"You're barking up the wrong tree," Ernest said.

"Be quiet," his sister told him.

"We weren't anywhere near here when Harvey was killed," Ernest went on. "When Morris got home —"

"Shut up, Ernest," Josephine shouted.

281

"Why?" Ernest asked. "Why don't we just tell them about how we spent a quiet evening at home, worrying about Harvey and ordering in Chinese? I bet the delivery guy from the Hunan Palace —"

"We'll tell them all that," Josephine snapped. "But not without our attorney."

She lifted her head and straightened her spine slightly — although not quite enough to erase her resemblance to a praying mantis — and strode out.

"Waste of time and money," Ernest muttered, and followed her.

We all watched in silence as the Haverhills got into their car and drove off.

"I think right now Ernest is my favorite Haverhill," I said. "Of course, that's rather like saying Lucrezia is my favorite Borgia."

"You'd think they didn't want their cousin's killer found," Vern said. "And —"

The door opened, and we all turned. I was half expecting to see one or both of the Haverhills back with a lawyer in tow.

But it was Tabitha Fillmore who walked in and stood dripping copiously onto the linoleum and looking cranky and impatient.

"What can I do for you, Ms. Fillmore?" the chief asked.

Instead of answering, she reached into her sodden black suede purse and drew out a damp folded sheaf of papers, which she handed to the chief.

He unfolded them and read, frowning slightly. Finally, he looked up.

"Thank you," he said. "May I keep this or —"

"No!" she said. "I don't have another copy. Not with me."

"I'll have a photocopy made, then." The chief gestured to the copy machine that stood behind the reception desk. "Vern, if you wouldn't mind."

He handed the paper to Vern, who obediently ambled over to the copy machine. Tabitha watched him as if she expected him to run away with her papers. I could see Vern trying to read the document as he copied. His eyes grew wide.

"So can I have the key now?" Tabitha asked.

"The key?" The chief gazed at her placidly.

"The key to my house. You read the will. It's mine now."

"That's as may be."

Vern returned with the original and the copy and handed both to the chief, who passed the damp original back to Tabitha.

"It says so in the will," Tabitha said. "He left it to *me*. He left *everything* to me. I want the key to *my* house!" She stamped her foot and pouted in what would probably have been an adorable expression of girlish petulance if she were still in her early teens.

"Ms. Fillmore," the chief said. "It doesn't work that way. Before I can turn anything of Mr. Dunlop's over to you, that will would need to be probated — which means that the court would have to authenticate that it was really his will, and moreover that it was the most recent will he'd made. If you want to go down to the courthouse and start the process rolling, go right ahead. An even better idea would be to hire yourself a lawyer to handle the process — including the hassle that's going to happen when Mr. Dunlop's family finds out and tries to contest the will. If you don't know a lawyer, Vern can lend you our copy of the yellow pages."

"But —" she began.

"But on top of all that, right now Mr. Dunlop's house is part of my crime scene," the chief said. "And even if you'd already had that will probated and it was your house, it would still be my crime scene. So unless you have some bit of information that will help me figure out just who killed Mr. Dunlop, I'd appreciate it if you'd stop wasting my time."

Tabitha looked hurt. She made a sound that was a cross between a tortured sob and a cat bringing up a hairball. Then she batted her eyes as if trying very hard to hold back tears. When she realized her visible sorrow wasn't having much effect on the chief, she glanced at Vern and then at me. Evidently we didn't look any more sympathetic. She choked back another even more dramatic sob, turned on her heel, and ran out of the station.

We stood for a few moments staring after her. Vern was the first to break the silence.

"You think that thing's legit?" He craned his head to take another look at the photocopy the chief was holding.

"I have no idea," the chief said. "I'm going to make a call to the state crime lab. We're going to need a forensic document examiner."

He turned and headed for the corridor that led to his office. Then he turned back.

"Meg, you think the crew we're sending can pack up the rest of Mr. Dunlop's papers tonight?"

"I think so," I said. "Josh and Jamie got close to half of it all by themselves yesterday afternoon."

"How much was that?"

"A little over a hundred boxes."

He winced. Then he nodded.

"While y'all are packing everything up,

keep an eye out for examples of Mr. Dunlop's signature."

"Can do, Chief," Vern said. "Or anything that looks like another will, I guess."

"Or anything that looks like correspondence between Mr. Dunlop and an attorney," the chief said. "Or anything that might have anything to do with this old-time bank of the Dunlops. I have a hard time thinking that has anything to do with his murder, but stranger things have happened."

"Chief, if we're going to be looking through the papers —" I began.

He frowned, but cocked his head in a question.

"I can think of two town employees who'd be a big help in spotting relevant documents," I said. "What Ms. Ellie Draper doesn't know about this town probably isn't worth knowing — and she's on the town payroll. The same for Judge Jane Shiffley — does she count as an employee?"

"More like an authority," the chief said. "But yes, like Randall, she'd be acceptable."

"So what if we enlist them to help out?"

He thought for a moment.

"I don't want either of them toting and carrying boxes," he said. "And you know they'd insist on trying."

"Why don't I let Vern and company handle the packing," I said. "I'll go over to Harvey's house and help them figure out where the relevant stuff is. And then I can invite Judge Jane and Ms. Ellie to join me over at the furniture store to work on the boxes that are already there. I can kind of postpone mentioning that there are more boxes coming."

"Good plan. And I'll send over Aida to supervise at the furniture store. Keep it official." He smiled, then turned and disappeared into his office.

"I guess the chief has his doubts about Ms. Tabitha," I said to Vern as we started putting on our rain gear. "What's the penalty for forging a will?"

"Forgery in general's a class five felony," Vern said promptly. "One to ten years, and possibly a fine. No idea if there's any special penalty for forging a will, though if you ask me there ought to be. Chief!" he called out. "You want me to call someone to mind the desk?"

The chief came out, talking on his cell phone, and sat behind the desk where Vern had been.

"No, not yet," he was saying on the phone. "But I think she intends to."

He waved at us, so Vern and I pushed

open the front door of the station and dashed through the renewed rain to our vehicles.

I made a quick detour past Muriel's Diner for a carryout of chili and fries before heading over to Harvey's house. Was it only my imagination, or did the place look sadder and more dilapidated in the rain? In yesterday's sunlight you might not notice that the yard was more dirt than grass. Today, with the patches of dirt turning into mud and puddles, you couldn't help seeing it. Rain dripped off the roof in random places, including one just above the front door. At least the tarps all seemed intact. No feral kitten in the trap, but the little door into the crawl space was open, as it was supposed to be.

And inside, we were relieved to see that everything was still snug and dry.

"So far," Vern said. "But you were right to worry. Rain's stubborn and patient. If it can't get inside on a straight path, it'll keep burrowing around until it finds a roundabout way."

"I guess that means we should get everything that could be damaged out before the rain wins," I said.

"We should get everything out, period," Vern said. "Get it all safely locked up at the furniture store, slap a good security system on it, and that'll keep it safe until we get an expert in to evaluate it all and see if there's anything there that's valuable. Or anything that gives us a clue to who did him in and why."

Beau and Osgood arrived and started packing.

Vern strolled outside with me, although I suspected he actually wanted to check on what the neighbors were up to. Mr. Brimley wasn't on his porch, but you could see his face from time to time at one or another window. Mrs. Gudgeon's binoculars might have been glued in place.

"Probably a good thing I'm here to fend off those two," Vern said. "Especially her. Brimley's had enough run-ins with the department to know we won't put up with much of his nonsense — he'll back away if I mention 'interfering with a police investigation.' But what can you do about a little old lady who thinks it's her God-given right to know everything that's happening in *her* neighborhood."

"Hmm." I studied Mrs. Gudgeon's staring binoculars for a few moments. "Maybe I can help."

"How?" Vern looked dubious.

"I'll figure it out when I get in there. I'm

going to visit her. On official Helping Hands business, of course."

CHAPTER 22

I fished around in the back of my car —
which wasn't as horrible as the back of Tabitha's, but could use a good clearing out.
Then again, ever since the first time I'd
walked into Harvey's house, I'd felt the
almost irresistible urge to tidy everywhere I
went. I found a clipboard, a pad of lined
paper, and a pen that the dogs hadn't yet
used as a chew toy. Then I locked the car
and strode down the street and up Mrs.
Gudgeon's front walk.

A distinct improvement over Harvey's
front walk. The thought saddened me. Why
couldn't the killer have waited until after
we'd finished clearing out and repairing
Harvey's house? So he'd at least have a little
time to enjoy it. For that matter, why did
the killer have to go after Harvey at all?

I focused back on Mrs. Gudgeon's walk,
which was completely devoid of cracks or
crumbled bits, and not a single fallen leaf

or twig marred its surface. In fact, I couldn't see so much as a stray dead leaf anywhere on her property. The bushes flanking her front stoop had been pruned into rectangles so perfect that from a distance I wondered if they were fake. They weren't, but the blooming geraniums in pots on either side of her front door certainly were.

I put on my most officious look and rang her doorbell. A harsh buzzer sounded somewhere inside.

I kept my expression neutral and business-like during the several minutes in which I was sure Mrs. Gudgeon was peering at me through her peephole. I began to wonder if I'd flunked her inspection and she was planning to ignore me indefinitely. But I didn't want to betray impatience by ringing the doorbell again. And it might be interesting to see how long she was capable of ignoring someone standing on her front stoop.

Eventually I won our strange game of doorbell chicken. Mrs. Gudgeon opened the door and scowled at me.

"I'm busy," she said. "And I already talked to the police."

She didn't actually say "go away" but I got the message. Got it, and blithely ignored it.

"I know this has been very inconvenient

for you, Mrs. Gudgeon," I said. "I'd just like to ask you a few questions about the proximity impact, so we can complete or at least schedule any mitigating work."

She frowned as she tried to decipher that deliberate chunk of bureaucratese. A gust of wind sprang up, carrying with it some errant fallen leaves that swirled near her stoop — obviously from someone else's yard. She shuddered and looked alarmed.

"You'd better come inside and explain that in English," she said. "Wipe your feet and leave your shoes by the door."

I stepped inside, wiped my feet on a doormat almost the size of a twin mattress, and deposited my shoes alongside the regimented row of Mrs. Gudgeon's footwear — a pair of black lace-up shoes, a nearly identical tan pair, and some utilitarian boots. She was wearing a pair of slippers that looked as if they got a lot more wear than any of the outdoor shoes. I could feel her disapproving eyes, but resisted the temptation to adjust my shoes so they were in perfect alignment with hers. Then I turned and saw that she was standing in the middle of the hallway, as if protecting the rest of the house while she waved me into the living room. I followed her directions, making sure I kept to the two-foot-wide path of plastic matting laid down to protect the spotless white shag carpet. Was this a temporary accommodation to the bad weather or a permanent feature? It seemed pretty firmly anchored.

The plastic motif continued in the living room — covers on the chairs, the sofa, the lampshades. She motioned me to the sofa, whose thick plastic cover crinkled and squeaked as I sat down, and perched herself on the straightest and most uncomfortable-looking chair in the room.

"So what is it you've come to bother me about?" she said. "I already told you that I don't have need your charity."

"No, ma'am." I took out my pen and held it over the clipboard. "But I would like to get a statement about any negative impact Mr. Dunlop's hoarding has had on your property. Obviously we can't proceed with the cleanup at his house until the police investigation is over and the issue of the house's new ownership has been resolved. But part of our project is to ensure that we do everything we can to address the legitimate concerns of neighbors who have experienced hardship as a result of the situation we're resolving."

It didn't sound all that plausible to me, although I said it with a straight face. But

Mrs. Gudgeon, clearly a woman with a grievance, swallowed the bait.

"Hardship," she exclaimed. "Yes, he's caused me plenty of hardship, but I don't know how you can possibly make up for most of it. Do you realize what it's been like, living next to that eyesore for years?"

I nodded with unfeigned sympathy. I knew I'd have found Harvey a trying neighbor — and I liked to think that more than a decade of living with lively twin boys had given me higher than usual tolerance for chaos. For someone like Mrs. Gudgeon, with her obvious need for neatness and organization, living beside Harvey must have been hell.

"How long have you been here?"

"Sixteen years."

"Before his father's death, then," I said, remembering the dates on the tombstones at Trinity.

"That's correct. And before you tell me that we should have known what we were getting into, it wasn't that bad when we moved in. Not the yard, at least. It was a little messy, but I just assumed it was because he was distracted by his father's illness. But then the old man had his heart attack and died, and I went over to drop off a casserole, and as long as I was going I thought I'd take a business card from my yard service and suggest he give them a call if he couldn't handle it himself, and I got a look at the inside of that place."

She shuddered and looked pale.

"It must have been a shock." If I'd been in my own house I'd have fetched her a glass of water, but I got the distinct impression that she'd rather pass out than have me barging into other parts of her lair.

"It was two months before he gave back my casserole dish, and by that time, after what I'd seen — well, I ran it through the dishwasher a couple of times and then donated it to Goodwill. The idea of eating out of it turned my stomach. And after that his yard got progressively worse. The house, too, from what little I can see. Cleanliness is next to godliness, you know."

From the angry look on her face, I suspected she was still bitter that Moses had come down off the mountain without an eleventh commandment about cleanliness.

In fact, it went beyond anger. What I saw on her face was naked hate. For a moment, I had no doubt whatsoever that she could have killed Harvey. He'd been there for sixteen years, his hoarding and the condition of his house and yard steadily growing worse, spoiling her enjoyment of her own pristine home. And she'd finally had enough.

Vern had called her a little old lady, and maybe she was in his eyes. By my reckoning she was probably well short of seventy, and not the least bit frail. What if Harvey, too, had seen her as a harmless old lady? Annoying, but harmless. Maybe that was the answer to the puzzle of how the killer had lured Harvey out of his locked house and into the garage.

I'd mention that theory to the chief later. Meanwhile I listened to her rant about Harvey for a while, ending with "and I don't care if you think I'm heartless, but I'm not sorry he's gone."

"I understand how you feel," I lied. "Of course, we all want the chief to catch whoever did it. You can't let a murderer get away with his crime."

"I'm not holding my breath," she said. "Look how long it took them to do anything about his squalor."

"You can help, you know," I said.

Her face didn't suggest that she was all that interested in helping.

"I bet they have to keep their eye on his house, in case the killer returns to the scene of the crime," I said.

"We need better police protection in this neighborhood anyway," she said.

"And you'll definitely get it for a while, because obviously anyone who goes over there could be the killer — even if they seem to have a good reason. They're definitely going to be interrogating anyone who shows up. So I hope you won't be shy about telling them when you spot anyone."

"I never am." She sounded a little unsettled, as if she'd just realized how what I'd just said would cramp her style.

"Well, I shouldn't take any more of your time," I said. "But please do give a little more thought to the question of whether you're owed restitution. Odds are they'll end up taking it out of his estate, you know, so it's not like it would be charity."

I hoped she wouldn't think that last bit through too much. Time to take my leave. I stood, marched along the assigned plastic path to the front hall, thanked her for her hospitality, donned my shoes, and left.

I found Vern fetching another stack of flat moving boxes from the Shiffley Construction Company truck Beau and Osgood had arrived in.

"Piece of work, isn't she?" he said, nodding toward Mrs. Gudgeon's house.

"I hope the chief hasn't taken her off his suspect list." I related my conversation with Mrs. Gudgeon. Vern nodded thoughtfully when I described the look of hatred and malice that had crossed her face. And cracked up when I got to the part about the police suspecting anyone who showed up at the house.

"You know, that just might keep her out of our hair," he said. "Good work."

"She might make a few more calls to nine-one-one after you leave," I said.

"And some of them might actually be useful," he said. "See you over at the furniture store. Oh — by the way. Chief told me to give you these. New keys for here and the furniture store."

"Roger." I slid the keys onto my key ring and headed for my car. "Keep your eyes on the cat trap," I called over my shoulder.

I put in the calls to Judge Jane and Ms. Ellie on my way over to the furniture store, and as I expected, both were not only willing but downright eager to join the paper chase. I must have made it sound like fun — if only I could do as well when trying to coax the boys into doing chores or homework.

The store didn't look nearly as festive as it had during our party the night before. The tree was still in the front window, and garlands decked the walls, but the long lables with their bright red and green covers

299

had gone back to Trinity, and whoever had brought the red and green throws that had covered all the boxes had taken them home again.

I found Aida at the store, setting up a few of the card tables and folding chairs we'd used for overflow.

"I don't know about you folks," she said. "But if I'm going to spend a perfectly good afternoon sorting through Harvey Dunlop's junk, I am not sitting on the floor to do it. I shoved all the boxes with papers in them over to this side. Is this all?"

"No, Vern's got a crew to fetch the rest of it."

"There's more?" Judge Jane said, frowning slightly at the rows of boxes.

"This is probably about half of it," I said.

"Well, let's not waste time," Judge Jane said.

"Remember, nothing gets thrown away," Aida warned us. "Not even a paper napkin. We can start a box of probable trash, but nothing actually gets pitched. And while we're sorting, we keep our eyes open for anything that might give us a clue to why someone would bump Harvey off."

Aida set up Harvey's little radio and tuned it to the college radio station — during the winter break they could usually be relied on in the afternoons for long, uninterrupted programs of instrumental Christmas music. Then we each grabbed a box, hauled it to a table, and dived in. After a while Randall turned up, and we got him started with a table and a box of his own.

I very quickly realized how much more satisfying this would be if we were allowed to throw away trash, because so much of this overwhelming mass of paper was very clearly trash.

We started filling one box with out-of-date coupons and advertising flyers. However interesting it might be to know how much the Caerphilly Market was charging for turkeys and fresh cranberries back in 1987, we had a hard time imagining that information could have any bearing on Harvey's murder. Still, we didn't throw the coupons and flyers out — just scanned them for any cryptic notes and tossed them in the ad box. Make that ad boxes. We'd filled one box and started a second. I'd be delighted when we could toss them all in the recycling bin.

And the same for the newspaper and magazine articles. Mostly clippings from the *Clarion,* although apparently for a while back in the seventies and eighties the household had also taken the *Richmond Times-Dispatch.* After much discussion, we sorted the clippings into a small — well, smaller — collection of articles about aspects of town history or local notables, and a larger collection of ones that seemed completely random and unlikely to be related to the murder, like cartoons, recipes, gardening columns, book reviews, and articles about celebrities.

At least a dozen boxes were filled with nothing but old magazines. We ruffled the pages to find any papers that might be hidden between the pages, and Ms. Ellie sorted them into two collections — magazines the Friends of the Library might be able to sell if whoever inherited them wanted to donate them, and magazines that were no longer of any use to anyone — old computer magazines, particularly — and should just be recycled.

We were also rapidly filling a box with user manuals for appliances and electrical devices, some of them so ancient that it would be a miracle if we found the items themselves still in good working order. Although the vintage 1940s KitchenAid mixer we'd found in Harvey's kitchen hadn't looked in such bad shape, so you never knew.

Judge Jane got excited when she came across a stash of genealogical papers, and I had to admit that they might turn out to be useful. Were there any other distant cousins lurking about who might have had designs on Harvey's property? In a burst of optimism we created a genealogy box, but it wasn't filling up very fast. And Judge Jane's cursory study of the box's contents weren't encouraging.

"Looks as if Harvey was the last of the Dunlops," she said. "And it doesn't look as if his three Haverhill cousins are doing much to replenish the earth. No children listed for any of them."

"If you ask me, that's not such a bad thing," I said.

We were also well into our second box of family photographs — everything from ancient black-and-white or sepia portraits of stiff-backed ancestors with fixed smiles or stern frowns on their faces to fading fifties-era Polaroids of people who bore a vague resemblance to Harvey. As soon as I saw the pictures of him as a teenager I recognized Harvey, as awkward and diffident then as when I'd met him. Nothing more recent than that, of him or anyone else. I took an immediate if irrational dislike to his father, Aristede Junior — and I knew it was him because, to our delight, most of the photos had the names of their subjects neatly inked on the back. Aristede looked as stiff and scowling as the worst of his ancestors, and at least they'd had the excuse of having to hold still for an ungodly length of time to have their pictures taken. I couldn't offhand think of any way the pictures were going to be useful to the chief's case, but you never knew.

Around five o'clock two workmen from the Shiffley Construction Company arrived and began installing wireless cameras and motion-activated lights at both doors and all three of the ground-floor windows.

"I'm going home and tackling my basement after this," Aida said. "Not that I'm planning to be a homicide victim, but if I ever am, I damn well don't want the chief and Vern and Horace pawing through my things like this, trying to figure out who did me in."

"Amen," Ms. Ellie said.

"I don't know — stuff can have a positive effect sometimes," Judge Jane said. "Once or twice a year I get a case so annoying that it makes me wonder if it's time for me to retire. Let someone younger and less cranky deal with some of my repeat customers. Then I look around my chambers and think about what a pain it would be to pack up and move out, and I say the hell with it. I'll die on the bench, and someone else can clean out my chambers after I'm gone."

"You could hire Meg to do it," Ms. Ellie said. "If she wasn't already juggling three or four careers, I think Meg could do an excellent job as one of those people who comes in and declutters someone's house."

"I'd do a good job at the clearing out part," I said. "Someone else would have to do the therapy. The first time one of them said 'But it's a perfectly good something or other,' I'd lose it."

"Bingo!" Randall shouted. "I've got financial stuff here!"

CHAPTER 23

We all crowded around to take a look. Bills and bank statements from around the turn of the millennium, so neither old enough to give information about the family bank or new enough to give us much of an idea about Harvey's current financial state. Still it didn't look as if he'd thrown out a single bill or canceled check from that time period. Who knew what else we'd find?

Around 3:00 P.M., as we were working on the last few boxes we had, Vern, Beau, and Osgood came in with another hundred and fifty or so boxes.

"Good gracious," Judge Jane said. "How much more is there?"

"This is most of it," Vern said. "A couple more boxes from the office, and we think there might be some paper in the far end of the living room. We should be able to get it all in the next load."

When they left to go back to Harvey's, we

all exchanged a look, took deep breaths, and dived into the next set of boxes.

And these boxes took us farther into the past. Aida was unearthing canceled checks from the seventies and eighties. Judge Jane was sorting through phone and utility bills from the forties and fifties. Ms. Ellie came across a copy of Aristede Dunlop's last will and testament, which she immediately handed to Judge Jane for an expert evaluation.

"Perfectly solid will," Judge Jane said after scanning it. "But not very illuminating. Left everything he died possessed of to Harvey, without saying whether that everything was a king's ransom or a pile of debts. Still, knowing the father went to Homer Billingsley to get his will done might help us find out if Harvey had one."

"This was signed in 1971," Aida said. "Do we even know if this Homer Billingsley is still alive? I've never heard the name."

"No, he's long gone, but his granddaughter's running the firm now. Kate Warren. I'll just ring her up and see what I can find out."

Unfortunately, about all she could find out at the moment was that Counselor Warren was spending Christmas in Arizona.

"More delay," Aida grumbled.

"Don't worry," Judge Jane said. "I asked

her to call me back as soon as she gets the message. Lawyers tend to return my phone calls pretty quickly."

We went back to sorting until Aida hit pay dirt.

"Hey, I think I've got something about that bank."

Again we crowded around. There were actually several boxes full of papers from the bank. Ledgers. Typed financial reports. Boxes of blank letterhead.

And an old-fashioned ledger with a gray canvas cover and red leather corners. Inside someone with elegant old-fashioned handwriting had written on the first page, "Repayment of outstanding obligations of the Farmers and Mechanics Bank. Aristede Charles Dunlop, Sr."

"That's it," Judge Jane said. "Just what Mrs. Diamandis was telling us."

The first page had a list of twenty-three names with amounts beside them. Seven of the names, the ones with smaller amounts beside them, had a neat line drawn through them — repayments in full was my guess.

The rest of the book contained pages for each of the twenty-three, headed by the name and address and followed by columns of numbers. From 1933 through 1942, the only entries were quarterly additions of interest, and I found myself wondering if Aristede ever despaired of seeing the totals begin to shrink. Then in March 1942, he started slowly but steadily whittling down the totals. All entries stopped in November 1965.

"I expect that would be when Aristede Senior died," Judge Jane said, with a nod.

"Yes." I had pulled out my notebook and flipped to the page where I'd copied down all the Dunlop family dates. "According to his tombstone over at Trinity."

"I bet the chief would find it interesting if we could figure out which of these people still have kin here in Caerphilly," Judge Jane said.

Randall, Aida, and I went back to sorting while Ms. Ellie and Judge Jane worked on the names in the ledger. It helped a little that Aristede Senior had updated the names, addresses, and telephone numbers over the years, usually by pasting a new slip of paper over the old address on a ledger page as needed. But the last repayment entries were in 1965, so there was still the fifty-five-year gap to be crossed between Aristede Senior's death and now.

Judge Jane finally pushed the faded ledger away and rubbed her eyes.

"Fascinating as this is," she said, "my eyes

are crossing. And if I don't leave now, I won't get over to the college theater in time for Michael's performance."

"Good point," Ms. Ellie said. "I have an idea — let's the two of us meet at the library tomorrow morning and finish figuring this ledger out."

"Ledger has to stay here, Ms. Ellie," Aida said. "Evidence."

"We wouldn't need the ledger." Ms. Ellie handed it over to Aida. "If someone could take pictures of the pages, we could work with that."

"I'll do that," Aida said. "I should be able to get it done before I have to take off for the theater, and if not I'll drop by here after the show."

She cleared off one of the card tables, set the ledger down in the middle of it, and started methodically taking pictures with her phone.

I made sure all the doors and windows were locked.

"You want me to set the security system?" I asked.

"No need," she said. "I won't be long, and I'll do it when I leave."

I left her to it.

Outside I noticed that the Shiffley work-men had posted a NO TRESPASSING sign by the back door. In fact, several that I could see, and I suspected there were others along the sides and in front. I wasn't sure how much good they'd do to protect the premises against a determined burglar, but we had the security system for that. At least the signs would probably reduce the number of nosy people who set off the alarm.

There was a lull in the rain, but the temperature was hovering just above freezing and the wind was rising, making for a miserable night. Thank goodness Michael's show would start at seven — early, by theatrical standards, but the better for children's bedtimes. And it only ran a little over two hours, so even allowing for a reasonable amount of post-show backstage celebrating we should be home by ten. Hosting a large noisy cast party, of course — but home.

Back at the house, everything was chaos. About half of the relatives staying with us were going to tonight's sold-out opening night. The rest had reluctantly settled for later performances. And where was Michael? He had to get to the theater much earlier than his audience members, so I was planning to throw on my dress, drop him off, and then come back to ferry one or more carloads of family members. Unless he'd already gone.

More likely he'd gone outside to get a little peace and quiet. Much as Michael seemed to like my family, when they showed up en masse like this he sometimes had to get away. I'd probably find him cocooning in his office. Or, better yet, leaning on the fence of the llama pen, listening to them hum.

I stepped out of the hot, crowded kitchen and scanned the yard. No Michael. The llamas looked up expectantly when they saw me. I felt a pang of guilt. I should probably take them a few apples for a treat.

Then again, my relatives seemed to find the llamas almost as entertaining as the llamas found us. Odds were the guys were already stuffed with bits of apple, carrot, broccoli, and who knew what else.

I was about to go back inside again when I noticed a black-and-white bird sitting on the railing at the other end of the back stoop. He also seemed to be staring at the llamas.

Was this one of Grandfather's magpies? I took note of his markings. Black head and neck. Long, mostly black tail. Patches of black on the wings. White belly. And then it occurred to me that I could do better than describe him. I pulled out my phone and opened the camera to take a picture.

Just as I snapped the shot he turned around and I saw he was holding something in his bill. Something black and slightly iridescent. Then he uttered a harsh cry, sounding something like "Ack-ack!" and took flight. The object he'd been holding fluttered to the ground.

I walked over to where it had fallen and picked it up. A fragment of black butterfly wing. Just like Rose Noire's. Or was it the same bit of wing, stolen back from Rose Noire and redelivered to me?

"Creepy," I muttered. The magpie — or one of his friends — was still saying "Ack-ack! Ack-ack!" somewhere nearby.

If it was a magpie. I hesitated. I could send the photo to Grandfather, but he'd only chide me for not capturing the poor bird. I texted "Is this a magpie?" to Caroline and sent her the picture.

"There you are." Michael came out of the back door. "I need to get to the theater."

"I can take you any time," I said. "Just —"

"No, you relax," Michael said. "Rob's going to run me in. I just wanted to let you know I was taking off."

Rob followed him out onto the stoop.

"I'm meeting Delaney there to take care

313

of the dog thing," Rob said.

Good — I assumed that meant they'd been able to print some glamour shots to display in the lobby.

"The tickets?" I asked as they were crossing the yard toward the driveway.

Michael slapped his pockets.

"I think — no, I left them on my desk. I can go and —"

"I'll find them," I said. "Your desk is probably messy, but it's nowhere near Harvey level. Go!"

I waved good-bye. And then realized I was still holding the butterfly wing. I let it go and watched as a breeze caught it and whisked it out of sight.

My phone vibrated. I glanced down to see a reply from Caroline: "Yes. Free-range magpie all right."

I went back in to brave the family chaos.

Still, I managed to escape the kitchen and get dressed in a more leisurely fashion than I'd expected. Then I made my way down the long hall to the library and Michael's adjoining office to collect the tickets.

There were still game players in the library — a Dungeon & Dragons group at one end, and a session of Ticket to Ride, a railroad building game, at the other. Jamie was watching the D&D crew. To my surprise, I found Josh in Michael's office.

"Hey, Mom." His tone was matter-of-fact, but he was frowning and staring around. I suspected I knew why. But I'd ask anyway.

"What's up," I said, as I scanned the top of the desk and spotted an envelope marked "CC tickets."

"You guys have a lot of paper."

"Colleges make for a lot of paperwork," I said. "And you know how busy your dad is during the semester. Once Christmas is over I'm sure he'll do his usual office cleanout."

"Yeah," Josh said. "But he doesn't throw it all out. He puts most of it in the attic."

I couldn't actually argue with him.

"And you have a lot of paper up there, too."

"Yes, I do," I said. "And I should take the time to sort through it all, to see what we should still save and what can be thrown out."

"Cousin Eric says you could scan it all and get rid of the paper, and it would take up a lot less space and you'd be able to find things easier."

"He has a good point," I said. "Is he volunteering to come down and do the scanning? Because that's a lot of work."

He nodded but he didn't seem to be reacting to what I'd said.

315

"Is this how Mr. Dunlop's house got that way?"

"Don't worry," I said. "I think we're a long way from turning into Mr. Dunlop. But I tell you what: after the holidays are over, let's start a family project. Let's go around the whole house and figure out any spots, like your dad's office and the attic, that are starting to look even a little like Mr. Dunlop's house. And then we'll figure out a schedule for fixing them."

"Yeah," he said. "I guess that would work. If you really do it."

I pulled out my notebook and entered it on the page where I was collecting things to do in January.

"Duly noted," I said. "Is that what you're wearing to the show?"

He glanced down at the sweater and jeans he was wearing and rolled his eyes.

"Of course not," he said. "I'm getting dressed up."

"Well, go change, then," I said. "We only have half an hour."

At that he started and then walked out, pretending nonchalance. He didn't start running till he turned the corner.

I glanced around Michael's office. Yes, it could do with a good cleanout, as he himself would say if he had time. But he always did clean it up at the end of every semester. And while it was true that we had rather a lot of paper in the attic, I was pretty sure all of it was all neatly organized in file folders and the files themselves stored in carefully labeled boxes. Should I explain to Josh — and Jamie, if he shared this worry — that there was a big difference between this and the vast mountain of undifferentiated paper that had once filled Harvey's office.

Then again, maybe Josh had a point. Well-organized clutter could still be clutter.

I'd worry about it after the holidays.

I checked to make sure the relatives Mother had recruited to make preparations for the cast party needed no help from me. Then I returned to the living room to relax in a way that was — well, probably not unique to me, but still somewhat unusual. I was tending my notebook-that-tells-me-when-to-breathe. Crossing out things I'd done — yay! Things other people had done for me — double yay! Things that had turned out to be unnecessary, things whose time had passed, things that there just wouldn't be time to do, no matter how worthwhile they were. And —

"Mom?"

It was Jamie. I was about to ask why he wasn't ready to go to the play, but I realized he looked troubled about something. Not, I hoped, his parents' surfeit of paper.

"What's wrong?" I asked, closing my notebook.

"It's *Christmas,*" he said.

"You say that like it's something bad," I said. "Like 'homework' or 'spinach' or something."

"Yeah. And it's supposed to be fun, right?"

"Among other things. It's also supposed to be a time for thinking about the meaning of the season. And spending time with the people you love."

"Yeah." He frowned. "It was kind of fun working with you and Josh and Rose Noire and Gran-gran yesterday. Helping out with Mr. Dunlop's stuff. I wish we'd started it sooner, so we could have finished and he could have enjoyed it for a while."

"Me too," I said.

Was that it? Was he upset about Harvey? Understandable. He and Josh were probably both upset, in their own ways. I was figuring out the best way to tackle the subject when he spoke again.

"He had a lot of magazines. Only I don't think they were his. They were all addressed to someone named Aris-something."

"Aristede," I said. "That was his father's name. And also his grandfather."

"I don't think his father ever read any of those magazines," he said. "There were dozens of them, and some of them were still in the plastic wrappers they came in. And some of the others, if you picked them up, a bunch of postcards would fall out — you know, the ones that always fall out the first time you open the magazine."

"Yeah." I nodded. "They probably hadn't been read."

"Why?" he asked. "Why would someone buy all those magazines if he wasn't going to read them?"

"I'm sure he intended to read them," I said. "Remember how last summer you were going to do a little bit of your summer reading every day, and then in July we figured out that in spite of all your good intentions you hadn't done any of it yet?"

"And you put me on a schedule, and I got it done," he said. "Mr. Dunlop's father should have done something like that for himself. Only — what if he didn't want them? What if Mr. Dunlop gave them to his father for Christmas and his father was too polite to say he didn't want them, and then he never read them, so every week a bunch of magazines would come in the mail and remind Mr. Dunlop how he sucked at picking out presents."

319

Okay, now I definitely knew where this was going.

"It's possible," I said. "Yes, I could very easily see that happening."

"How are we supposed to figure it out?" He sounded glum, and I knew it wasn't over any unappreciated presents Harvey had given his father.

"Did I ever tell you about the most unusual present I ever gave your Grandpa when I was a kid?"

He shook his head.

"I gave him an ashtray that I made myself."

"An ashtray?" He frowned in puzzlement. "Grandpa smoked?"

"No, neither he nor Grandma ever smoked. But it was a really cool ashtray. I made it myself in school, out of clay. It was a relief map of the state of Virginia, about this big." I held out my hands a foot apart. "And I painted it just the way we used to color in maps of the state, with the Tidewater in green, the Piedmont in yellow, and the Appalachian mountains in orange. And — now this is the cool part — the mountains were made of little cones of clay, with spaces between them that were just the right width to hold a cigarette. And the country around Richmond was kind of hollowed out a little, which wasn't true to life, but it meant there was someplace to flick the ashes."

"That's kind of. . . . weird, Mom." Jamie grimaced. "And I bet you're going to tell me that Grandpa loved it anyway because you made it."

"Actually, he did," I said. "He kept it in his office, and stored paperclips in the little hollow around Richmond, and stuck pens and pencils between the Appalachians, and he'd probably still have it if your uncle Rob hadn't knocked it off and broken it a few years later."

"And that was a great present." His voice sounded flat.

"No, it was a terrible present," I said. "But I was only six or seven, and I didn't know any better. It gets harder when you get older. And yeah, it's pretty horrible to be surrounded by the Ghost of Bad Christmas Presents of the Past."

"Yeah." He grinned at that. "So what do we do? 'Cause there are still a lot of people on my Christmas list that I haven't thought of anything really good for. And I don't want to give them stuff that'll just sit around and be a waste."

"That's good thinking," I said. "Look, maybe I'd have a different answer if I hadn't been spending so much time in Mr. Dunlop's house, but maybe we all need to think a little more about how to give each other more intangible presents. Presents that aren't actual physical things," I added, since I wasn't entirely sure he got "intangible."

"Like what?"

"Remember the year your uncle Rob couldn't think of a good birthday present, so he gave you and Josh a promise that he'd take both of you and two of your friends to Kings Dominion the first weekend it was open in the spring?"

"That was actually kind of an awesome present." Jamie grinned at the memory.

"But what if you were tired of Kings Dominion?" I asked. "What if you'd been so often that just the thought of going again made you sick?"

"That's kind of hard to imagine."

"But what if?"

He thought.

"Well, we could go just to be polite." He didn't sound very convinced.

"Yes," I said. "Or you could ask if maybe he could take you someplace else that you weren't tired of — like Busch Gardens or Virginia Beach or skiing some place. Either way, you wouldn't be stuck forever with something you didn't want — like those giant teddy bears Aunt Catriona gave you last year — and may I say again, you both did a great job of pretending to be thrilled."

"Is she coming for Christmas? Because if she is, we should probably get those out of the attic and put them out in our rooms."

"I have a better idea — why don't we get them out of the attic and take them down to the women's shelter and leave them there for some younger kid to play with."

"Good deal. But what if she asks about them?"

"Then I will explain that you made a great sacrifice and decided the children at the shelter needed the bears more than you did."

He looked thoughtful.

"That would probably work," he said. "But we should get Dad to tell her. He's better at telling polite whoppers like that."

"Yes, he is." I had to grin. "And getting back to the present situation — if you haven't thought of something someone would like, give them a gift certificate. Use your laptops and make really awesome gift certificates."

"For what?" He looked discouraged again. "Like Dad, for instance — what could I give him?"

"How about a booklet of coupons, each good for one llama feeding or one llama pen cleaning."

"We do that anyway sometimes. And I think Dad likes feeding the llamas."

"He likes doing it most mornings. But what about when he knows he has an early meeting and has to set his alarm even earlier than usual. Or if he has a cold and would like to sleep a little late the next morning. And I doubt if he'd ever object to a pen cleaning. And that's just one idea. Heck, you could give him a blank check. A coupon worth one hour of whatever chore he doesn't feel like doing."

"Yeah." He looked thoughtful. "I can work with that. Thanks, Mom."

He gave me an absentminded peck on the cheek and wandered off, clearly considering the possibilities.

I went back to my notebook and added a few more to-do items. A reminder to check with Michael and see if he actually had expressed an interest in getting a subscription to a magazine, and if so, which one. A reminder to find out if Grandfather still needed a new pith helmet or if he'd already replaced the one his elephant stepped on. And a note to drop a hint to Mother about how much I liked Mrs. Dinwiddie's quilt.

"Isn't it about time to leave?" Cordelia stood in the doorway, not only dressed in her theatergoing finery but already putting on her coat. "Rose Noire and Caroline already went out to the car."

"Yikes." I slammed the notebook closed. "You're right." I walked out into the hallway, rang the dinner bell, and bellowed, "Anyone who wants to go to *A Christmas Carol* should already be in the Twinmobile!"

CHAPTER 24

A thunderous stampeding sound followed, and the boys managed to beat me to the driveway without knocking their grandmother over. Caroline and Rose Noire were already in their seats.

I hadn't expected the boys to react quite so rapidly, so I decided we had time to take a slightly longer way around and show Cordelia and Caroline some of the more notable town decorations.

Like the *Nightmare Before Christmas* house, whose eccentric owner decorated lavishly for Halloween and then made minor concessions to the subsequent holidays as an excuse to leave his spooky decor in place. In the few weeks leading up to Thanksgiving, all the pumpkins and skeletons wore pilgrim hats and appeared to have sinister designs on the life-sized ceramic turkey that had taken its place among them. Now, with Christmas approaching, the house's roof sported a glossy black sleigh and eight skeletal reindeer, and all the pumpkins and skeletons wore Santa hats. The owner had also added black bows and ribbons to all the headstones in his faux graveyard, and decorated the fir trees flanking his front door with tiny bats and witches' hats.

And then there was Crèche Lady, who'd taken a ceramics class at the college a few years ago and then bought an enormous kiln so she could make her own life-sized nativity scene. The first year it had been a slightly minimalist nativity — a solitary shepherd and his single sheep gazing at Mary, Joseph, and Baby Jesus, who were clearly still awaiting the arrival of the Magi. The second year she'd added two more shepherds, a dozen sheep, and a hovering angel. The wise men on their camels had appeared the third year. This year there had been much speculation on whether she'd declared the project finished or if she'd continue expanding it — and if so, how.

"Look. She's not just doing a nativity this year," Cordelia said. "She's added some other biblical scenes."

To the left of the nativity, in a separate tableau, three standing wise men, holding the reins of their camels, appeared to be wrangling with a figure seated on a throne and wearing a golden crown. King Herod and Magi, presumably. To the right, Joseph appeared to be striding briskly toward the shrubbery at the edge of the yard, leading a donkey on which Mary and Baby Jesus were riding, while what appeared to be a trio of spear-carrying Roman centurions peered in the wrong direction. And the angel hovering over the stable now had company, in the form of two smaller angels holding hymn books and singing.

"I like this," I said. "She could be just getting started. She's got the scope to keep doing this for years."

We also passed close enough to the town square that they could peer down the streets to see the Ferris wheel, the merry-go-round, and the delightful chaos of the Christmas Carnival that surrounded the official Caerphilly Christmas tree in the town square.

"We'll take you there while you're here, Gran-gran," Jamie told Cordelia.

"The Ferris wheel is pretty scary," Josh advised. "But you'd like the merry-go-round."

From the look on her face, I suspected Cordelia planned to show them that she wasn't a bit scared of any old Ferris wheel. They'd see.

As we approached the drama building,

Jamie and Josh lapsed into one of their perennial debates over the proper rendition of a line from tonight's performance — Tiny Tim's famous "God bless us, every one!" Since the boys had appeared in the full cast performance of *A Christmas Carol* several years ago, each alternating between Tiny Tim and Scrooge as a boy, they both had strong opinions on the optimal way of reading it.

"God bless us EV-ry-one," Josh exclaimed.

"No, you have to hit the last syllable, too," Jamie countered. "God bless us EV-ry ONE!"

They bickered amicably about it the rest of the way. Each was convinced that Michael would read the line his way, so at least this was a dispute that would soon be resolved.

I dropped Caroline, Rose Noire, and the boys off on the front steps of the drama building. Cordelia preferred to ride with me around the back, where I would be taking advantage of Michael's faculty parking privileges.

"So you won't have to walk alone in the dark, dear," she said.

I suspected it wasn't really a question of my safety. The drama building wasn't located in a bad section of town — in fact

Caerphilly didn't really have anything you could call a bad section of town, apart from a few blocks near the bus station that made timid souls ever so slightly nervous at the dark of the moon. She was probably trying to avoid having to look at the large, elegant brass sign on the front of the building, proclaiming it "THE DR. J. MONTGOMERY BLAKE DRAMATIC ARTS BUILDING." It worked both ways — Grandfather always scowled when he saw the plaque thanking her for funding the town's much improved baseball fields.

We arrived in the lobby to find the usual preshow festivities in place. People were wandering about oohing and ahhing at the decor — done by Mother, of course. Before long she'd have cornered every Christmas decorating project in town. The highlight was the twenty-foot tree in the soaring glass-walled lobby. It was festooned with gold ornaments in the shapes of dancers dancing, lords leaping, and all the rest of the "Twelve Days" crew, and instead of a star it was topped with a large gold representation of the comedy and tragedy masks.

Students in Dickensian costume were selling cider, mulled wine, and gingerbread in one corner of the lobby, and a costumed string quartet serenaded us with carols from another. And at the far side, I spotted people crowding around something.

When I got closer I realized that the main attraction was a collection of Clarence's newly groomed dogs: a slender, languid dog who wasn't quite a saluki but clearly had the attitude; several large, friendly dogs that showed signs of Labrador or golden retriever ancestry; a nice assortment of small, lively dogs. Delaney was hovering nearby, snapping candid shots of the dogs and theatergoers interacting. A tuxedo-clad Rob was on his knees, facilitating an introduction between two little girls in velvet party dresses and an excitable terrier of some sort.

I almost didn't recognize Clarence Rutledge without either his denim and leather biker's gear or his white veterinarian's coat. He wore a blue sports coat over new-looking black jeans, and his emerald-green tie featured pictures of dachshunds in Santa hats. He was chatting with a young couple, presumably about the happy-looking dog they were all three taking turns petting.

"Ah! Meg!" My friend Ekaterina Vorobyaninova, general manager of the five-star Caerphilly Inn, greeted me, as she often did, with air kisses to both cheeks, in the European fashion. "You will know. You always know everything."

She pointed to where Clarence's glamorized dogs were lolling on velvet pillows or wagging their tails eagerly while being petted by members of the crowd. Clearly Clarence had done a good job of picking dogs that wouldn't freak out at the crowds. In fact, all of these dogs had to be either complete hams or total exhibitionists.

"Some of these dogs are quite attractive." Ekaterina, whom I knew to be a staunch cat person, sounded quite surprised. "Where do they come from?"

"All over," I said. "Some of them were picked up as strays or surrendered here in Caerphilly, but many of them come from shelters all over the place — Virginia mostly, but also West Virginia and North Carolina. Wherever there are shelters struggling with overcrowding. Especially kill shelters. Clarence will travel for hours to rescue animals from a kill shelter."

"No, I mean who brought them here tonight to be adopted — it is Clarence, then?"

"Yes." I pointed down the hall to where Clarence was standing. Why was Ekaterina so interested in the dogs? I didn't think her two aristocratic Russian blues would appreciate a canine sibling.

"We could do this at the Inn." She flung

her arms open in an expansive gesture. "Guests are always petting my cats and saying how much they miss their own cats. And only the other day I asked a guest who was returning from a run if he'd had a good workout, and he said the only thing he missed was having his dog to run beside him. We could try having a few dogs at the Inn, and allow guests to take them out for walks or pet them or whatever else people do with dogs. And some of them would fall in love with the dogs and want to take them home, and even when that didn't happen, both the dogs and the people would be happier."

"Sounds great to me," I said. "Talk to Clarence."

"Thank you." She strode off briskly. I hope Clarence liked her idea of fostering dogs at the Inn. Because if he didn't, he was in for a battle.

I found a corner where I could stand, sip my cider, and watch the dogs. A few people noticed where I was and came over to say hi. Michael's students. Michael's colleagues. Assorted family members. The occasional high-muck-a-muck from the college. I wasn't feeling antisocial. I liked being here, surrounded by people who were clearly full of holiday spirit.

I was just tired of having to be coherent.

"Hey, Meg!"

I looked up, already bracing in case it was another college dignitary whose name I would have to remember, and was relieved to see Clarence Rutledge ambling my way.

"You look festive,"

"Thanks." He glanced down at his Santa-dachshund tie with a look of satisfaction.

"Did Ekaterina tell you about her idea of featuring shelter animals at the Inn?"

"Yes!" His face lit up. "Rob's going to take her over to the shelter tomorrow to pick out the first batch. I wanted to ask you for a favor — I'm heading out before dawn to pick up a load of animals from a kill shelter on the far side of West Virginia."

"Where are you going to put them all?" I asked, and then hoped I hadn't accidentally volunteered to help with the solution to that problem.

"Your grandfather's got some vacant habitats at his zoo — he reintroduced a whole passel of black-footed ferrets into the wild this fall, and the new batches of kits won't arrive till May or June. So he's going to let me use them for the time being."

"Great," I said. Actually, I wondered what Grandfather would do if Clarence's new rescues were still around when the new kits began arriving. I'd let him worry about that.

"But if all goes well, I'll be gone at least twelve hours," Clarence said. "Longer if there's much weather in the mountains. Any chance you could drop by Harvey's occasionally to check on the cat trap I set up there? Because the weather's going to be nasty tomorrow, and if that feral kitten goes into the trap, she'll be out of the rain — I set it up in the crawl space under the house — but it could get pretty cold, and she'll be cut off from wherever she's been sheltering. I told everyone to leave the little door into the crawl space open, so she can get to the trap, so check on that, too, when you go by."

"Of course," I said.

"If you find her in the trap, just take the whole thing home and call Manoj out at the zoo," Clarence said. "And he'll come by to pick her up as soon as he can."

"Can do," I said.

"Thanks. Ooh — there's that professor from the German department — the one who likes Weimaraners. There's an alleged Weimaraner in the batch I'm collecting tomorrow — I should see if I can get him interested. Do you remember his name?"

"No one remembers his name," I said. "It's about fifteen syllables long. Most people call him Professor Grimm, like the fairy tales, which happens to be his academic specialty. But just 'professor' will do."

"Thanks!" Clarence dashed off to greet the tiny white-haired and -bearded figure.

I sipped my cider and half closed my eyes. It was nice, being here in the festively decorated lobby of the drama department, listening to the hum of conversation. It would be even nicer when the show started, and I could sit back in my seat to watch and listen, free from the occasional need to make coherent conversation with people.

"Dammit, those are my magpies!"

CHAPTER 25

I opened my eyes to find Rose Noire and Grandfather glaring at each other a few feet away.

"They're wild creatures," Rose Noire said. "They don't belong to you. They don't belong to anyone."

"They're a valuable part of my research!" Grandfather snapped.

"The value of a species does not lie in its utility to mankind," I said, raising my voice so they could hear me. They both turned to glare at me.

"Humanity," Rose Noire said.

"It was a quote," I said. "And just for the record, I support the magpies' right to freedom."

Rose Noire looked smug. Grandfather glowered at me.

"But I also think it's important to consider Grandfather's point of view. When he brought them here from their native habitat, he made himself responsible for their well-being. For keeping them safe and healthy while they are participating in his experiment, and then returning them to their proper habitat when the experiment is over."

"Actually —" Grandfather began.

"And consider what this experiment could do for the entire species," I said, interrupting Grandfather, who was probably going to have an inconvenient moment of candor and say that he had no intention of returning the magpies to the wild. "If he can actually prove that their intelligence is as high as he thinks it is, it could significantly improve the way they're treated! It could actually help their survival as a species!"

I glared at Grandfather, willing him not to pipe up and explain that magpies were not even on the outer fringes of the endangered species lists.

To my relief, Grandfather assumed what we all referred to as his heroic crusader pose, as if to suggest that he was ready to go into battle to defend the magpie. Rose Noire frowned and looked uncertain.

"I'll think about it." She sailed off, head high.

Grandfather took a step to follow, but I caught his arm.

"Leave her alone for now," I said. "Mother

and I will work on her."

He nodded and strode off in the opposite direction.

I closed my eyes and tried to regain my peace of mind.

"There you are, dear." Mother appeared, dressed in a long, elegant fitted gown of deep red velvet, and gave me a kiss on the cheek. "How are you tonight?"

"Dog tired." It seemed like a good moment for honesty. "Can you do something for me?"

"Of course."

"Make Rose Noire give Grandfather's magpies back." I related what I'd said, since it seemed to have made at least a small dent in Rose Noire's stubborn determination.

"I'll take care of it, dear. Anything else?"

"Talk for me if anyone comes over and wants conversation."

"Of course, dear. Did I tell you the good news about Mrs. Dinwiddie's quilt?"

"Good news?" I had the feeling I wasn't going to like her definition of good news.

"Apparently it's not really her style," Mother said. "So while she wanted it finished, in honor of her grandmother, she doesn't want to keep it. She's donating it to the Helping Hands, and we're going to raffle it off to raise money for future projects."

"Damn," I said. "I was hoping to talk her into selling it. To me, I mean."

"Oh, dear." Mother sounded genuinely sorry. "I wish I'd known that. I'd have tried to talk her into selling it and donating part of the proceeds. But don't worry. We can all buy lots of tickets."

"Buy me a whole bunch," I said. "As many as you can. Do you want me to give you some money now?"

"I'll trust you, dear."

"And also take lots of photos," I said. "Because if none of our tickets pay off, I want to find someone to make me one just like it."

"I'm sure that can be arranged." Mother was using her most soothing voice. "And — they're blinking the lights. Time to take our places."

As I settled into my seat, I felt a pleasant and rather surprising sense of anticipation. Surprising because this wasn't the first time I'd seen Michael's one-man performance of *A Christmas Carol*. How many years had he been doing this each Christmas? I couldn't quite remember. A few years ago we'd escalated to a full-cast production, with Michael directing and a well-known actor imported from Hollywood playing Scrooge. And that had been well-received, and made a satisfactory amount of money for that year's charity, but most people had been perfectly happy when the word went out that we were going back to the one-man show the following year. Not that we wouldn't ever do the bigger production again — we were thinking maybe once every ten years or so. And maybe next time Michael could play the lead — I liked his Scrooge better, anyway.

But for now, we were back to the one-man show. And not only had I seen at least one and sometimes several of his performances every year, I got to hear him rehearsing at home. Christmas in the Waterston/Langslow/Hollings-worth family played out with a soundtrack that included both Christmas music and Dickens's prose, in what sometimes seemed like equal measure.

And yet every year words from the book would hit me with sudden freshness. It happened now in the first few minutes, when Michael read the line about Scrooge being Marley's *"sole executor, his sole administrator, his sole assign, his sole residuary legatee, his sole friend, and sole mourner."*

Harvey, locked away in solitude all those years. As solitary as Marley, or as Scrooge himself. Though at least he'd had Clarence as a friend. If only we'd known. And at least Clarence wasn't his sole mourner.

We'd failed Harvey. But we could help others. Mrs. Diamandis. She wasn't the first person who'd started out as a Helping Hands client before becoming a volunteer herself. Mrs. Dinwiddie, who seemed to enjoy her quilting lessons. Maybe doing the Helping Hands project at Christmas wasn't a totally stupid idea after all.

"At this festive season of the year, Mr. Scrooge," Michael was saying, *"it is more than usually desirable that we should make some slight provision for the poor and destitute, who suffer greatly at the present time."*

Yes. Most of the Helping Hands clients weren't destitute, but more than one were poor. Poor, yet embarrassed to ask for help. Or unable to ask. Like Harvey, sitting in his increasingly cluttered and uncomfortable house. By making the project open to anyone, regardless of whether they needed it or not, we'd probably increased the odds that someone in real need would reach out to us.

But before he shut his heavy door, he walked through his rooms to see that all was right. He had just enough recollection of the face to desire to do that. Sitting-room, bedroom, lumber-room, all as they should be. Nobody under the table, no-body under the sofa; a small fire in the grate; spoon and basin ready; and the little saucepan of gruel (Scrooge had a cold in his head) upon the hob. Nobody under the bed; nobody in the closet; nobody in his dressing-gown, which was hanging up in a suspicious attitude against the wall. Lumber-room as usual. Old fire-guard, old shoes, two fish-baskets, washing-stand on three legs, and a poker.

Just like Harvey, checking his house last night when we took him home. Had he missed something — an open window, an unlocked door, an intruder hiding behind some pile of clutter? No, Aida had checked, too. Between his visible nervousness and her professionalism, I was sure they hadn't missed anything. And besides, he hadn't been killed in the house.

But how had someone lured him out of the house and into the garage?

Maybe that meant the killer was someone he trusted. Which would leave out all our main suspects except Tabitha. Maybe. If you bought her story that they'd formed a friendship online, and I wasn't sure I did.

Or someone he didn't find physically threatening. That seemed more plausible. Which would whittle it down to Mrs. Gudgeon and Tabitha.

Maybe no one had lured him out. Maybe he'd just wanted something that was in the garage. If he'd carefully checked and felt sure no one was there . . .

I forced my attention back on Scrooge.

"It is required of every man, that the spirit within him should walk abroad among his fellow-men, and travel far and wide; and if that spirit goes not forth in life, it is condemned to do so after death."

Required of every man? I had a sudden image of a transparent, spectral Harvey, hovering protectively in his house as we dismantled the clutter that had imprisoned him, box by box, paper by paper. Did he resent our interference? Would he be freed when we finished his de-cluttering? Or would he follow his stuff and haunt the furniture store?

You're getting fanciful, I told myself.

Still. I couldn't shake the feeling that we owed it to Harvey to finish the project. Sort his papers — and not just to see if there were any clues that would help the chief solve his murder. Find the proper home for all of his stuff, even if most of it went to a junk shop or the dump. Get his house fixed up so whoever moved in would have a happier life.

And then I tried to banish Harvey from my mind, to focus on Michael's show. There would be time enough to think about him tomorrow.

Like Mrs. Cratchit's pudding, the show was universally acclaimed to be a great success. Which meant that between the ticket sales, and the refreshment sales, a decent sum of money would make its way to CAWF.

Though probably not enough to solve its problems in the long term. But we'd worry about that after the holiday.

Back at the house, what we called the cast party was underway. Technically, with a one-man show, even inviting the posse of backstage techies who made everything happen would result in a fairly small cast party. So Michael generally extended an open invitation to anyone in the Drama Department, student or faculty, who was still in town. When you threw in our family — the relatives who were staying with us, the ones who were staying with Mother and Dad, the ones who had found rooms at the Caerphilly Inn or one of the many bed-and-breakfasts in town, and the ones who had come to town for just for the show and were hoping to find sofas to crash on — it made for a large and lively event.

There was caroling in the living room. Competitive cooking in the kitchen. Board games in the library. And food everywhere.

To my astonishment, I spotted my nephew Kevin — in the dining room, of course, where he could refill his plate whenever he liked. How like him, not even mentioning that he was in town either of the two times I'd been talking to him. He was deep in conversation with Josh and Jamie. They were probably consulting him about their Christmas present dilemmas. That significantly increased the odds that many of us would receive strange software or tech devices for Christmas. And most of them would be just peculiar, but a few would turn out to be phenomenally useful, once Kevin or one of Rob's tech gurus could be persuaded to set them up for us.

If it solved the boys' holiday stress, I was prepared to be enthusiastic about anything. Even a repeat of the electronic Rubik's Cubes Kevin had gifted some of us with a few years ago.

I ran into Dad sitting in a far corner of

the living room, slowly and morosely eating his way through a plate of food. And it occurred to me that I hadn't seen much of him in the last day or so.

"What's wrong with you?" I settled down into the chair next to him.

"The case." He sighed heavily. "Apart from the initial news that it couldn't have been an accident, I haven't been able to give the chief any information that will help him solve it."

"Sometimes that happens," I said.

"I suppose it's still possible that the time of death will help," he said. "Since we were able to narrow it down to a fairly small window, thanks to having such specific information on what and when he last ate."

"How narrow?" A dangerous question, I knew, since it could inspire him to share all sort of medical details that he found a great deal more fascinating than I did.

"Most probably between six and seven thirty," Dad said. "We might know better once we do the autopsy. Certainly not before five, and Deacon Washington got there at seven thirty with the Not Just Tacos Truck, and would have seen any activity by the garage after that. So at least it's a fairly narrow window."

At least I could stop worrying that Aida

and I had left him to the mercies of his killer when we thought we were leaving him safely locked up in his house.

"But that hasn't yet given the chief any help, I guess," I said.

"No." He looked morose. "Awkward time of day when it comes to alibis. And I've been doing my best to find out more about hoarding — both in general and as manifested in Mr. Dunlop's case. But even though the chief is very polite about it, I don't think he finds what I've learned very useful."

"You never know," I said. "It's always possible that he'll come across a new bit of evidence, remember a fact you told him, and have the solution to the case."

Dad sighed again. Clearly he wasn't very hopeful.

"So what have you learned?" I asked. "Do they know what causes hoarding?"

"They actually don't." The question seemed to cheer him up a bit. "Which is astonishing when you consider that some sources estimate that between two and five percent of the population suffer from it. The most common hypothesis is that it's a reaction to some kind of loss or trauma, and there may be a genetic component. It's more common in people who suffer from depression, anxiety, or attention deficit hyperactivity disorder. And sometimes associated with alcoholism, paranoia, or schizophrenia."

"Harvey didn't strike me as paranoid or schizophrenic," I said. "And I think if he were an alcoholic we'd have found a whole lot of empty bottles, and we didn't. But anxious or depressed, maybe. Ms. Ellie thinks maybe his father was the real hoarder, and Harvey just didn't know how to deal with the stuff. And he was probably a bit agoraphobic."

Dad nodded.

"And did you hear about his family's bank?" I asked.

"Bank? No. Tell me!"

As I'd hoped, hearing everything I'd learned about Harvey and his family improved Dad's mood significantly. Although it didn't give him any new ideas about who had committed the murder.

"But never mind," he said. "You're making great progress! I'm sure you'll have the solution in no time."

"I'm not," I said. "And anyway, I'm not the one who has to solve it. If you come up with any brilliant ideas, let me know."

His shoulders fell again.

"Not sure that's possible."

An idea struck me.

"Why don't you come over to the furniture store tomorrow and help us sort through Harvey's papers? It's a long shot, but there could be some bit of useful information in them."

He brightened again.

"If you think I could be of some use."

"You could be a lot of use," I said. "Meet us there at ten."

"Good. It will certainly be an improvement over trying to referee between Rose Noire and your grandfather. Two of the stubbornest human beings on this planet." He glanced at the nearby clock. "And if I have to get up in time to get there, it's about time I got your mother and your grandfather home."

He dashed off, looking much more cheerful.

I shooed the boys up to bed at eleven, and everyone else seemed to take the hint and began making their farewells. By midnight, everyone had either gone home or gone to bed — with the exception of the Dungeons & Dragons players, some of whom had been in the library for days now.

"Any exciting plans for tomorrow?" Michael asked as we settled into bed.

"Continuing to sort Harvey's papers," I

said. "And supervising any other Helping Hands projects that haven't already knocked off till after Christmas. And you? More manure?"

"No, the forecast is for rain on and off all day," he said. "The boys and I are going down to Trinity to help with the shelter photography project. They're moving on to the cats."

"Awesome," I said. Or maybe I just thought the word. Fine either way. Michael was already uttering his not-quite-snoring noises, and I could feel myself sinking into slumber.

CHAPTER 26

Wednesday, December 23

When I arrived at the furniture store the next morning, already soaked from rain blowing in under my umbrella, I found the chief and Aida already there, poking around.

"Nothing wrong, I hope," I said as I shed my rain gear.

"Everything seems okay now," Aida said. "But someone set off the security system three times last night, all between one and four a.m."

"Yikes," I said. "You'd think they'd learn their lesson the first time."

"It might not have been the same would-be intruders," the chief said. "And there's also the possibility that they were hoping we'd decide the alarm was malfunctioning and turn it off."

"No sign that anyone actually got in, though," Aida said. "All the stuff seems to be exactly the way we left it."

"I will be interested in finding out if any of my suspects have alibis for last night," the chief said. "But I'm not optimistic. Most of the folks on Beau Street would have been fast asleep at that hour. And Mr. Brimley and Mrs. Gudgeon both keep their cars in their garages, so unless someone happened to get up and glance outside at the exact moment they were coming or going, we won't get anything there."

"What about Tabitha?" I asked. "Is she still in town?"

"She has taken refuge in the Clay County Motel," the chief said. "A place with a long history of turning a blind eye to suspicious behavior. I'm not expecting any particularly reliable information on her movements. They claim she was in her room all night, both last night and the night of Mr. Dunlop's murder —"

"Wait — she was in town already Monday night?"

"Yes." The chief shook his head. "And while your nephew Kevin hasn't yet found any conversations between her and Harvey, he can't prove that they never talked. And she seems to know things she could only have gotten from Harvey. So she's still very much a suspect, both for the murder and last night's attempted break-ins."

"And the Haverhills?" I asked. "Is there some reason they're not at the top of your list?"

The chief sighed.

"I took a close look at the Haverhills," he said. "Particularly Morris, since he was the one who hung around the longest the day before Mr. Dunlop was killed. After I'd been interviewing Morris for a while, he got a little excited, said how dare I suspect him, and after quite a bit of useless vituperation, he finally said something useful — that he'd left Caerphilly at four in the afternoon and driven straight home, although it took him longer than usual because of the traffic, and did I want to inspect his thingie to prove what time he went through all those tollbooths around Richmond."

"His thingie?" I echoed. "He means his E-ZPass transponder, I suppose. Can you inspect those to find out where someone's been?"

"Not that I know of," the chief said. "But you can request the records on a particular transponder. Which I did — and that confirmed his story. He left here early enough to hit a series of tollbooths in the Richmond area between five fifteen and five forty-five. And didn't return here until the following morning. While I was at it, I got the records on his brother and sister. Both of them went home even earlier than he did and came back later the following day. And remember the Chinese delivery Mr. Ernest Haverhill made such a point of mentioning?"

"Because they were hoping it gave them an alibi."

"Yes." He chuckled. "I called the restaurant and got an earful about the Haverhills. Apparently, when the driver arrived, Ms. Haverhill was short on cash, so she started yelling for her brothers to find her some. First one brother then the other comes running up to empty his wallet, and they finally had to raid their spare change jar to make the last couple of dollars. No tip, of course, though apparently that's not unusual. So we have pretty solid confirmation that they were all there in Farmville at ten thirty p.m."

"Which doesn't help with their alibis, since Dad thinks he was killed between five and seven thirty in the morning," I said. "One of them could have driven back any time after the deliveryman left and got here in plenty of time to kill Harvey. Taking a roundabout way here to avoid the toll readers. Or taken the transponder out of their car."

"Possibly," the chief said. "But the Chinese restaurant owner steered me to a neighboring doughnut shop that can alibi them for the morning. Apparently after I called to notify them, they dropped by for three coffees to fuel their trip down here, and were, in the words of the doughnut shop owner, "even nastier than usual" over a slight mistake in their order. If the autopsy shows that Harvey was killed a little earlier than your father's preliminary estimate, it might just be possible for one of them to have done it and gotten back to Farmville in time — but only just."

"A pity," I said. "I think they're the least likable suspects you've got, and considering the competition, that's saying something."

"Yes." The chief shook his head. "So if any evidence comes up to invalidate their alibis, I will gladly move any of the Haverhills back to the top of my suspect list. For the moment, Ms. Fillmore and Mr. Dunlop's neighbors are looking much more plausible."

Just then the bell over the door opened and Judge Jane and Dad strode in.

"There you are," Judge Jane said to the chief. "Debbie Ann thought you'd be down here. Ellie and I have been up since dawn, working on the information we found in that ledger — about people who might hold a grudge against Harvey because of their family losing money in the Farmers and Mechanics Bank failure."

"A fascinating bit of local history," Dad said, with great enthusiasm.

"But does it have anything to do with my murder case?" the chief asked.

"No idea," Judge Jane said. "I can tell you who's still around here whose family was damaged by the Dunlops' bank failure. If this murder had happened back in the thirties, you'd have your suspects."

"But it happened yesterday, and the bank failure was more than eighty years ago." Chief Burke had raised one eyebrow as if to express doubt.

"Yes, and I agree that it might be a little farfetched, someone still holding a grudge after so long."

"This is Virginia," Dad said. "There are people still arguing over who did what to whom in the Civil War."

"True," Judge Jane said. "At any rate, no idea if the bank failure had something to do with the murder. But if it did, we can tell you some of the people you'd need to look at."

"Only some of the people?" The chief didn't look happy at that.

"The ledger contained twenty-three names representing nineteen individuals or families," Judge Jane said. "Ten of them still have descendants in town."

"What happened to the other nine?" the chief asked. "People don't just disappear."

"For all practical purposes, some of these did," Judge Jane said. "We're talking eighty-four years, remember? In four cases the family died out. The other five just drop out of the town records over the years. Two of them right after the bank failure, so I'm betting they're people who lost everything they had and went elsewhere in search of work. Anyway, we're going to keep looking and see what we can find out about those missing five. Here's the scoop on the ten who are still around."

She handed the chief a sheet of paper and he studied it for a few moments.

"Some pretty respectable families here," he said.

"Who probably had nothing to do with Harvey's demise," Judge Jane said. "Which means this probably isn't going to do a thing to help solve your case — unless we come across some sign that one of these folks has been bad-mouthing the Dunlops or making threats or . . . whatever."

The chief nodded.

"Sorry, Henry," Judge Jane said. "I know so far all I've done is add to your workload.

We'll keep looking. If there's something useful, we'll find it. I have to admit, though,
this is pretty interesting. Ellie and I are
thinking we might write a little local history
book about this, once we finish researching
it. Those were interesting times. We could
add in the Feds seizing everybody's gold.
That had some interesting local ramifica-
tions."

"Seizing everybody's gold?" The chief
looked curious. "For real? I thought they
mostly seized moonshine."

"That, too." She chuckled. "Apparently
the economists figured out that one of the
things causing the Depression — or maybe
making it worse — was people hoarding
gold. Don't ask me how — I'm no econo-
mist. But there probably was a lot of gold
hoarding — people squirreling away gold
coins because they didn't trust that their
paper money would still be worth anything
if things got any worse. So about the time
he closed the banks, Roosevelt told the U.S.
Treasury to stop minting gold coins, and he
sent out an order that anyone who had more
than a token number of gold coins had to
turn them in for paper money."

"I can't imagine that being popular," the
chief said.

"It certainly wasn't," Judge Jane agreed.

"The bank closure didn't hit my family too hard, because there weren't but a few of us high-falutin' enough to have a bank account. Most of the old-timers, at least in my family, liked to be able to put their hands on their money at a moment's notice. And none of this paper nonsense. But then when the government made everyone turn in their gold — well, I had an uncle who did hard time because of that."

"For hoarding gold coins?" I asked.

"Well, that and taking a potshot at the Fed who came to arrest him." She shook her head. "The Feds take a dim view of such goings-on. And —"

Evidently her phone had buzzed. She glanced at it, then did a double take and looked at it more closely over her glasses.

"Now this is interesting," she said. "Ms. Ellie found an article from ten years ago about the Farmers and Mechanics Bank closure."

"I don't remember seeing anything about it," the chief said. "And I tend to read the *Clarion* pretty closely."

"It wasn't in the *Clarion*." Judge Jane shook her head. "The Caerphilly Historical Society's newsletter."

"Well, that explains it," I said. The now-defunct society, which locals had nicknamed the Pruitt Mutual Appreciation Society, had been more about social status than history, and had fallen apart when the Pruitts had been ousted from power and left town.

"Hardly anyone actually read the Historical Society's newsletter," I said. "Not even their members."

"I didn't know they even had one," Dad said.

"I've never seen it before, myself," Judge Jane said. "Then again, if this is anything to go by, we weren't missing much. I'll send you a copy."

My phone dinged and I pulled it out to look at what she'd sent. I saw Dad and the chief doing the same.

If the article was typical of the literary output of the Caerphilly Historical Society then she was right — it was no surprise that their newsletter went largely unread. The article was wordy, convoluted, and occasionally even ungrammatical. It was marred by racism, anti-Semitism, misogynism, classism, and every other ism I could think of. The author — a Pruitt, of course: Mrs. J. R. Pruitt — was clearly fighting a futile rearguard battle against Roosevelt and the New Deal. For that matter, she was arguably still touting Robert E. Lee for sainthood. But I'd have just rolled my eyes and muttered "consider the source," except for a little bombshell hidden in the last few sentences.

" 'Who knows where the millions local citizens lost after the Farmers and Mechanics Bank closed went?' " I read aloud. "Ugh."

"Badly constructed sentence, I agree," the chief said.

"And she conveniently fails to mention all the money people lost when the Pruitts' own bank closed," I pointed out.

"And there's no way the Dunlops' bank had millions," Judge Jane said. "It was a small backwater bank in a small backwater county. No offense, but we are. The Pruitts' bank was much larger, and I don't even think it had millions to lose."

"And yet she goes on to say 'Are Wilberforce Dunlop's descendants still squatting on wealth stolen from the hardworking citizens of Caerphilly?' " Dad quoted. "You'd think she was trying to stir people up against Harvey."

"Doesn't actually name him," Judge Jane said.

"Doesn't have to," I replied. "It mentions the Dunlops, and he's the only one in town. Everyone knew who they meant."

"Who knows the whereabouts of the millions local citizens lost in the closure of the Farmers and Mechanics Bank?" the chief said. "Sorry; that sentence really bothered me. Getting back to the business at hand — yes, I can see that the article would have been inflammatory. But it was published — and largely ignored — ten years ago. Why would it inspire someone to kill Harvey now?"

The same question had occurred to me, and I was texting a question to Ms. Ellie.

"Good point," Judge Jane said. "If I thought someone had stolen millions from my family, I wouldn't brood over it for ten years and then bean them with a spittoon. I'd go over and have it out with them. So I'm not sure I buy the revenge angle. But greed works. Doesn't have to be someone whose family lost money. Anyone who thinks there's loot for the taking might go after it."

"Aha!" I said. "The Historical Society newsletters were only added to the library's collection a few weeks ago. A bequest from a Mrs. Wilhelmina Pruitt Blaine, who died earlier this year."

"It would be a Pruitt," Judge Jane muttered.

"Were there any Blaines on your list of

people who lost money to the Dunlops?" I asked.

Judge Jane nodded. The chief suddenly sat up straight.

"I remember her," he said. "Old Mrs. Blaine, I mean. Up until a couple of years ago, when she went downhill, she used to sneak out of the nursing home regularly and shoplift decorating magazines from the drugstore. *Architectural Digest* and *Better Homes & Gardens,* mostly. And now I remember where I've seen Mrs. Gudgeon before. She's the old lady's daughter. We used to have her down at the station right regularly, picking up her mother and taking her back home."

"So maybe Mrs. Gudgeon was brought up believing the Dunlops ruined her family," Dad said. "That would give her a motive."

"More probably she only found out about it when she cleared out her mother's belongings and took the newsletters to the library," I suggested.

"Either way, she had a reason to hate Mr. Dunlop, and it could explain the timing." The chief looked happier. In fact, his expression reminded me of the way Lurker and Skulker, our barn cats, looked when they'd finally pounced on a particularly elusive mouse. "Convey my compliments to Ms. Ellie. I think I'll drop by the library right now to take a look at these newsletters in person and get the specifics about when the library took possession of them. And then I'll go have another chat with Mrs. Vera Blaine Gudgeon."

He left, looking more cheerful. Judge Jane, Dad, and I settled in to get some work done on Harvey's papers.

"I'm only going to do a little of this," Judge Jane said. "I'm hosting the big family Christmas Eve all-day potluck and barbecue, and I need to get home in time to clean up a bit."

"And Christmas Eve is tomorrow." I looked at the boxes still left and shook my head. "I can't stay too long, either — Michael and I are helping chaperone the middle-school sleepover at church. I need to get home and pack for the four of us."

"If I weren't here I'd be trying to make peace between Rose Noire and your grandfather," Dad said. "I can put in as many hours as you want."

"Mother would object if you stayed out too long," I said. "Let's put in a few solid hours and then knock off till Boxing Day."

They both agreed, and we buried our noses in the file folders.

"I've found something!" Dad exclaimed, leaping up and almost knocking over Judge Jane's card table.

CHAPTER 27

"Must be darned exciting," Judge Jane grumbled, although she also hurried over to see what Dad had found.

"Here." Dad held out a sheet of yellowed paper for us to read.

"A threatening letter," I said.

"An unsigned threatening letter," Dad corrected. "Although I think we can guess who sent it from this part: 'I want the money you owe me — my mother's share of the money your father stole.'"

"Not for certain." Judge Jane shook her head. "Always possible it could be from someone who lost money in the bank failure. But given the wording, my money would be on the Haverhill's father. From the research Ellie and I did, Aristede Senior only had the one sister, Irma. She married a man named Buford Haverhill and left town."

"A pity the Haverhills are alibied," I said.

"They could have hired someone to knock off Harvey," Dad said. He pointed to part of the letter. "Look at that bit — where it says 'I know someone who can make you sorry you ever crossed me.' "

"Sinister," I agreed. "But wouldn't that take a lot of money?" I asked.

"Hiring one of those suave assassins who leaves no clue behind and takes his secrets to the grave would take a lot of money," Judge Jane said. "Wouldn't cost very much to find a thug to lean on someone — you might even know someone who owes you a favor. But dolts like that aren't usually very good at getting away with murder, and they don't have a lot of incentive to keep their traps shut."

"We should show that to the chief," I said. "Along with these."

She and Dad drew closer to inspect the papers I held out.

"Bank statements," she said. "Dating back to the nineties — Harvey's?"

"Aristede Junior's. He never kept a big balance. Didn't write a lot of checks, either, usually just a handful at the end of the month. And a few days before he wrote his checks, he'd deposit enough funds to cover them."

"Probably keeps most of his funds in

another account," Dad suggested. "A savings account, perhaps."

"So far this is the only account of his we've found," I said. "And those are cash deposits."

Dad took a closer look.

"So they are. Not sure what it means, but it's interesting." I could tell from Dad's expression that he found these financial clues rather tame compared to medical ones.

"It could mean that at least when Harvey's father was alive, people were right to suspect he had treasure hidden here," I said. "The bank's staff would gossip. Although if you ask me, he probably kept the bulk of his money in another bank. He was a traveling salesman, remember? He wouldn't find it all that convenient to use a bank with only the one branch here in Caerphilly."

"Then why have an account here at all?" Dad asked.

"So people in town wouldn't think he was disloyal to the local bank?" I suggested.

"More likely so people in town would know as little as possible about his financial affairs," Judge Jane said.

"Regardless of what the real reason was," I said, "everyone would assume he kept his money under the mattress."

"Which would be a great motive for murder if these were current bank statements," Judge Jane said. She stretched. "We've been here for three hours. I vote we close up shop for the day."

I suspected Dad was about to object,

"Yes," I said. "We can take these finds over to the chief. See what he makes of them."

"Good idea." Dad sounded much more cheerful.

Judge Jane had already loaded the papers into an empty box and was putting on her coat.

"Raining cats and dogs again," Dad said. "Let's find something waterproof to put over that box."

"I'll lock up," I said, heading for the front doors. "Meet you there."

The chief wasn't bowled over by our latest discoveries.

"Interesting," he said. "No, I mean that," he added — no doubt remembering that Mother had trained her family to use "interesting" when we couldn't think of any other polite adjective to use. "The letter certainly sheds light on the . . . strained relationship between Mr. Dunlop and his cousins."

"Only second cousins," Judge Jane pointed out.

"And the bank account makes it credible

that at some point, people might have had good reason to suspect Mr. Dunlop's father of hiding his money under his mattress," Dad added.

"But it's not exactly evidence," I finished.

"We'll keep looking," Dad said.

"Though we're going to take a break until after Christmas," I said. "If you're okay with it."

"I'm fine with it," the chief said.

Just then the power went out. The chief's windowless office became very, very dark.

"Drat," the chief said. "The generator should come on in a few seconds."

We waited in silence.

The chief sighed.

"Then again, sometimes we have to call Randall so he can coax the blasted thing into —"

The lights came on again. Some of them.

"That's better," the chief said. He glanced up at the ceiling, where only one of the four overhead fixtures was on. "We mostly worry about the phones and the heat and the electronic locks on the jail cells," he explained. "After that, we just need enough light not to bump into the furniture. And then —"

"Chief?" Vern had appeared in the doorway. Evidently the intercom wasn't something they worried about. "Got a call from Aida, out on the Richmond road. Couple of eighteen-wheelers almost collided."

"Why is 'almost collided' a problem?" the chief asked, although he was already standing and reaching for his coat.

"Because of what happened after they avoided each other," Vern said. "One plowed into the power substation and knocked it to smithereens and the other fell over and is blocking both lanes of the highway."

"On my way," the chief said. "Vern, can you see if you can get someone to fill in for you at the desk?"

"I can watch the desk for as long as you like." Dad sounded as if he'd actually enjoy it. "And I'll find someone reliable to take over for me when I need to leave. You go on, Vern."

"Thank you," the chief said.

"What about the furniture store?" I asked. "If the power's out, so's the security system."

"Drat." The chief paused on the threshold.

Dad looked torn, no doubt wondering if he should volunteer to babysit the furniture store instead of the police station. Which would be the most exciting post?

"Maybe we could recruit some folks to camp out there tonight," he said.

"With no heat?" the chief said. "Randall hasn't gotten around to fixing the insulation yet. Not to mention the fact that whoever's trying to burgle it might be our murderer."

"I'll bring the dogs in," I said. "Spike and Tinkerbell. It won't get cold enough to bother them, and the two of them should have a pretty good deterrent effect."

"It'll have to do," the chief said. "Thanks. And I'll have my officers cruise by as often as possible."

Although we both knew that if the chief and his troops were dealing with the toppled eighteen-wheeler, the ruined power substation, and all the other complications that would arise with heavy rains and gale force winds, they wouldn't be able to swing by all that often.

"Just lock the door between the front room and the rest of the station if you have to leave the desk for any reason," the chief said.

We left Dad sitting behind the desk, looking excited at his new assignment.

The fact that the chief, who knew Dad's enthusiasms and eccentricities all too well, had accepted his help so readily underlined how perilously thin the department's resources were stretched.

I'd have felt guilty for not volunteering

myself, but I had a lot to do to get ready for the overnight at Trinity. Packing a backpack for myself wouldn't take much time. Making sure Michael and the boys were packed would take much longer. And I'd been putting off fixing anything for my contribution to the potluck supper, on the theory that by this point in the holiday season I could pull together enough food just by raiding the leftovers from all the various family festivities. Foraging would be faster than cooking, but would still take time. And then there was packing up the dogs.

I expected to find the house in turmoil, as the visiting relatives adjusted to the lack of power. But things were humming along nicely. In spite of the rain, several visiting uncles had fired up our grills and were standing around in their rain slickers, grilling or warming up things.

Inside, half a dozen relatives had found the Coleman lanterns and were quietly reading by the Christmas tree, while an aunt sat at the piano, softly playing Christmas carols by way of a replacement for the iTunes playlist that would normally be emanating from all the tiny speakers hidden in the greenery.

In the kitchen, various aunts and cousins were expertly assessing which foods needed to be eaten soon, which would keep till tomorrow, and which would be taken out to the overflow refrigerator in the barn, where they'd keep indefinitely, since the temperature out there was already at or below the temperature inside the fridge. And brewing pots of hot tea over a small one-burner camp stove.

I successfully delegated the job of gathering dinner and snacks for the boys and their friends and went upstairs to pack. Michael's backpack was there, and seemed complete. Okay, mostly complete. I tucked a few things I suspected he'd miss into my own backpack.

"Hey, Mom!" Josh bounced into the bedroom, with Jamie trailing close behind him. "We figured out what we're giving Dad."

"Great," I said. "Do I get a hint?"

Jamie shoved a piece of paper in front of me. A picture of a piece of electronic equipment of some sort. A rather familiar-looking piece of equipment. I peered at the text below the picture.

"A scanner." My heart sank — I was going to have to break some bad news to them.

"It's a very good scanner," Josh said, rather importantly.

"According to Cousin Kevin," Jamie

added. "He knows about stuff like that."

"Yes, I know," I said. "But your dad already bought a scanner — pretty sure it was that exact scanner, because it was the one Kevin recommended."

"Well, we know *that*," Josh said. "He got it after Kevin convinced him that it would be a great idea to scan all those old papers you have in the attic."

"But Dad hasn't started doing that," Jamie said. "He hasn't used it at all. He hasn't even set it up, and he's had it almost two years now."

He was probably right. Michael's zeal to declutter our files had suddenly vanished when he was faced with the task of actually setting up the scanner, and even if he had done the setup, I wasn't sure when he'd have found the time to use it.

"We're not giving him the scanner," Josh said. "The present is that we're setting it up for him."

"That's why Kevin's here — he's going to help us set it up," Jamie explained. "And show us how to use it."

"And then we'll scan all that paper for you," Josh said. "I think that will be a pretty cool present."

"I think it will be an awesome present," I said.

"Cool beans," Jamie said. Was that still a fashionable phrase, or was he using it because he knew I'd get it?

"We just thought we'd tell you so you could stop racking your brain to think of something good for us to give Dad," Jamie explained.

I decided not to tell him that I'd been too busy worrying about Harvey's stuff and then his murder to do much brain-racking.

"And isn't it nice that we thought of something that gets rid of useless stuff instead of adding to our stuff?" he added.

"It's fabulous," I said.

"Oh, and we thought of a good present for you, too," Josh said. "And Dad agrees that it's cool, so you can stop worrying about dropping hints."

He gathered up the picture of the scanner and I could tell they were about to dash off.

"Are you all packed for the sleepover?" I asked. "And if so, could you pack up what Spike and Tinkerbell need for their own sleepover?"

"Are they coming to the sleepover?" Jamie sounded dubious, as if sure this was against the rules.

"They're going to guard Mr. Dunlop's stuff while the power is out," I said.

"Awesome," Josh said.

"Won't they be in danger?" Jamie asked.

"Not really," I said. "Anyone who sees Tink or hears Spike will probably change their mind about trying to break into the furniture store. So pack their food and bowls, and some dog blankets for them to curl up in."

"Right!" They dashed out.

I hauled the backpacks down and left them in the front hall. I trekked down the long hall to the library. More Coleman lamps were set up here, and more people than ever were playing board games, role-playing games, or card games. I liberated a few of the boys' favorite games just in case the kids needed distraction at the sleepover.

About the only person in the room who didn't look perfectly contented was Kevin. He was sitting at one of the long mission-styled tables playing a game called Escape from Colditz. It was always a shock to see him in person and realize how much he'd changed since his pudgy adolescence. His long, wiry frame was slouched in a chair and he was hiding a discontented expression behind a long lock of his disheveled dark-blond hair. He was tapping his fingers lightly on the side of his Diet Coke can, waiting with visible impatience while the less-seasoned player whose turn it was dithered.

"You need a generator," he said without looking up at me.

"Sorry," I said. "Had we known you were coming, maybe we'd have taken care of that."

He shrugged.

"Are you going into tech withdrawal?" I asked. "Because if so, you could always go down to the police station after the game and mind the front desk. The chief's down four officers and so desperate for help that he left your grandfather doing that."

"They have power there?" He didn't try to hide the eagerness in his voice.

"Emergency generator," I said. "And probably some means of communication with the outside world. For that matter, Trinity has a generator, too. You could come help with the sleepover."

"No thanks. But I'll go down and relieve Gramps when this game is over. Which should be sometime between now and Easter," he added, raising his voice.

"Sorry, sorry," the slow player muttered.

"Has the chief caught his killer yet?" Kevin asked.

"Alas, no."

"I'm betting on the Haverhills," he said.

"They're low on the chief's suspect list," I said, and explained about the transponder evidence.

"Bummer," he said. "Good thing I didn't actually have money on it. Although —"

The other player finally made his move, and I let Kevin go back to the game. It was probably bad form for chaperones to be late.

CHAPTER 28

It was already growing dark when we set out for town. The dogs settled in nicely — especially after I checked the refrigerator and bribed them with some bits of chicken left over from the party. I left a battery-powered camping lantern on in the main room, at its lowest setting, less for the dogs than for the convenience of the deputies who'd be cruising by.

Trinity was warm and cozy, thanks to the generator. Although it only powered the essentials — the heat or air-conditioning, the kitchen, and emergency lighting — it was an improvement over what most people had at home, so half a dozen parents had decided to bring their air mattresses and join the ranks of the chaperones. Which was fine by me — we had plenty of food, and sharing the work made it more relaxing for all of us. One mother had even brought several dozen homemade pizzas, which we could heat up thanks to the generator.

And all the extra chaperones made me feel less guilty about slipping out to check on the dogs. I waited until we'd finished with dinner, the post-dinner cleanup, the caroling, the board games, and all the other scheduled activities. The kids were having such a good time that they hardly noticed the howling of the wind outside. With luck they'd be tired enough to fall asleep quickly — and if not, there were plenty of other grown-ups there to cope.

If it had been a pleasant night, I'd have been happy to walk the dozen or so blocks over to the furniture store. But the temperature was dropping, the wind was rising, and it was raining steadily. So I fought down the guilty feeling that I was being lazy and wasteful and climbed into my car.

While I was out, I dropped off half a pepperoni pizza at the police station — where I was relieved to see that Kevin had taken over from Dad at the front desk.

"This is more like it," he said. "Power, Internet, pizza — it's almost like civilization."

I left before he could complain that I should have brought a whole pizza.

I parked in back of the furniture store and used my key. I was surprised not to hear barking as I drew near — was my confidence in Spike and Tink as watchdogs misplaced?

"Spike? Tink?"

Spike gave a short, sharp bark, but didn't appear. Tink merely growled, a deep bass sound that you felt as much as heard.

Something was definitely up. I instinctively reached to turn on the lights in the back room — which had no effect, of course. But the door to the main room was ajar, and I could see that the battery lantern was still on there. So I turned on my phone's flashlight so I wouldn't trip over anything in the back room and hurried into the main room.

First I spotted Tinkerbell standing nose-to-nose with Mr. Brimley, who had his back against the side wall, not too far from the front door. He shifted his body slightly. Tink growled, and he froze again.

"Help," he said weakly.

I moved the beam some more to the right and illuminated Spike, who was sitting outside the bathroom door, staring at it.

"Help!" said a loud voice from inside. Mrs. Gudgeon.

Spike barked a couple of times, rounded off with a long, ferocious growl, and continued to stare at the door.

"Good dogs," I said. "At ease, Tink."

Tink backed a few steps away from Mr.

Brimley and sat down, though without taking her eyes off him. Her nose was still nearly level with his.

"Those dogs attacked us," Mr. Brimley said.

"You don't appear to be bleeding," I said. "Trust me, if either of them had actually attacked you, there would be bleeding. Just what were you doing in here, anyway? Was it too dark to read the 'no trespassing' signs outside?"

"I saw a light on here in the furniture store," Mr. Brimley said. "And I looked in and saw her rummaging through things." He pointed toward the bathroom door, so I deduced that he meant Mrs. Gudgeon.

"He's a liar!" came the voice from the bathroom. "I saw *him* rummaging in here! I came in to warn him that if he didn't clear out, I'd go for the cops."

"Oh, listen to her," Mr. Brimley said. "I never did anything of the kind!"

"Don't listen to him!" Mrs. Gudgeon shouted.

Spike began barking, which didn't drown out the sound of their voices, but made it pretty impossible to decipher what they were saying.

"Shut up!" I yelled.

Mr. Brimley and Mrs. Gudgeon obeyed,

and once they were quiet, Spike calmed down, too.

Meanwhile, I was trying to dial 911, and not getting a signal. Drat. Cell phone coverage was eccentric in Caerphilly at the best of times and usually gave out entirely in any kind of bad weather. I gave up trying to call and sent texts and emails to the chief, Horace, and Aida. I'd seen that emails, especially, could sometimes go through on less signal than a call.

And worst case, the police would be checking on the store periodically, right? They weren't just going to rely on the dogs.

"Just what were you looking for?" I asked. "Because believe me, if we'd found anything valuable, we wouldn't have brought it here — we'd have turned it over to the police."

Mr. Brimley set his jaw, as if to suggest that even siccing Tink on him wouldn't make him talk. I couldn't see Mrs. Gudgeon's expression, but she certainly wasn't speaking up.

Suddenly Tink glanced over at the front door and growled. Spike strutted over toward it, stiff-legged and growling.

The door swung open a foot or so.

"Call off your dogs or I'll shoot them," came a voice. "I mean it. I hate dogs anyway."

Tabitha.

I reached down to scoop up Spike and grabbed Tink's collar.

"Now put them in their crates."

"I can put the small one in his crate," I said. "They don't make crates big enough for Irish Wolfhounds."

"Put the small one in his crate, then. And control the big one. It's your fault if I have to shoot him."

I didn't like the idea of trapping Spike. She could shoot him just as easily in the crate, and I wouldn't put it past her. So I did what I could. I shoved him in and pulled the door closed, but instead of latching it I shoved the whole crate close to the nearest wall. He could work his way out over time if he tried, but he couldn't come barreling out in the middle of whatever was about to happen. But I could also grab the crate and unleash him. Options.

Tabitha stepped into the room. Her gun was pointed at me and Tink, but she also had an easy shot at Mr. Brimley.

"Hands up!" she snapped.

Mr. Brimley complied. I glanced down at my hands, both of them holding Tink's collar.

"You can lock the big dog in the bathroom," she said.

"Mrs. Gudgeon is already locked in the bathroom," I pointed out.

"Come out of the bathroom now!" Tabitha shouted.

The door remained closed.

Tabitha stared at me for a few seconds, then flicked her gaze over to the door and fired a shot through the top half of it. I heard glass breaking.

Mrs. Gudgeon shrieked. In fear or pain? I had no clue.

"Come out of the bathroom, now," Tabitha said. "I've got lots more bullets."

The bathroom door flew open and Mrs. Gudgeon stepped out with her hands in the air.

"In with the dog," Tabitha said.

I led Tink to the bathroom door and stopped at the sill.

"There's broken glass all over the floor," I said.

"Broken mirror," Mrs. Gudgeon muttered. "Seven years of bad luck for *someone*."

"I don't care," Tabitha said. "Do it."

I used my foot to shove as much of the glass as possible aside before leading Tink in.

"Sit," I said. "Stay."

Tink looked unhappy, but she obeyed. I

closed the door.

"So where is it?" Tabitha demanded.

"Where is what?" I asked.

"The money," Tabitha said. "Harvey's money."

Mr. Brimley and Mrs. Gudgeon seemed just as eager as Tabitha to hear my answer.

"I have no idea," I said. "If he had any money — which I doubt — we haven't found it yet."

"But it has to be here somewhere!"

"What makes you think he had money?" I asked.

"He told me!"

She must have seen the look of disbelief on my face. I'd pretty much decided her friendship with Harvey was as fake as the will she'd tried to pawn off on the chief.

"He did." She stuck her chin out as if defying me to doubt her. "I was texting with him one day, and he was upset because he'd found out the local historical society had run this article about how his family had stolen all the money from people and kept it."

"Did he also tell you that the article was a big fat lie?" I asked.

"Yeah, but I didn't believe him." Tabitha tossed her head for emphasis. "He was really upset — and why would he be that upset unless he was afraid someone would try to steal his money?"

"Maybe he was upset because whoever wrote the article was telling lies about his family," I suggested. "Ruining their reputation in the town."

"Yeah, right." She was shooting glances over at the rows of boxes. "Get that roll of tape," she ordered, jerking her head toward one batch of boxes.

Mr. Brimley, Mrs. Gudgeon, and I all three glanced and saw a roll of packing tape lying on top of one of the boxes.

"Only one of you. You." She waved the gun at Mrs. Gudgeon.

Drat. If, as I suspected, she was going to use the packing tape to immobilize some or all of us, I wanted to be the one wielding it. Mrs. Gudgeon scowled, then walked over and picked up the tape.

"Tie him up," Tabitha said.

"It's tape, not rope," Mrs. Gudgeon said.

"Don't argue with me," Tabitha said. "You."

She pointed at me. I went over, relieved Mrs. Gudgeon of the roll of tape, and walked over to Mr. Brimley.

If I'd thought there was a decent chance Mr. Brimley would fight on my side if push came to shove, I'd have tried to figure out how to tape him up loosely enough that he could escape. But I suspected he was more likely to turn on me if he could get hold of the gun for himself, so I trussed him up nicely.

"Now start opening those boxes," Tabitha said. "I want to see what's in them."

Mrs. Gudgeon shuffled slowly toward the stack of boxes Tabitha was indicating, a surly look on her face, and began picking at the strip of tape that held one of the boxes closed. I followed suit, though I worked at the picking a little more energetically, in the hope that one of the boxes would contain something I could use to turn the tables on Tabitha. Or, if I was lucky, I might find one of the half-dozen box knives that had disappeared over the course of yesterday's packing. I could have sworn I'd seen one earlier, when I opened a box of Harvey's papers.

Unfortunately, the first box I opened contained only Harvey's grandmother's good china. I unwrapped plate after plate, holding each one up for Tabitha's inspection, and shaking the packing paper to prove that there was nothing valuable hidden in it. By the time I got to the bottom of the box, the floor was covered with dishes and crumpled sheets of paper.

"Shove the paper back in the box," Tabitha ordered. "And stack the plates on those shelves."

I did as I was told. The shelves were farther from Tabitha and the gun. Surely Mrs. Gudgeon and I could somehow use that to our advantage. Get the drop on Tabitha when we were as far apart as possible and it was harder for her to cover us both.

Of course, that would require getting Mrs. Gudgeon to work with me. At the moment, she seemed to be ignoring me entirely. She had finally succeeded in pulling the tape off her box and was lifting out assorted kitchen items — a saucepan, a cookie jar, glass pie plate, several vintage Texas Ware mixing bowls. Following Tabitha's orders, she was carrying the items over to the shelves in batches. I'd found one of the boxes I'd seen Joyce Grossman packing, and was filling the space around me with the set of pink china elephants.

Suddenly Mrs. Gudgeon uttered an unearthly shriek and began running toward Tabitha with a box knife in her outstretched hand. Of course, idiotically, she started her run from the shelves, where she had apparently found the knife, instead of waiting until she was back at the boxes, so she had about twice as far to run.

"Stop that!" Tabitha shouted. And when Mrs. Gudgeon paid no attention, Tabitha fired at her.

She'd have had a hard time missing at that range, except that just then Mrs. Gudgeon slipped on some of the fallen packing paper. She yelped, went sprawling, and then began scrambling away on her hands and knees.

When Mrs. Gudgeon had started her attack I had been unwrapping the hideous knob-covered china vase, so while Tabitha was distracted I lobbed it in her direction and managed to hit her gun hand with it. She shouted "ow!" and dropped the gun, which landed somewhere in the litter of the wrapping paper and china fragments that now covered the floor. I lobbed pink elephants at Tabitha to keep her off balance while inching closer in the hope that I could grab the gun before she found it.

"Ow!" she shouted again, and I could see that while searching for the gun — or possibly reaching for it — she had sliced her hand open. And then she screamed even more loudly as a furry missile aimed itself at her face. Apparently in scuttling away Mrs. Gudgeon had knocked Spike's crate away from the wall and set him free.

Tabitha jerked away and Spike's lunge fell short of her face, but he fastened his sharp little teeth on her right arm and began growling as loudly as he could with his mouth full.

I heard a crashing noise behind me and glanced over to see that a ragged wolfhound-sized hole had just appeared in the flimsy wall between the bathroom and the main part of the store. Tink herself was now looming over Tabitha, adding her deep bass growl to Spike's soprano one. Tabitha froze, staring into Tink's eyes with such intensity that she almost seemed oblivious to Spike's grip on her forearm.

I carefully poked through the crumpled paper and shards of pink and white china until I found both the knife and the gun. Then I grabbed the packing tape and strolled over to where Mrs. Gudgeon was crouching. I showed her the gun — not really pointing at her, just hinting that it could come to that if need be.

"Turn around," I said.

She obeyed, and I taped her arms behind her back. After that, I did Tabitha, and pried Spike off her arm.

Then I sat back to wait for one of the deputies to show up. Tabitha, Mr. Brimley, and Mrs. Gudgeon weren't very good at following my orders to shut up, but about the time it occurred to me that the packing tape would work on mouths as well as wrists, Vern Shiffley came through the doorway.

"Well," he said as he surveyed the chaos inside the store. "Y'all have been having quite a time here this evening."

CHAPTER 29

Vern was soon followed by the chief, then Aida, and eventually Horace, at which point the chief dispatched one prisoner with each officer and stayed behind himself to finish getting my story.

He sat, frowning into space when I'd finished.

"A penny for them," I said.

"I was thinking, what a pity it is that none of those wretched people said anything that enables me to wrap up the murder investigation."

"Yes," I said. "It would have been so much more helpful if one of them had said something like 'dammit, here I go to all the trouble of killing Harvey and so far I haven't gotten any loot out of it. This just isn't my week!' "

"Something like that." He smiled.

"Doesn't it help that you have the chance to hold them for other crimes?" I asked.

"Not a lot," he said. "I doubt if I could hold Mrs. Gudgeon and Mr. Brimley for anything other than trespassing, and that won't keep them long. There's a satisfyingly broad range of things I can charge Ms. Fillmore with, but still — none of it proves anything about Mr. Dunlop's murder. The only positive note is that tonight's events should make it a lot easier to get any warrants I need to investigate them, and the truth will turn up in time. I should go." He stood, looking rather weary.

"You have a long night ahead of you."

"Probably not," he said. "They'll probably all refuse to talk until they get lawyers, and that could take till morning. But what with all the red tape involved in booking them, I probably won't get home all that early, and I'll have a long day ahead of me. You headed home?"

"Back to Trinity for the middle-school sleepover," I said.

"Sleep as well as you can, then." He chuckled at the thought. "I'll see you safely out."

I made sure the dogs had food and water, gave them each another well-deserved treat, and locked up. The chief walked me out to my car and drove off in his sedan.

I locked the car doors and sat for a few

minutes, taking deep breaths. I picked up my phone, thinking I'd call Michael. No. It was past midnight now. With luck, he was asleep. If he wasn't asleep, he'd have his hands full, wrangling restless middle schoolers who ought to be asleep. I could fill him in when I got back. Or in the morning.

In the morning would be better. If I wanted anyone at the overnight to get any sleep, I should probably wait till morning to tell the boys that not only were the dogs just fine, they were heroes. They'd caught two burglars and a killer. At least if Mrs. Gudgeon and Mr. Brimley were telling the truth. If Tabitha was telling the truth, did that mean the dogs had caught two killers and a burglar? Time would tell. Either way, good for the dogs. The chief would probably have it sorted out by morning.

I was about to head back to Trinity when I suddenly remembered something: Harvey's feral kitten. I'd promised Clarence to check his trap as often as I could, and I hadn't been there since early afternoon. And the weather was getting worse — what if the kitten was in the trap, prevented from taking refuge in whatever warm spots she'd found to survive the cold?

So I headed for Harvey's house. It wouldn't take long just to check the trap and haul it into the car if the kitten was in it. Harvey's house was on the other side of town, but at this time of night — and in this weather — I could go straight through the center of town, the area that would be so choked with tourists as to be impassible in the daytime or early evening.

Definitely not a night for man or beast to be out. The wind howled ceaselessly. There wasn't that much rain at the moment, but what there was traveled horizontally. After parking in front of Harvey's house, I stayed in the car long enough to zip up my coat and don my gloves and hat.

Hunched over to stay warm, I half ran to the right side of the house. The little door that gave access to the crawl space was open and I bent down to peer inside. Blackness. I pulled out my phone and turned on the flashlight. I could see the trap, baited with something. The smell hit me — canned tuna. But no cat.

At least not in the cage. As I stood up, I heard a noise, like something being knocked over. Was that the noise the trap made when it snapped shut? I bent down again. No, the trap was still sitting empty.

Had the noise come from inside the house? I played the flashlight beam around and saw, a little to my right, splintered wood sticking down into the crawl space. Of course — it must be the place where Horace's foot had gone through the floorboards. I remembered Randall shouting through the hole into the crawl space.

Was the hole large enough for a cat to slip inside? Yes. Especially a small cat, a kitten still young enough to be socialized.

I quietly pulled the little door to the crawl space closed, so the kitten couldn't easily escape if it ran out through the hole again.

Then I hurried around to the front door, tiptoed up the front steps, and unlocked the front door, making as little noise as possible.

I swung the door open, stepped in, and shut it behind me as quickly as possible, to keep the cat from running out.

Then I moved my flashlight around and — yikes!

Something had done a number on the living room. Great holes had been gouged in the walls. We'd only left one piece of furniture — a sofa so decrepit that we'd have no trouble convincing Harvey it needed replacing. The sofa's guts were ripped out and lying on the floor.

"It's you."

Morris Haverhill stepped out of the kitchen. He was holding a long-handled sledgehammer in his right hand and a chunk of cinder block in the other. The look in his face wasn't particularly friendly. I tried to reassure myself that he couldn't be the bad guy. He had an alibi for Harvey's murder, didn't he? Or had he faked it somehow? I had a bad feeling about this. Probably wiser to hide that and pretend everything was normal.

"Damn, I thought you were the kitten," I said. "You haven't seen it, have you?"

"Kitten?"

"A stray kitten Harvey was feeding. I gather you haven't seen it. Ah, well. There's a trap in the crawl space — if you notice the kitten going into it, call the shelter and they'll come take it off your hands. Merry Christmas."

I turned and reached for the knob. The chunk of cinder block crashed into the door, barely missing my hand. I leaped back — tactical mistake. Morris darted forward and was now between me and the door.

When in doubt, keep talking, I told myself. Pretend you don't suddenly suspect that the chief has all the wrong suspects locked up.

"No need to take your frustration out on me," I said. "It's not my fault the chief hasn't let you into your cousin's house. But there's good news. Chief Burke has arrested

Tabitha Fillmore for Harvey's murder. And proven that the will she's been waving around is a fake. So once the paperwork is finished, the place will be yours."

"Nice try," he said. "But you don't really think I'm buying that crap about rescuing a kitten, do you? You came here for the same reason I did — to find the gold."

"Gold?"

"The gold coins our great-grandfather hid away when the Feds tried to seize them," he said. "Thousands of dollars' worth. Hell, the way the price of gold has grown, maybe millions by now. Harvey claimed there wasn't any gold, but I knew he was lying. His grandfather kept it all. He was supposed to give half to my grandmother, but he was a cheapskate and a crook and he never gave her a penny. I want it, and you're going to tell me where it is."

"I have no idea," I said. "Do you think if Harvey had a bunch of gold coins he'd be living like this?" I gestured at the house — which actually looked a lot worse than it had before, thanks to him and his sledge-hammer. Evidently he'd been searching the walls.

"Tell me where it is."

He took a step toward me, raising the sledgehammer.

I turned and fled. Maybe I could make it into the kitchen and out the back door or —

Whack! The sledgehammer hit the kitchen doorframe. I veered in the other direction and kept on going. Past Harvey's bedroom and into the office. I spotted a hammer lying on the floor — only a claw hammer, unfortunately, but maybe I could use it to break a window and climb out.

I leaned down to get it and slipped on a patch of damp floor, falling face forward and knocking the hammer out of reach in the process. I scrambled onto my back and found myself looking up at Morris. He had gripped the sledgehammer handle with his right hand just below the head, which he was tapping into his left hand.

"I got rid of Harvey — my own cousin," he said. "You think I'm gonna be squeamish about getting rid of you? Where is it?" Tap. Tap. "I know you know." Tap. Tap. "I can smash your knees." Tap. Tap. "And then smash your elbows." Tap. Tap.

Years ago I'd taken martial art lessons, learning just enough to be dangerous, mostly to myself. But every so often, bits of what I learned came back when I needed them. I took my eyes away from the hammer and focused on his face. His eyes. His mouth. If I could predict when he was going to strike, I could roll sideways, and maybe wrest the sledgehammer away from him. I had to try, anyway.

And I spotted the moment when he tensed to raise the sledgehammer, and was in the act of rolling aside when the head of the hammer hit the low ceiling, smashing a huge hole in it.

Gold coins started pouring out onto his head. Dozens of them. Maybe hundreds.

Morris was so astonished that he stood there for a few moments, looking up at the ceiling and watching the gold coins hit him in the face. Then he dropped the sledgehammer with a thud and began catching the coins as they fell and shoving them into his pockets.

I rolled to my feet and felled him with a tackle. Then I snatched up the sledgehammer and thrust it up under his chin, in much the same way people were always holding swords to each other's throats in historical dramas. I wasn't sure how effective this would be, but it was either that or bash his skull in. I liked this option better.

"Don't move," I said. "Or I'll smash your windpipe."

He froze.

"Just for the record," I said. "Not only did I not know there was gold here in Harvey's house, until those coins started falling out of the ceiling I thought you were completely bonkers for thinking so. You have my apologies for doubting you."

He made a growling noise.

I started when from somewhere behind me, a cat meowed.

"It's okay, Meg." Clarence. I heard his footsteps coming down the hall. "I came to check the cat trap and noticed there was something going on here. Why don't you stand down and let me take over guarding him?"

Clarence loomed into the room, six feet four and almost as wide, even without the bulk added by his puffy down jacket. He set down the cat trap he was holding and held out his hand. I took the sledgehammer away from Morris's throat and handed it to Clarence. I could see Morris considering the idea of making a break for it and thinking better of it.

"What happened to your face?" Clarence asked. "Are you okay?"

"My face?" I put my hand up to touch it and felt something damp. And realized that my left cheek and temple hurt. "I think I scraped it when I fell. Nothing major. Want me to call nine-one-one?"

"I called before I came in," he said. "On

my police radio."

Was it just my imagination, or was I hearing sirens in the distance?

I sat down beside the cat trap and looked inside. At first all I saw was what looked like a wad of dark matted fur, and I wondered if Clarence had caught something else by mistake. Like a small rat. Then the kitten opened her enormous blue eyes and hissed softly at me.

"She's sopping wet," I said. "And shivering. I think we left a couple of hand towels in the bathroom for convenience — I'm going to dry her off."

"She's feral, remember," Clarence warned, without taking his eyes off Morris. "She'll scratch and bite."

She tried, briefly, but long experience of wrapping our two barn cats for their trips to see Clarence had made me a reasonably adept cat wrangler. By the time the sirens came to a stop outside and Vern burst into the house, she had stopped struggling against the towel and was even purring softly.

She continued to purr all throughout the dramatic arrival of most of the Caerphilly police force and the reading to Morris of his Miranda rights — which he interrupted more than once with loud and unprintable

405

insults. She didn't much enjoy being put back into the trap so Clarence and Vern could finish demolishing the ceiling and the chief could take all of Harvey's hidden gold into custody. I could understand how she felt. I fought the idea of being dragged down to Caerphilly Hospital to be checked out.

"I don't like the look of those abrasions on your cheek and forehead," Clarence said. "If you fell hard enough to do that, you could have a concussion."

"I didn't even notice them until you pointed them out," I said. I wasn't lying — I'd been much too busy trying not to get killed to worry about a few minor scratches.

"Clarence is right," the chief said. "Even if the abrasions are only minor, a hoarder's house isn't the most hygienic place to be injured in. Last I heard, your dad was down at the hospital visiting his patients. I'll just take you by there, let him check you out, and then I can run you back to Trinity. And I'm sure he'd like to hear about this evening's events from you."

"Okay," I said. "But I want to stay until they're finished bashing in the ceilings."

It was nearly one o'clock before we arrived at the hospital, and I was actually hoping Dad had gone home to bed. I was perfectly happy to let whoever was on duty in the ER check out my minimal injuries.

To my surprise, the chief didn't pull up to the ER entrance. He just parked in one of the staff parking slots near the front door and led the way in.

"We'll just drop in on your dad and his patient," he said.

We took the elevator up to the second floor. The chief nodded to the nurse on duty and then led the way down to the far end of the hallway, past quite a few empty rooms. Puzzling — why would they stick either of Dad's patients so far away from the nurse's station? If they'd had something contagious maybe it would make sense. The only other reason I'd ever seen them exile someone like this when there were closer rooms available was when Grandfather had been in the hospital. He'd been so loud and unruly that they'd had to move him as far as possible from the other patients. But I couldn't imagine either of the police casualties being that annoying.

I could ask Dad. Meanwhile it was nice to see how happy the chief was, now that he'd caught his killer. He was grinning ear to ear as he knocked on the open door of the last room along the hallway. I glanced in, but although the door was open, the privacy curtain inside was closed.

"Okay to come in?" the chief called. "I've brought Meg."

"Bring her in," Dad answered.

The chief bowed and waved me in.

I slipped through the privacy curtains and glanced curiously toward the bed to see which of Dad's patients was here — George, the newly appendix-free desk clerk, or the concussed deputy.

My mouth fell open when I saw who was in the bed.

Harvey.

CHAPTER 30

"You're alive!" I exclaimed.

"Not so loud," Dad cautioned. "Only a few people know he's here."

Harvey was sitting up slightly. The top of his head was swathed in bandages, as if someone had set out to wrap him up like a mummy and then given up when the ears proved complicated. He looked pale. But he was grinning.

"I guess I have a pretty hard head," he said.

"He's lucky to be alive," Dad said. "If you hadn't found him when you did —"

"And if you hadn't hauled him off to the hospital as fast as you did," the chief added.

"It was still touch and go at first." Dad gazed at Harvey with satisfaction. "But he's a fighter."

"And you decided to pretend he was dead," I said. "I assume that was to protect him."

"Yes." The chief sighed. "I was worried that if word got out that he was alive — alive, but still unconscious — whoever had tried to kill him might come back to finish the job. Even if we put out the word that he couldn't identify his attacker, they'd want to get rid of him, just to be sure. And I was already so shorthanded that it would have crippled the department if I had to put someone here round the clock to guard him."

"So we announced that he was dead," Dad said. "And recruited Sammy to help out."

I hadn't noticed him before, but Sammy, the deputy who'd broken his leg, was sitting in an armchair in the far corner of the room with his leg up on a footstool and his service weapon on a small table beside him. He waved and grinned at me.

"And even after Harvey woke up, he couldn't tell us who'd done it," the chief said.

"Retrograde amnesia?" I guessed.

"No," Harvey said. "I remember everything that happened — even the part that hurt like the dickens. I just didn't see anything useful. It was maybe five in the morning — still dark, and I heard mewing outside. I thought maybe the feral kitten

410

was hurt, so I went out to check, and the noise seemed to be coming from the garage. I went inside, and was looking around, and then something hit me on the back of the head. I never saw who it was."

"We're going to keep the fact that he's still alive quiet a little longer," the chief said. "Just until I can locate the rest of his cousins. Mr. Morris Haverhill may be the one who struck the blows, but we can't discount the possibility that the other two were accomplices."

"I won't say a word," I said.

"I hope you find them soon," Harvey said.

"I'm sure you'll feel safer when we do," the chief said.

"Yes," Harvey said. "And the sooner I can come out of hiding, the sooner we can finish with my house. That is still on, isn't it?" He turned to me with an anxious look.

"Absolutely," I said. "By the way, we caught the gray kitten you were feeding. Clarence seemed to think you might be interested in adopting her."

Harvey frowned.

"I hate to disappoint him," he said. "I mean, cats are okay. But what I really want is a dog. A big friendly one I can take on long walks."

"I'm sure Clarence can help you find

one," I said. "And don't worry — I already have a plan for the kitten."

"We should let Mr. Dunlop rest," the chief said. "And get your injuries checked out so you can head back to Trinity. Remember, mum's the word!"

I nodded. And I noticed he didn't actually order me not to tell anyone. Which was a good thing. I knew I'd burst by morning if I couldn't tell Michael about this.

CHAPTER 31

"No, we're not keeping the kitten," I said, for about the twentieth time since my brother had arrived at the furniture store. I looked up from my sweeping — I'd mainly come in to clean up the mess the various burglars had made in the store. And to do a little planning about what came next. Just because I couldn't share the good news about Harvey yet didn't mean I couldn't get a plan ready.

Across the room, Rob was playing with Shadow, as we'd provisionally named the rescued kitten.

"Two barn cats are enough," I added. "And I don't think it's a good idea to bring a kitten into the house with Tink and Spike."

"Tink wouldn't hurt her," Rob protested. "She wouldn't hurt a fly."

"Spike would," I said. "At least he'd try, and they'd both end up the worse for wear.

413

For that matter, mild-mannered as Tink is, I'm not sure what Shadow would do to her if you left them in a room together."

"Oh, Shadow's not that bad." Rob reached out to pet the kitten, who retaliated with yet another set of tiny lacerations.

"Keep an eye on her, will you?" I said. "She could do a lot of damage if she got into some of those boxes."

"So if you're not keeping the kitten, why is she here?" I had half a mind to answer "why are *you* here if you're not going to help clean up things?" But no sense taking out my brief but cranky reaction on Rob. Although it was useful to let myself feel just a little bit cranky. I was finding it hard work keeping from grinning at the thought that Harvey was alive. Would be coming back here to the furniture store to claim all his family treasures — the slab of marble that used to be a bank counter, the mourning brooch with the dead children's hair in it, and the antique blown glass Christmas ornaments his great-grandmother had brought over from England. Claiming his treasures, but almost certainly letting us get rid of the lion's share of the junk.

I forced a solemn look on my face.

"Mother is dropping by any time now," I said aloud. "She might be ready for another cat, and I'm hoping if she sees Shadow she'll fall for her, and Clarence will have one less mouth to feed."

"Great idea," Rob said. "I know she misses old Boomer."

"Sebastian," I corrected mechanically. "You know she hated the 'Boomer' nickname. Anyway, keep playing with Shadow, will you? Tire her out, so Mother will think she's a quiet, docile, well-behaved little ball of fluff, not the hyperactive homicidal ninja we already know her to be."

"Does Mother know you've invited her here so you could play feline matchmaker?" Rob asked, as he led Shadow a merry dance with the cat toy — a tuft of feathers on a resilient wand.

"No — she and Mrs. Whatzit from the antique store are going to look over all the china and vases and stuff. Identify anything that might be valuable." She'd be delighted when she heard the good news about Harvey, and knew she'd be doing her sorting and appraising for him, not for his wretched cousins.

We heard a car stopping outside.

"That could be Mother now," I said aloud.

The old-fashioned bell over the furniture store door had jingled. We both looked up to see Judge Jane Shiffley entering.

"Hard at work already — good! And in such a good cause."

"I'm not so sure about that," I grumbled. "I'd much rather be organizing stuff for Harvey than for those wretched cousins of his — don't Ernest and Josephine end up with all of this? And what about all of Harvey's gold?"

"The gold he probably never knew he had," Judge Jane said, shaking her head sadly. "I bet if he'd known he had a ceiling full of gold he'd have given Clarence a lot more money for the shelter."

He probably would. Not smiling at that idea was hard.

"Still — it was in his house," I insisted. "Unless someone can prove otherwise, I'm assuming whoever decides these things will say it was his. I hate to see the praying mantis people get their claws on it. And Morris Haverhill doesn't get any of it, does he?"

"I doubt it," Rob said. "Like most states, Virginia has a slayer statute."

There were times when I forgot for weeks on end that Rob had graduated from law school before finding his true vocation as an inventor of computer games. For that matter, I suspected Rob forgot about it for months on end.

"So what happens under a slayer statute?" I asked.

"They treat it as if the murderer died before his victim," Rob said. "Right, Your Honor?"

Judge Jane nodded.

"So it goes to Morris's heirs," Rob said. "Whoever they are."

"The other two Haverhills — as I thought." I sighed. "Pity. Harvey didn't like them much better than Morris. Although if the chief is right that they were aiding and abetting Morris —"

"Actually, nothing goes to any of the Haverhills," Judge Jane said.

I gave her a sharp look — had word about Harvey's survival leaked out?

"If Harvey had died intestate, it all would have gone to the cousins," Judge Jane went on. "But he was smart. He made a will."

She sounded as proud of Harvey's foresight as if he were one of her own kids.

"Smart move," I said. "Given how much he supposedly hated his cousins. Do we know who does get the loot?"

"The Caerphilly Animal Welfare Foundation." Judge Jane beamed with approval. She'd adopted more than a few of her dog pack from Clarence's shelter. Any hunting dog, no matter how old or sorry looking —

or for that matter any dog that looked as if it might have hunting blood somewhere in its ancestry — ended up at her farm if no one else wanted it. "I found out this morning and let Clarence know as soon as I heard."

"Good for Clarence," Rob said. "I know the shelter can use it."

"We should probably keep that quiet for now," I said. "We have no idea how much the gold's going to be worth, and we don't want people thinking the shelter's rolling in dough and doesn't need donations or adoptions."

"Good point," Judge Jane said.

"And besides, are we sure the will will stand up?" I asked her.

"Odds are good," she said. "I never say 'of course' because strange things can happen in a court of law. But Kate Warren's very solid. Got a nice way with a will. Then again, as I told Clarence, if I were him I'd hire me a good litigator to fend off all the nonsense that's going to come his way, from the Haverhills and that gun-crazy woman from the hoarder site and who knows who else."

Oh, dear. She'd already told Clarence. Well, at least with him, the disappointment of learning that the shelter wasn't getting a windfall would be more than made up for by the joy of learning that Harvey was still alive.

Judge Jane looked up as the bell over the door jingled again. "In fact — ah, there he is now. Clarence, did you take my advice?"

"Of course." Clarence ambled in, looking a little stunned. "I called the only attorney I could think of."

"You didn't call me," Rob looked indignant.

"Okay," Clarence rolled his eyes. "I called the only attorney I could think of who'd actually ever represented anyone in a courtroom. Meg, your cousin Festus says hi, and can he stay with you when he comes down tomorrow, because the Caerphilly Inn's completely full?"

"I'll call him and tell him he's very welcome." While we had many lawyers in the family, most of them pretty darn competent, if I were in any kind of real trouble, Festus would be the one I'd call. Clarence was batting a thousand in the common sense department so far. And it would be nice to see Festus, even if Clarence probably wasn't going to need his help. I was beginning to feel grateful that Dad and the chief had kept the secret of Harvey's survival from me as long as they did. Keeping my mouth shut was driving me crazy.

"I'm not going to keep all the money, you know," Clarence said. "I'm going to give some of it to those poor people whose families lost everything when the Dunlops' bank failed. Pay them back what they lost, plus interest. I'm sure I can find someone to figure out what the numbers would be."

"You know, that was over eighty years ago," I said. "I think by now they've all gotten over the loss." And did he have any idea how much the interest would have added up?

"There's no proof the gold came from the bank," Judge Jane pointed out. "For all we know, Harvey's father could have bought those coins over the years and squirreled them away. He sure didn't spend much on anything else."

"I know all that," Clarence said. "But I think it's what Harvey would want me to do. I know he felt bad about the suffering his family bank's failure caused people. I'm pretty sure he had no idea that money was up there, or he'd have made restitution himself."

"Just let Festus work out all the legal details," Judge Jane said.

"And don't tell anyone you're planning to give them money until you're sure there aren't any hitches," I said.

"Of course." Clarence nodded. "And I'm not counting chickens for myself either — by which I mean for the shelter. I hope there will be enough left over to make some improvements to the shelter, but in the meantime, we have to make do with what we have. And keep up that adoption program."

"Good thinking." I breathed a sigh of relief and made a mental note to point out to the chief that the longer his deception went on, the more complications like this would result.

"Speaking of the adoption program," Clarence said. "Rob, you and Delaney are hired. Last night Kevin posted the first batch of dog glamour shots on that new website he made for us, and we've already got a dozen people coming by today for possible adoptions."

"Awesome," Rob said.

"Any chance you could drop by for a while and help keep the dogs in a good mood?" Clarence suddenly sounded a little anxious. "Because I can't be everywhere, and you're so good at getting them to relax and open up to people."

"Can I spend the day playing with your dogs?" Rob laughed. "No problem. Opening at ten, right?"

Clarence nodded.

"As long as you're all here," I began.

Just then the bell over the front door tinkled. We all looked up to see Ernest and Josephine Haverhill.

"Speak of the devil," Rob muttered.

Shadow hissed and arched her back.

My latest encounter with Morris had left me wary of Haverhills. I pulled out my phone and dialed 911.

"Anything wrong, Meg?" Debbie Ann asked when she answered the phone.

"Can we help you people?" Judge Jane asked the new arrivals.

"Ms. Haverhill," I said, looking up from the phone but keeping it near my ear — and mouth. "And Mr. Haverhill. How nice to see you."

"Try and keep them there," Debbie Ann said.

"Your police chief has arrested our brother," Ernest Haverhill said. "I would assume that means we can have our stuff."

"And you'd be making an erroneous assumption," Judge Jane said. "Your brother's only arrested — not even arraigned, much less convicted. So at the moment Mr. Dunlop's house is still a crime scene and its contents still potentially constitute evidence.

But even if that weren't the case, you can't just walk in and take possession. The estate has to go through probate. It's a lot faster and easier when there's a will — do you know if he left one?"

The Haverhills hunched slightly more than they were already and exchanged a glance.

"We're his family," Josephine said.

"His only family," Ernest added. "I expect he didn't think he needed a will."

"If it turns out there's no will, you'll get his property once you go through the probate process." Judge Jane managed to keep a straight face as she said it.

The bell over the door rang again and Chief Burke stepped in. The Haverhills turned in unison and their faces lit up with a pleased though predatory expression, as if he were a hummingbird coming within range. Clearly they didn't know him yet.

Vern followed him. I heard a noise at the back door and saw Aida slip in.

"Ms. Josephine Haverhill. Mr. Ernest Haverhill. You're under arrest for the attempted murder of Harvey Dunlop. You —"

"Murder! What are you talking about?" Josephine shrieked.

Ernest made a dash for the back door, and Vern gave chase and tackled him.

"Attempted murder?" Judge Jane murmured.

"That's the most ridiculous thing I ever heard!" Josephine was saying. "We didn't murder him. Apparently you think Morris did, which is almost as ridiculous — were you not listening when —"

"Quiet!" The chief didn't often raise his voice, but when he did, the results were impressive. Josephine shut up. Ernest stopped struggling and let Vern put the handcuffs on him.

"Your little trick with the transponders was ingenious," the chief said. "It could easily have fooled us."

"Trick with the transponders?" Judge Jane asked.

"Those things in your car that let you breeze through tollbooths," Rob explained.

"I know *what* they are," Judge Jane said — probably sounding more patient than she felt. "I want to know what trick the Haverhills played with them, and how the chief saw through it."

"Mr. Morris Haverhill made a point of suggesting that we check his transponder," the chief explained. "Since, as he pointed out, it would show that he left Caerphilly in time to pass through several tollbooths in the Richmond area between around five fifteen and five forty-five, then returned along the same route at around ten o'clock yesterday morning."

"So far, so good," Judge Jane said.

"E-ZPass confirmed those times," the chief went on. "And while we were at it, we checked his siblings' transponders, which showed that they passed through Richmond on much the same route several hours earlier and didn't come back the next day until sometime even later than Mr. Morris."

"Then how can you arrest us for murder if none of us were anywhere near here when Harvey got killed?" Ernest demanded.

"Your brother's transponder may have been passing through Richmond between five fifteen and five forty-five on Monday," the chief said. "But his cell phone never left Caerphilly that night."

"Bingo!" Rob exclaimed. Judge Jane nodded.

"And Ms. Haverhill's cell phone records show that after passing through a series of tollbooths in and around Richmond, she then proceeded to circle back on non-toll roads so she could take the same route through the tollbooths, this time with her brother's transponder. And then you pulled the same stunt in the morning to make it look as if he came back here."

"We were just trying to help him get out of trouble," Josephine said.

"Not the way I see it." The chief looked stern. "The texts and emails we've retrieved from his phone show that the three of you actively planned to murder Mr. Dunlop and were in constant communication before, during, and after your brother's attack on him."

"But we erased those," Ernest said.

"Shut up, you fool!" Josephine snapped.

"I'll be taking you down to the station for booking," the chief said. "The attorney you retained for your brother is already down there, although it's up to you whether you want to retain him or whether you each want separate attorneys to protect your interests."

From the suddenly suspicious looks Josephine and Ernest were giving each other, I predicted that two more attorneys from Farmville would be trekking down to Caerphilly soon.

The chief stood watching as Vern and Aida led the Haverhills outside.

"Good work, letting us know they were here," he said to me. "I was just about to issue a BOLO on them after the phone records came in this morning. And thanks for sending young Kevin down to the station last night — he was actually the one who figured out the phone thing."

"Henry, you arrested them for attempted murder," Judge Jane said. "Just what aren't you telling us?"

The chief glanced at me, and I deduced that he was giving me permission.

"Harvey's alive," I said. "He was badly injured and unconscious for a while, but he's awake now, and going to be okay."

"Hurray!" Clarence shouted, and for a few minutes we all cheered, laughed, or even cried a little.

Shadow went over and sniffed delicately at the chief's trousers.

"Don't try to pet her," I warned, seeing him lean down. "That's the feral kitten Harvey was feeding."

"Ah." The chief put his hands on his knees and peered down at Shadow, who stared up at him, unblinking. "You have a lot to answer for, little lady."

"How is that?" Judge Jane asked.

As if resenting the chief's accusation, Clarence scooped up Shadow and took her into the back room.

"Sandbox time," he muttered.

"Morris Haverhill used her to lure Harvey outside," I said. "It wasn't her fault."

"Apparently, while the decluttering was

going on, Mr. Haverhill managed to slip into the garage long enough to unlock the one window," the chief added. "He returned and hid in there. And at some time in the early morning, he imitated a kitten in pain to lure Harvey out there."

"The wretch," Judge Jane muttered.

"Incidentally, don't be shocked if you hear the Haverhills trying to shift some of the blame on the Helping Hands project," the chief said, turning to me. "Apparently the reason they were trying to get the building inspector and Adult Protective Services to come down hard on Harvey was so he'd turn to them for the help he needed to get his act together."

"I have a hard time imagining him trusting them that much," I said. "He's afraid of them."

"Yes," the chief went on. "And it came as a nasty shock when they found out someone outside the family was going to help him declutter. They realized that they had to do something quickly to keep a bunch of 'nosy, interfering outsiders' from finding the family treasure."

"A treasure I bet Harvey didn't even know about."

"You're right," the chief said. "It was his father who hid the gold. Harvey was only ten or eleven when the false ceiling went up. Anyway, after attacking Harvey, Morris took his keys and spent some time searching the house. Horace has already found his fingerprints inside."

"Will that hold up?" Judge Jane asked. "After all, they were cousins. He could claim he was visiting Harvey."

"The fingerprints were on some of the moving boxes delivered to the site by the Shiffley Construction Company Monday morning," the chief said. "Harvey tells us that he did not let his cousin in to the house at any time after that. And Mr. Haverhill claimed the key ring he had was one Mr. Dunlop had entrusted to him years ago, but given the presence of a key to the furniture store, I don't think that explanation will hold up." He chuckled.

"But maybe we caused it," I said. "Their attempt on Harvey. If we hadn't —"

"No." He sounded fierce, and shook his head. "This is on them. I'm pretty sure they'd have tried to get to him eventually. At worst, having the Helping Hands come in drove them to act sooner than they would have, but they were heading that way. And maybe if they'd had more time to plan, they'd have succeeded in killing him. And gotten away with it. But now . . . all's well that ends well."

"What about Tabitha?" I asked. "And Harvey's neighbors?"

"Ms. Fillmore's still down at the jail, conferring with her defense attorney," the chief said. "She could very well see prison time. Dangerous use of a firearm — that's a class four felony, which means up to ten years in prison. Even if her attorney does a good job — well, our local juries generally take a dim view of people taking potshots at their fellow citizens. Mrs. Gudgeon and Mr. Brimley, now — they're out on bail. I'll let the D.A. decide if she thinks she can get them on breaking and entering or if she has to settle for trespassing."

"Busy holiday season for you," Judge Jane said.

"But at least I don't have a lot of unsolved crimes to worry about," the chief said. "And if you'll excuse me, I'm hoping to have some interesting conversations with the Haverhills before I start my holiday. Merry Christmas!"

He exited, although I heard him exchanging Christmas greetings with someone outside.

A few seconds later, Mother sailed in with Rose Noire trailing behind her.

"Merry Christmas!" Mother trilled. "Meg,

I heard you helped the chief capture the culprit last night. And they tell me Harvey is alive. How wonderful! Now we can all relax and really enjoy our Christmas."

"Culprits, actually," I said. "I'll fill you in later." I noticed that Rob had caught Rose Noire's eye and pointed dramatically toward the back room before slipping into it himself. To get Shadow ready for her introduction, I suspected. "So did you bring me any raffle tickets?"

"Raffle tickets?" Mother looked blank.

"For Mrs. Dinwiddie's grandmother's quilt."

"Oh, dear." Her face fell. "I'm afraid I didn't manage to get any. They were all bought up before I got a chance. But don't worry. I took a lot of pictures."

"Don't worry," Rose Noire echoed, before disappearing into the back room.

"And by the way," Mother went on, "Robyn's come up with a lovely idea for expanding the Helping Hands program."

Yesterday I might have growled at her. But now, in spite of my disappointment about the raffle tickets, I was sufficiently cheered by Harvey's survival and the arrest of the remaining Haverhills that I merely made a mild protest.

"I think the current program's going to

keep us pretty busy for the holidays," I said. "And possibly some time into the New Year."

"Oh, yes," Mother said. "Especially given all the publicity about how the program was helping Harvey before the poor man was attacked. We've gotten a dozen new requests today alone. But we've started to notice that perhaps the most common reason people give for not being able to do these projects themselves is consumer debt. They don't have the money to hire someone, and they've already maxed out their credit cards. And Robyn found the loveliest article about how several churches have organized projects to help everyone pay off their debts."

As Mother nattered on about seed money, cohort groups, and financial counseling, I pulled out my notebook and jotted a quick to-do item: ask Robyn to show me this lovely article. And talk to her about what she had in mind. Because it sounded like a wonderful idea, but it also sounded a lot more complicated than simply showing up to build a ramp or finish a quilt.

Of course, it also sounded as if it could have even more impact on the Caerphilly community than what we were doing this year. So it might be worth doing.

"I've made a note to talk to Robyn," I

said. "So we won't forget about it." Not that there was much chance of Mother forgetting about anything that got her this excited. "For now let's concentrate on this year's agenda, shall we? Do you have any information on these dozen new projects?"

Only on a couple of them, but they sounded small and doable. Possibly doable before Christmas — but not so urgent that we had to squeeze them in. Which was good, because I was hoping to take a few days off. The rest of today and tomorrow, at least.

"But we can worry about that after Christmas," Mother said. "Right now. . . . ooooh! Who is this?"

Rob and Rose Noire had returned. Rob was holding Shadow, who appeared to have fallen asleep in his hands. Rose Noire was gently stroking the kitten's shiny fur.

"One of the cats Clarence needs to unload to make room in the shelter," Rob said.

"So precious," Rose Noire cooed.

"May I?" Mother held out both hands. Rob deposited Shadow in them. Mother held the sleeping kitten to her chest and Shadow snuggled closer and began purring.

"What a darling!" Mother whispered.

Behind her back Rob was doing fist pumps. Rose Noire contented herself with beaming at what was clearly a case of love at first sight. Well, at least on Mother's part.

Rose Noire slipped closer to me. I must have looked a little less than happy.

"For goodness' sake, don't worry about the quilt," she whispered. "I cut a deal with your grandfather. I told him I'd give him back his magpies . . . but only if he bought every single raffle ticket and gave them all to Josh and Jamie. But pretend to be surprised, okay?"

"You're amazing," I said, and gave her a fierce hug.

She returned to helping Mother pet Shadow.

The bell over the door rang, and Dad dashed in, pushing a wheelchair that contained a familiar figure.

"It's Harvey!" I exclaimed, and everyone gathered around to greet him. He seemed pleased but a little overwhelmed by the warmth of our welcome.

"Oh, never mind about me," Harvey said finally. "I've got more exciting news. Come and look! They were wrong!" He pointed behind him toward the door.

"Who was wrong?" I asked as we all hurried toward the front windows. "And about what?"

"The weather forecasters," Dad exclaimed, as he turned Harvey around and pushed him toward the windows. "As late as last night, they were forecasting nothing but more rain for today and tomorrow. And now look at it!"

Snow was falling. And not just a few scattered flakes. The sky was full of the kind of tiny flakes you only see when a snowstorm means serious business.

"Now that's more like it," Rob said.

"Yes," I said. "It looks as if we'll be having a white Christmas after all."

ACKNOWLEDGMENTS

Thanks once again to everyone at St. Martin's / Minotaur, including (but not limited to) Joe Brosnan, Lily Cronig, Hector De-Jean, Paul Hochman, Andrew Martin, Sarah Melnyk, and especially my editor, Pete Wolverton. And thanks to David Rotstein and the art department for yet another beautiful original cover. You've all got me spoiled.

More thanks to my agent, Ellen Geiger, and to Matt McGowan, and the staff at the Frances Goldin Literary Agency — they take care of the practical stuff so I can focus on the writing. Many thanks to the friends who brainstorm and critique with me, give me good ideas, or help keep me sane while I'm writing: Stuart, Aidan, and Liam Andrews, Chris Cowan, Ellen Crosby, Kathy Deligianis, Margery Flax, Suzanne Frisbee, John Gilstrap, Barb Goffman, Joni Langevoort, David Niemi, Alan Orloff, Art Taylor, Robin Templeton, and Dina Willner. Thanks for all kinds of moral support and practical help to my blog sisters and brother at the Femmes Fatales: Alexia Gordon, Aimee Hix, Dean James, Toni L.P. Kelner, Catriona McPherson, Kris Neri, Joanna Campbell Slan, Marcia Talley, Elaine Viets, and LynDee Walker. And thanks to all the TeaBuds for two decades of friendship. I'd like to give a special shout-out to all my friends who struggle with clutter, like Harvey — and me. You know who you are! And above all, thanks to all my readers. You're the ones who make this possible!

ABOUT THE AUTHOR

Donna Andrews is a winner of the Agatha, Anthony, and Barry Awards, a *Romantic Times* Award for best first novel, and four Lefty and two Toby Bromberg awards for funniest mystery. She is a member of MWA, Sisters in Crime, and the Private Investigators and Security Association. Andrews lives in Reston, Virginia.

The employees of Thorndike Press hope you have enjoyed this Large Print book. All our Thorndike, Wheeler, and Kennebec Large Print titles are designed for easy reading, and all our books are made to last. Other Thorndike Press Large Print books are available at your library, through selected bookstores, or directly from us.

For information about titles, please call:
   (800) 223-1244

or visit our website at:
   gale.com/thorndike

To share your comments, please write:
   Publisher
   Thorndike Press
   10 Water St., Suite 310
   Waterville, ME 04901